First Printing

P.P.M.

by

GARY NAIMAN

Cover art by Todd Aune, Spokane, Washington

www.fidelipublishing.com

Dedicated to the living spirit of Rachel Carson…

Chapter 1

Somalia

Twin beams of polarized light radiated from the metal ceiling, their pale glow illuminating the two men working below. The men wore surgical gowns, gloves, and caps, with protective masks covering their noses and mouths. The only sound was the air rushing through the recycling vents on the grated floor. The shadows flickered with colors from the electronic instruments racked on the metal walls.

The men sat at a table arrayed with test tube racks, slide boxes, and culture dishes. A microscope occupied the space in front of them, with a centrifuge and ice chest off to the side.

One of the men placed a glass slide on the scope's viewing platform. He leaned forward and peered through the twin eyepieces, his gloved hand slowly turning the focus knob. He stiffened, his eyes trained on the unexpected filament of protein floating on the sea of dead blood.

"You have something?"

The man ignored his colleague and continued turning the knob, his eyes fixed on the bronze strand.

Nihalla leaned closer. "Mr. Frankton?"

Karl slumped on the stool, his bloodshot eyes glaring at the microscope. He plucked the slide off the scope's viewing platform and handed it to Nihalla. "Eyelash, sorry."

Nihalla raised the slide to the light and squinted at the amber fluid trapped inside the slide's transparent seal, and at the red "84" scribbled beside it. He frowned and snatched the lash with a tweezers before placing the slide in its white-plastic box.

Karl glanced at the box. "That's it?"

1

"Yes, last one." Nihalla closed the box and applied a tape seal. He slipped an insulated glove over his right hand and reached for the ice chest. When he lifted the lid, a rush of white vapor spilled down the chest onto the table. The vapor crept across the table like a freed spirit before disappearing into the conditioned air.

Nihalla's frown deepened as he lowered the box into the ice chest. "Maybe I missed something."

"Missed?"

"When I checked the spinals."

Karl gave him a puzzled look. "We both checked the spinals. Everything normal. No anomalies."

Nihalla ignored him while lifting a frost-covered box out of the chest. He held it up and watched the vapor drift down his glove.

"You okay, Doc?"

Nihalla didn't respond.

"How about a break?"

"I'm fine, Mr. Frankton."

Karl slipped off the stool and stretched his aching back. "Want anything?"

"A cup of tea would be nice."

"No problem, but you should take a break. Give you a chance to clear your head."

Nihalla didn't hear him. He'd peeled the tape off the frosted box and lifted out the first slide. It would take three hours to recheck the spinal fluids.

"Well...back soon with that tea." Karl patted Nihalla's shoulder and shuffled across the van's grated floor to the rear door, taking care not to brush against the racked vials on the lab table. He gripped the door's metal handle and looked back at Nihalla hunched over the microscope's twin eyepieces.

The Somali physician had been at it for two days without a decent break. No food, no rest, not even a cup of his precious chamomile tea. Dedication was one thing, but the poor guy was killing himself. Take a breather for Christ's sake.

2

Karl started to speak, but the words jammed in his throat. Watch it, chum. He's not like you. This is his country, his village, his people. And don't call him "Doc." It's Dr. Nihalla, the very best. Hell, you're not good enough to be his scrub, so take your sorry ass out of this van, clear your muddled head, and get back with that tea.

Karl yanked the handle and pushed out of the Vickers Mobile Lab into the blinding daylight. He closed the door and felt a blast of crushing heat. After four hours in the van's conditioned air, he'd almost forgotten where he was.

He pulled down his surgical mask and squinted at the sun floating in the haze. If there was a hell on earth, he was standing in it. Unbearable heat, dead trees, parched savannah grass, swarms of flies, and that oppressive haze. A real paradise, southwest Somalia in July. Smack in the middle of the *hagaa* drought.

He brushed back his surgical cap and ruffled his blond hair while studying the cluster of brown shacks on his left. The only sound was the unnerving drone of flies.

He stared at the yellow plastic tape encircling the shacks. Suspended by wire stakes, the tape stretched nearly fifty yards before disappearing around the last shack. It reminded him of an enormous crime scene investigation, except for the tri-pincered International Biohazard Symbol stamped across the tape in black. The warning was clear. Cross that tape without proper gear and your next step might be your last.

He eased down the van's metal steps and placed his foot on a lever protruding from a white-plastic container. He popped open the lid and ripped off his surgical gown, followed by his mask, cap, and latex gloves. He dropped them in the container and pulled his foot away. The weighted lid plopped shut.

In a few minutes, Crumley would snatch the container's plastic bag and dump it in the incineration pit at the far-end of the village. A quick "bleach-n-burn" to eliminate any

3

contamination risk and Crumley would be done with his grim chores for the day.

God, he was tired. If he could just close his eyes. No sense working like this. Might overlook something. Maybe already had.

Where the hell was the breeze? Not even a rustle. Nothing but burned grass, scrub, and that damned sun. He tugged at his khaki shirt and shuffled through the faded savannah grass toward the white tents on the slope above the village.

He was nearly to the tents when he stopped to look down at the village. The drone had grown louder, more like a steady hum. A bead of sweat trickled down his forehead.

He stared at the pavilion at the north end of the village. Swarms of flies darted under its rusted, corrugated metal roof, their tiny bodies engulfing it in black haze.

He squinted at the shadows beneath the metal roof and felt his stomach churn. There was no tree to grab, nothing to lean against. He bent over and clutched his knees.

This was different than peering at death through a microscope's sterile eyepiece, or studying gruesome photographs in an air-conditioned Atlanta briefing room. This was the real thing and it was more than he could stand.

He could barely make them out in the shadows. Eighty-four silver bags, each containing the remains of a human being, neatly placed beside one another in four tight rows, their ID tags stamped "1" through "84." The same numbers as on the slides.

And that gut-wrenching smell. The acrid stench of bleach. A final bath for the dead administered by agent Terwood Crumley as he stepped through the plastic bags in his white biohazard suit, a spray tank strapped to his back, a silver nozzle in his gloved hands.

Karl fought the nausea while recalling the moment their chopper touched down two days ago. They were warned it would be rough, but nothing could prepare them for the shock when they stepped off the chopper in their biohazard suits.

He'd seen death before. A year ago in Zaire. A dozen corpses in a small village below Mt. Elgon, their bodies liquefying from the latest outbreak of Ebola. Another two dozen fighting for their lives, their skin splattered with ominous red blotches, blood leaking from their noses and mouths, a look of hopeless lassitude in their eyes. A hard day, but not like this.

The landscape was different than Zaire. No dense, green jungle shrieking with colubus monkeys. No Mt. Elgon rising above the haze, its stepped ridges shaded silver-green in the morning sun.

This was southwest Somalia and there was no emerald jungle. Only burned savannah grass, dead trees, and that merciless sun.

To the north, rugged highlands rose toward the Karkaar Mountains, but here everything was flat and barren. The only water came from two rivers flowing down from Ethiopia. One of them, the Jubba, managed to reach the Indian Ocean at the port city of Chisimayu.

But Chisimayu lay three hundred miles to the southwest. The only water up here came from the Shabeelle River, or what was left of it. A trickling stream fading south toward the parched sand dunes below Mogadishu, the Somali capital.

Karl wiped the sweat off his face and looked north. Hell, if you want to see a river take a look at the flood of refugees pouring into Mogadishu from the west, all of them fleeing Somalia's tribal wars and killer droughts.

What a hellhole. Poverty, civil war, drought, and death. An anarchist nation ruled by territorial clans and warlords. Names like *Dir, Daarood, Isaaq, Hawiye, Digil,* and *Rahanwayn* fighting to protect their turf while their women and children starved to death. And now, this.

He recalled the bodies strewn across the village, their frozen hands clutching their throats, their strained fingers

5

embedded in the clawed dirt. Mothers and children clinging to each other, their faces twisted in agony. But most of all, he'd never forget the terrified look in their glazed eyes. Like they'd seen the devil before gasping their final breath.

Yes, this was the nightmare Karl Frankton and his four colleagues dropped into two days ago. And still no answer.

He took a deep breath and continued up the slope. When he reached the tents, he paused for a final look at the village. From here, he could see tomorrow's work.

They hadn't cleared away the dead animals. Goats, dogs, and birds lay in the dirt beside the huts, the relentless insects and vultures tearing at their carcasses. Tomorrow, he and the others would don the bio-suits and perform the gruesome task of collecting tissue samples. Maybe they'd find something in the animal fat.

He eyed the cooking pots and bowls scattered around the burned-out campfire. The flies were having a feast on the spilled contents, as were the wild dogs that slinked between the huts, snatching the decayed food in their teeth before bolting into the tall grass. Yellow tape meant nothing to those starved creatures. Another day, and they'd start on the carcasses.

He rested his hand against a dead tree and stared at the morbid scene. Something was eating at him. Something very deep. Something missing, like an unfinished painting.

"What are you doing?"

Karl spun around and saw Jim Powell staring at him, his unbuttoned khaki shirt hanging limp over his trousers.

"Well?"

"I'm taking a break."

Powell's face twisted in a scowl. "Sorry, buddy. No time for that. Tom's sweating bullets. We have visitors in the morning. We work all night if we have to."

Karl flicked a bead of sweat off his forehead. "I'll get back to Nihalla."

"Hold it." Powell stroked his chin. "Since you're so interested in those dead animals, put on your suit and start taking samples."

"Now?"

"Better than working in the dark with those dogs hanging around. One of them might take a bite out of you. Lord knows what they're carrying." Powell nodded approvingly. "Yeah, you take care of the carcasses and I'll take care of Nihalla." He brushed past Karl and headed down the hill toward the van.

.   .   .

It was cooler now. Below ninety degrees. The haze had dissipated and the night sky flickered with stars. A light breeze had picked up from the southeast, flaring a few lazy embers into the darkness above their campfire.

Powell leaned toward the fire and rubbed his tired eyes. "Where the hell are we?"

"Up a creek without a paddle."

Powell glared at the attractive brunette sitting across from him, her tanned face glistening in the fire light.

Susan Cayman shrugged. "What do you want me to tell them?"

"The truth, dammit. We're on the verge of a breakthrough. Another couple days should do it."

"Sure you want to say that?"

Powell's face flushed. He snatched his spiked coffee and chugged it down. "No reason to alarm anyone. We just need more time."

"Tom agrees?"

Powell gave her a second dirty look. "Don't worry about Tom. He'll listen to me."

She nodded and sipped her coffee.

Powell dragged a silver flask out of his shirt pocket and took a swig. He wiped his mouth with the back of his hand and glanced at the stern-faced man seated on his left. "Shot?" He held out the flask.

7

Karl ignored him and stared at the fire, his arms wrapped around his knees. His mind was on the dead animals. He couldn't forget the look of terror in their bulging eyes when he knelt beside them. Just like the villagers.

Powell took another swig and leaned toward him. "You okay?"

"Yeah."

"Better take some dex. It'll be a long night."

Karl nodded and looked toward the village. "How's Nihalla?"

"Out on his feet in the van. Keeps going over the same damn slides."

"Sure he's okay?"

Powell stabbed the coals. "What do you care?"

Karl flinched. Things were getting a little tense on the Shabeelle. It had been building since the two men met in Atlanta four days ago. He started to speak, but Susan cut him off.

"I'll talk to Nihalla." She stood up and brushed off her khaki pants. "The poor guy knew those people in the bags. Probably brought them into this screwed-up world. It's gotta be rippin' him."

"Leave him alone."

"What?"

Powell swiped the coals. "We all have our little ghosts. No time to play nun out here."

"But—"

"Forget it. We have bigger problems." Powell waited for her to sit down before resuming his ritual with the coals. "Tom told me he picked up a broadcast from Mombassa. Sounds like it broke out down there."

"Mombassa?" Karl's head snapped up.

"That's what I said."

Karl snatched the flask and took a swig.

"Hey, I said a shot." Powell reached for the flask but Karl yanked it away. He took another swig and flipped the silver flask at Powell, nearly striking him in the face.

"Hey, watch it!"

Karl stood up and peered into the darkness. "How did it get down there so fast? That's five hundred miles?" He looked at Powell with stunned eyes. "The damn thing's airborne."

"Screw that. You just chugged half my scotch."

Karl wasn't listening. He stepped away from the fire, his eyes focused on the village. "God, if it's airborne—"

Powell jumped up and seized his arm. "Forget the damn bug. What about my scotch?"

"Take it easy, I'll pay you when we get back."

Powell's face twisted in a sneer. The booze had done its job. "You expect me to fall for that? I want my money now!"

Karl tried to pull his arm free, but Powell's grip was like iron. The last two days had taken a hard toll on the young pathologist.

"Now!" Powell jabbed his nose into Karl's face.

Karl noticed Susan backing away from the campfire. The commotion had awakened Crumley who was gawking at them from his tent. The man clutching his arm was on the brink of losing it. If things went any further, it could finish them both.

Karl yanked his arm away. "Snap out of it. You're acting like a kid."

"Damn you!" Powell lunged at Karl and threw a right cross, but his fist only caught air. He gasped from a sharp pain in his gut as Karl's right fist slammed into his solar plexus, dropping him like a rock.

Karl looked down at the young man doubled up at his feet. He lowered his fists and took a calming breath. "You okay?"

"Go to hell."

Karl reached down to help him, but Powell swiped his hand away. Karl crouched beside him and lowered his voice. "Come on, man. I know it's rough. None of us expected this.

We need to stick together. I'll get your booze. Just take it easy."

Powell glared at him. "How the hell did we end up with you? With all the good ones out there, how in God's name did we draw you!"

"You think I wanted this? I go where I'm told."

Powell took a painful breath and stood up, his hand clutching his stomach. "You talk like you're one of us. Think we don't know what happened at FDA? Think we're stupid? You're poison, Frankton. Poison!"

Karl clenched his fists. "There's a lot you don't know. Just let it go."

Powell picked up his flask and stuffed it in his shirt. "I know this. If you're not outta here tomorrow, I'm going to Tom with it. It's you or me, dammit. You or me!" He brushed past Karl and headed for his tent.

Karl scooped a handful of dirt and stared at the deserted fire. Through the darkness, he heard Susan's strained voice coming from Tom Buckley's tent. The dust hadn't settled and the ambitious bitch was already blowing the whistle.

He flung the dirt at the ground. Nice going, jerk. Picking a fight with a kid on the verge of a breakdown. The poor guy probably came from a wealthy New England family. A silver-spooned med school grad with guarantees of fame and fortune. Probably thought he knew it all after those dry runs in the Level 4 Lab.

He'd watched Powell perform the first three biopsies. Why in God's name did Buckley start him with a family? First the father. Nothing to it. Swab the skin with alcohol, point the scalpel away from your bio-suit, and make an incision in the abdomen. Forget the blood. He's dead, remember? Peel back the skin flaps until you find the liver. Shove in the biopsy needle, give it a good twist, and yank it out. Drop the sample in the plastic vial and you're done. Now for mommy and baby daughter. God...

He stood up and brushed off his khaki pants. Best to let the poor fool sleep it off. Nothing like a little sleep to ease the pain. He glanced at his watch. Better take that dex. And pin ten bucks to Powell's tent flap. Anything to keep the peace. He started toward Powell's tent and heard a shuffling in the darkness. Tom Buckley's stern face burst into the firelight. Buckley was a tall, gaunt man with charcoal hair and deep-set, black eyes that had a way of making you listen. He stopped and trained his black eyes on Karl. "Well?"

"No problem. Just blowing off steam."

"Susan tells me you started it."

"Me? That little b—" Karl caught himself and lowered his voice. "Jim's a good kid, but he's in over his head. He's going to snap. You better pull him out before he kills himself, and us too."

Buckley's black eyes burned into him. "You have a lot of nerve. Too much for your own good."

The two men stared at each other, their faces flickering in the firelight. The only sound was the crackling flames.

Buckley looked down at the folded paper in his hand. "I received this a few minutes ago from Atlanta." He handed the paper to Karl. "They want one of us back there."

Karl unfolded the e-mail printout and focused on the sender's name. Hampsted? He'd not seen that name before.

"Get your things together. A plane's leaving from Mogadishu at ten hundred hours. I'll have a jeep pick you up at seven."

Karl looked at him in disbelief. "Me?"

"You."

"Just like that?"

Buckley nodded.

"Are you nuts? You don't want to pull me out now. Not when we're so close."

Buckley snatched the e-mail out of Karl's hand and stuffed it in his shirt pocket. "Sorry, I have to think of the team." He looked down and forced out the words. "You're a troublemaker, Karl. We don't want you here. There's too much at stake. Besides, you're contracted. An outsider. We'll replace you with one of our own." He started to turn away and hesitated. "Better get some sleep. And keep away from the others. You're on pretty thin ice." He disappeared into the darkness.

Karl felt a tightness in his gut. He looked down at the fading campfire. Were they crazy? All he needed was another day. He'd find the answer in another day. For God's sake, just one more day!

He recalled his attorney's warning at the FDA hearing two years ago. His scientific curiosity had cost some powerful people a lot of money. They wouldn't rest until Karl Frankton was a name on a tombstone.

.   .   .

He took a shower in the portable facility behind the tents. The cool spray felt like nirvana splashing off his face and chest. He was just getting into it when the timer shut off the water. He cursed the timer and stepped into the darkness, a towel wrapped around his naked waist.

It was past midnight and the temperature had dropped into the seventies. The breeze had died down and everything was still except the faint gurgle of the river. A full moon bathed the village in shadowed light.

He was about to duck into his tent when he spotted Nihalla leaning against the olive-drab van, his arms hanging limp, the moon lighting his exhausted face. A discarded surgical cap dangled from the Somali's left hand. He was staring at the village.

Karl's eyes filled with tears. He wanted to go down there and put an arm around him. Maybe offer a kind word or two. Then it hit him. *The tea, idiot. You forgot his tea!* He shook his head and slipped through the tent flap.

His watch read 12:20. It would only take a few minutes to pack his gear. He laid out his last clean pair of khakis and a worn, blue denim shirt. A quick stroke of his stubbled chin told him he should shave, but he was too tired. No problem. Better to step off the plane with that rugged, weary look. It might make a difference when Buckley filed his report.

He'd nearly finished packing when he spotted the brown-leather toiletry kit protruding from his disheveled clothes. He unzipped the kit and lifted out a small, pewter-framed photograph of a blond-haired woman. She wore a black graduation cap and gown, the cap tilted slightly back, its black tassel brushing her right shoulder. She was standing in front of a black, wrought iron gate.

He collapsed on the cot and studied the sunlit face. The only sound was the gentle hum of the HEPA air sensors going about their sampling outside his tent. It reminded him of the cool breeze rustling through the trees on that beautiful spring day, so long ago.

His hand groped for the flask in his kit. He popped the cap and took a burning gulp. Then another. He switched off the electric lantern and fell back on the cot.

The tears were coming freely now, along with memories of a better time and place. He forced back a sob and guzzled the scotch.

The ghosts were strong tonight. Like those dead faces in the village. Staring at him. Crying out to him. And that smell of bleach and rancid flesh. And that stifling, sunlit haze. He pressed the picture against his heart and stared at the spinning darkness. The flask slipped out of his hand. He was going back to a better time and place...

Chapter 2

Columbia University

He braced against the stiff breeze and focused the camera on the Chrysler Building's stainless steel crown. "Always wanted to do this." He smiled and pressed the shutter button.

"Satisfied?"

"Yup."

Anne leaned against him and stared at the wall of sunlit skyscrapers. They were standing on a bluff overlooking Morningside Park and the Manhattan skyline. The sun beamed down on them from a crystal-blue sky. The cool, spring breeze carried the scent of fresh wildflowers. It was a perfect day. A day like none other.

Anne looked down at the blue-ribboned diploma in her hand. "Guess you're next."

He stiffened and looked away.

"What's wrong?" She grasped his cheek and gently turned his face toward her. His eyes were filled with tears. "Karl?"

"You made it, dammit. The whole nine yards."

"Oh, honey." She reached up and kissed him softly on the cheek. "We'll be okay. I'll do some part-time work at Roosevelt. Maybe—"

He touched a finger to her lips. "Just get that practice started. I'll figure something out."

She brushed his finger away. "You think I'll let you down now? After all you've done? The nerve." She wiped away a tear and kissed him on the lips with a wife's love. They clung to each other and listened to the wind rustle through the trees.

He eased away from her and looked down at the camera. "Come on, Doc. We still have two shots."

"The cap and gown, remember? They're due at one."

He stepped back and eyed her attire. "You're keeping the cap, right?"

She dragged off the flat, square mortarboard and stared at it while her blond hair ruffled in the breeze. "Never thought about it. They charge a lot for these things. Maybe just the tassel."

"Tassel? After seven years in hell? No way. Gotta keep the cap. Tradition and all that. Right, old chum?" He glanced at the nine-year-old shuffling toward them from the trees.

Jeremy tugged at his starched collar and gave his neck an angry twist. "I don't care about all this kissy stuff. Let's go to Gram's so I can get out of this suit. It's killing me." He leaned against his dad and looked up at him with pleading eyes.

Karl rested a hand on his son's shoulder. His wife's warm body pressed against him. He looked at the skyline and felt the breeze on his face, and for a moment, he was a king.

"Honey?"

"Yeah?"

"We should get going."

He nodded and kissed her softly on the forehead. "Anything you say, Doc."

They headed up 116th toward Amsterdam Avenue, passing Columbia's stately President's House and Greene Hall. When they reached the university's eastern gate, Karl paused and pulled out his camera.

"What are you doing?" Anne frowned while glancing nervously at her watch.

"Just one."

"Come on, honey. The reception's in an hour. I need to get into something decent."

"Only take a minute. We'll use the gate for a backdrop." He nodded at the opened wrought iron gate.

"Dammit, Karl." She was about to explode when she noticed Jeremy gawking at her. She let out a frustrated sigh and stormed through the entrance, her black gown flapping in the breeze.

"Come on, Dad. Take the picture already."

Karl smiled at his impatient son and shooed him through the entrance. The young man sauntered up the brick path behind his mom, his blond hair glistening in the sunlight, his right finger tugging at the starched collar.

God help the ladies. Ol' Jeremy had his dad's sharp features, blue eyes, and blond hair. He'd probably end up a surfer in Hawaii. Certainly not the physician type. Oh well, can't expect too much from Frankton genes. Karl smiled to himself and followed his son through the opened gate.

It only took a minute to line up the shot. He had Anne position the tassel so it brushed her right shoulder. The perfect graduation pose. He stepped back on College Walk's brick path and hesitated.

Hmmm, that view behind him looked pretty good too. The green quadrangle with Butler Library and Low Memorial to either side. Maybe take one on the steps of Low Memorial with those pillars stretching to the rotunda and French's statue of *Alma Mater* floating above her shoulder. Real profound.

"So help me, Karl!"

Oops. Don't want her mad this weekend. Got a lot of lovin' to make up for. Jeremy stays with Gram, and Mom goes to Cape Cod with dear ol' Dad. He smiled and lifted the camera. "All set. Just look up so we don't get any shadows on that beautiful face."

"That's it!"

"I love you." He centered her face in the eyepiece. "Once in a lifetime. You'll thank me someday."

She looked at him with pleading eyes. "For God's sake, honey. It's fifty blocks to the party. I still have to change and get fresh."

16

"We'll be fine. Lots of time. Think of the little gift I have for you this weekend. At-a-girl. Nice, sexy smile. Steady..."

He squeezed the shutter and listened for the click that never came. The picture froze in the eyepiece as if trapped in time. Anne's face glistened in the sunlight, and faded away...

.   .   .

"Frankton, you okay?"

Karl squinted at the blurred face peering down at him. He sat up on his elbows, trying to clear his throbbing head.

Buckley was standing beside the cot. He wore a white bio-suit with the helmet cradled in his arm. His face was twisted in a scowl. He held up the empty flask. "You know what this means?"

Karl blinked at the flask. "I'm not on duty. I'm relieved, remember?"

"You're drunk in the field! It goes on your report." Buckley threw the flask on the cot. "Get your gear together. The jeep leaves in ten minutes." He yanked back the tent flap and ducked through the opening.

Karl sat up on the cot and buried his face in his hands. Buckley's stinging words rang in his ears. Drunk on duty. The kiss of death, given his record of insubordination and recklessness. Or was it? Want to make a wager, Mr. Buckley? Bet the boys in Atlanta look the other way. Mustn't get the attorneys involved. Might cause a media flap. Most unwise, don't you think?

He spotted the photograph lying beside his foot. He reached down and picked it up while recalling the magic day three years ago when a proud husband celebrated his wife's triumph. With only a year remaining to his own graduation from Columbia's prestigious medical school, he would soon follow her down the road to fame and fortune.

Dr. Karl Frankton. It sounded so good. Not bad for a poor kid from York, PA. A real old-fashioned American dream. Only one problem. Three years ago, the dream became a nightmare because of a flashing computer screen and something called M-13. He jammed the photograph in his duffel bag and pushed off the cot.

The tents were bathed in sunlight and the humid air smelled from decay. Only seven a.m. and it was already ninety degrees. A quick check of the equipment locker revealed the bio-suits had been removed from their sterilized containers along with his own suit, a clear message his time was up in Somalia. He walked through the dead trees and looked down at the village.

There they were, prowling through the carnage in their white bio-suits, rakes in hand, their sample-collection boxes dangling from their waists. If he didn't know better, he might be looking at a 1970's TV shot of Apollo astronauts probing the moon's dead surface.

Buckley led the way, his rake clawing the dirt around the cooking pots. Can't blame him for being so stressed out. With the heavies flying in, it was important to stay busy, especially when no one had a clue. If the media discovered the outbreak before CDC isolated the invisible killer, the result would be chaos, and that would mean heads, starting with Mr. Buckley's.

Karl backed away from the slope. No sense waiting for an affectionate wave. They knew he was up here, but no one would look his way. Good riddance and all that. He hesitated and looked toward the pavilion.

What about them, Mr. Frankton? Eighty-four souls struck down in mid-stride, their breath snatched away by an invisible hand. So brutal. So frightening.

He recalled the numbered slides. Maybe Nihalla would find the answer. God, let him nail the damn bug before he killed himself with remorse. And someone please make him a cup of chamomile tea.

His eyes lit up. The tea! There was still time. Only take a couple minutes to boil the water. Hell, he'd brew it himself. A compassionate way to say goodbye to the only one he respected. A little late but—

"Mr. Frankton?"

Karl turned and saw Crumley staring at him with tired brown eyes. He wore a bio-suit with the helmet cradled in his arm.

Crumley nodded toward a jeep parked in the grass beyond the tents. "Gotta get going, Mr. Frankton. Those guys are kinda edgy."

Karl squinted at the two Somali soldiers staring at him from the jeep, their green camouflaged fatigues bathed in sunlight. "Which clan are they?"

Crumley shrugged. "Don't know. They're supposed to be government sanctioned."

"Government? That's a laugh."

Crumley extended his ungloved hand. "Good luck, Mr. Frankton. Wish I could go with you."

"Yeah...take care, Terwood." Karl shook Crumley's hand and started to pick up his duffel bag.

"Mr. Frankton?" Crumley held out a white envelope. "Maybe you can do me a favor? In case anything...well, you know what I mean."

Karl took the envelope and stuffed it in his pocket. "You'll be okay. Just use plenty of tape around those sleeves and ankles. And watch that rusted iron on the pavilion roof. It's sharp as hell."

Crumley nodded and glanced toward the jeep.

Karl forced a smile and patted his pocket. "I'll give this back to you in Atlanta." He snatched the duffel bag and walked toward the two Somalis and their CIA-issue jeep.

The jeep ride was the last thing Karl needed. The cursing soldiers had to pull over twice while their passenger staggered to the side of the road and heaved his cookies in the dried grass. The hard part was sitting in the open with all that high straw surrounding them, the perfect setting for an ambush. They were crossing *Hawiye* country and the clan was well-stocked with light arms and automatic weapons. Maybe even a "hand-held" or two.

Things got tense when Karl let fly the second time. The two Somalis backed away from their moaning passenger in horror. Had the young medic caught the dreaded disease that wiped out the village? Rumors of new outbreaks were rampant, even trickling in from Ethiopia and Kenya, and here they were escorting an infected American bureaucrat who had no business in their land, a useless intruder who might be more dangerous than any sniper. Better to shoot him and let the hungry dogs do the rest. One of them had his finger on the trigger when Karl crawled into the jeep and blurted out, "I'll be okay now."

A couple aspirins and Karl was almost feeling human when their jeep reached Mogadishu's bullet-riddled airport. He wouldn't forget the battered yellow and white buildings lining the roads through the town. The looted warehouses and stores. The young men on the rooftops, AK-47's dangling from their hands, their pockets stuffed with enough narcotics to dope them for a kill. And the faces of those starved, pathetic creatures huddled in the alleys and shadows, an army of refugees flooding the Somali capital in search of food, water, and shelter. The perfect breeding ground for the next HIV, Ebola, or Marburg virus.

The jeep skidded to a halt on the tarmac, a hundred feet from an ancient C-47 *Dakota* parked in the blazing sun.

"You're Frankton?"

Karl eyed the fatigue-clothed man staring at him from the opened cargo door. He nodded and swung the duffel bag over his shoulder.

"Gotta hurry, Mr. Frankton. We've got rumors of stingers in the area."

Great, nothing like getting blown away by some drugged kid with a hand-held. What the hell happened to spears? Karl climbed the ramp and felt a blast of hot wind as the engines came to life.

They hop scotched to Tel Aviv where Karl transferred to a C-5A. After a queasy ride through a line of storms, the massive jet touched down in Lisbon to pick up a special forces unit. From there, the huge transport headed over the Atlantic for the seven hour leg to Atlanta.

Karl tried to sleep, but his mind kept racing through the past forty-eight hours. He popped a sleeping tablet, but the platoon of green berets wouldn't shut up. Probably coming home from a rapid deployment exercise. Enough field equipment to launch an invasion.

He felt a little edgy sitting in the cavernous military transport with a unit of special forces personnel and their high-tech APC's. At one point, he struck up a conversation with one of the stern-faced grunts, but had to back off when the young warrior started questioning him about his assignment in Africa.

Since med school, Karl had gotten into the habit of keeping a journal. He spent the final hour going over his scribbled entries, particularly the ones he'd jotted down in the mobile lab.

In two years of face-to-face confrontations with Ebola, Marburg, Lassa, Hanta, Malaria, SARS, Alpha-Omega E, and a dozen other killers, he'd never seen anything so lethal, yet virtually nonexistent. Every test had proven futile. ELISA enzyme reactions—negative. HEPA air detection—negative, yet the virus appeared airborne. Blood, stool, urine, sputum, cerebrospinal fluids—negative. Organic samples—nothing. Protein analysis—zero. Impossible, dammit. There had to be something. Some trace of the virus. He closed the journal and jammed it in his duffel bag.

They touched down at Atlanta's Hartsfield International Airport at 6:15 a.m. Karl had reset his watch so many times, he was afraid the screw would come loose. In three years, he'd replaced the screw mechanism three times. Cheaper to throw the damn thing away, but Anne had given him the watch on his twenty-eighth birthday. Remember that day, old buddy?

Just a week before she graduated from Columbia. He twirled the screw and pushed it until it clicked.

The huge plane taxied to a secured terminal at the far end of the tarmac. When it rolled to a stop, an officer in a blue jumpsuit stepped to a console at the front of the cargo compartment. He pulled back a red lever and watched the nose ramp drop away. "This is where you get off, Mr. Frankton." He smiled at Karl and nodded toward the sunlit opening.

Karl stood up and swung the duffel bag over his shoulder. He exchanged well-wishes with the grunts and shuffled toward the officer. It had taken twenty-eight hours to cover the nine thousand miles to his destination.

"Watch yourself going down, Mr. Frankton. One of the mechanics will guide you clear of the plane. Good luck." The officer patted Karl's shoulder and watched him step down the ramp.

Karl barely cleared the plane when he heard a voice call out, "Mr. Frankton?" He stopped on the tarmac and squinted at the sunlit face staring at him from the opened window of a black sedan.

"You're Frankton?"

Karl nodded.

"Change in plans, Mr. Frankton. Hop in."

"You're?"

"Parker Hampsted, your new case leader."

Karl recognized the name from Buckley's e-mail. He stepped toward the car while eyeing the man's gaunt face and neatly-groomed charcoal hair. With those steel-blue eyes, Hampsted looked more like an FBI agent than someone from CDC. Karl forced a smile and asked the obvious question. "What's going on?"

"I'll explain on the plane."

"Plane?"

22

"We're headed for Seattle, Mr. Frankton." Hampsted watched Karl's stunned reaction. "Sorry, you're the only one available with the necessary qualifications."

Karl felt his shoulders drop. Twenty-eight hours for this? He opened the rear door and flung his duffel bag on the seat. "I need to take a pee."

"You can do that on the plane." Hampsted gave him the evil eye. "You clean?"

Karl shrugged. "They tested me on each leg. Nothing detected." He felt a rush of adrenalin. Nothing detected? What a laugh.

"Get in." Hampsted watched his passenger climb into the back seat. He nodded to his driver, a blue-suited man with black hair and sunglasses.

They drove across the tarmac to the charter terminal and pulled up beside a twin-engined *Gulfstream*. Hampsted slid out of the car and snatched a black attaché case off the front seat. He straightened his gray suit and gestured toward a ramp leading into the plane. "Never mind the duffel bag. We'll stash it in cargo." Hampsted climbed the ramp, followed by his stunned subordinate.

The small passenger compartment was deserted. Beams of sunlight lit up three rows of brown leather seats, one to each side of the blue-carpeted aisle. The compartment smelled from air-freshener. Not bad after two days in Somalia and nine thousand miles in a *Dakota* and C-5A.

Hampsted dropped into the first seat and gestured for Karl to sit across from him. As Karl sat down, a blue-uniformed pilot stepped out of the cockpit and pulled the exit door closed. The pilot flashed a smile and retreated into the cockpit.

Karl stared at the closed cockpit door. "So, what's up?"

Hampsted placed the black attaché case on his lap and frowned. "Get some rest, Mr. Frankton."

Karl's ears popped from a sudden rush of cabin pressure. The compartment vibrated from the throttled engines. He rested his head against the soft cushion and looked up at the white-plastic ceiling. The last thing he remembered was the plane taking off…

Chapter 3

Willapa Bay

He squeezed more suntan lotion on his palm and nudged the beautiful woman lying beside him. "How about the front?"

"Huh?"

"The front?"

Anne rolled on her back and smiled under her amber sunglasses. "You already did me there, remember?"

"Just a little more. Don't want you to get burned."

Her smile broadened. "You're going to get us kicked off this beach."

He leaned closer and rested his oiled palm on her bare stomach. "How about here?" His hand slid lower.

"Watch it, big guy. You're supposed to be studying."

"I am studying."

"I mean books."

He kissed her softly on the neck. "God, you smell good."

"Get some rest, Casanova. You'll need it when we're back in the room." She rolled on her stomach and rested her head on her arms. She hadn't worn a bikini in years and it was driving him mad. What a pair of legs. And the rest of her. Still warm and firm like the first night they made love. Hard to believe that was ten years ago.

He smiled and scanned the oiled bodies strewn across the sand. It was early June and the Cape was jammed with vacationers. Still a little cool, but quite comfortable after a hard Northeast winter. He squinted at the bright haze. The clouds were thickening. It would rain soon. No problem. The perfect excuse for staying in bed.

He could see the Harborside Inn through the corner of his eye, its majestic tinted windows overlooking Martha's Vineyard and Nantucket Sound. The air smelled sweet from roses and daffodils. Multicolored pennants streamed from the hotel's symbolic masthead. The perfect graduation gift for the woman he loved.

He closed his eyes and listened to the water lap at the shore. The mini-vacation had cost him eight hundred bills, but it was worth it. Epicurus was right. Live for the moment. The hell with tomorrow.

He felt a chill. Who was he kidding? Forget Epicurus, they were in big trouble. Tomorrow wasn't the problem. It would only be Sunday. Another day in paradise. It was the next day that scared him, and the day after when they were back at Columbia's Bard Haven Towers with a tuition bill the size of a house stuck in their mailbox.

He sat up on his elbows and gazed at the sound. He was flat broke with a jobless wife and growing son. Forget the dreams of grandeur, old chum. You just dropped to Maslow's Level One. You know—primal instinct—fear and survival.

He glanced at Anne. It would take her a year to get a practice started. She could always apply for interim work at one of the local hospitals, but the waiting lists were long and openings weren't plentiful for recent grads.

If they were alone it would be different, but they had to think of Jeremy. The poor guy didn't have a decent set of clothes. Even the suit he wore at his mother's graduation was borrowed, and school was only three months away. Nothing worse than being taunted by a bunch of spoiled kids. Karl knew that terrible feeling from his own impoverished childhood in York. He'd vowed that would never happen again. Now his son was going to live it.

He scooped a handful of sand and felt it pour through his fingers. Maybe they should ship Jeremy off to Gram's until things improved. They got along fine, and Jeremy would be safe there. He frowned and listened to a rumble of thunder.

Forget it, pal. Jeremy was already spending too much time at Gram's, and Anne's mom didn't have the money or stamina to handle him much longer.

They could try his sister in York, but she wasn't too keen on Anne or Jeremy, not to mention her own brother. Never forgave him for leaving the farm to pursue his fantasy of becoming a big-shot doctor. Blew up at him for being a dreamer. For not wanting to be like the other poor bumpkins in that boring town. Besides, he and Jeremy were too close to be separated. The guilt would tear him up.

The breeze was stiffening. A drop of rain struck his cheek. The approaching gray clouds flickered with lightning. He sat up and stared at the incoming storm.

Time to face the music, old buddy. You shouldn't have spent that last eight hundred bills on this little vacation. Talk about denial. You could have bought your family another few weeks while you tried to figure something out. Now you're in deep guano, and so are they. Nice going, jerk.

And how about the biggest laugh. Your tuition's due. Forget the student loan. You're so far in arrears, they'll probably drag you into court. Think about it, chum. You're a year away from graduation at one of the nation's finest medical schools and you're living on food stamps and a prayer, and the prayer just went south cause you got laid off from St. Luke's. He dug his fingers into the sand and recalled his supervisor's cold words…

Sorry, Karl. Damn budget cuts. Please don't take it personally. There's nothing I can do. I feel real bad because of your family situation. I tried to talk them out of it.

Hell, you're a good paramedic. Maybe you can come back when things improve. I'm sure you'll find something. Only another year to graduation. In a few years, you'll be rich and all this will be a fading memory.

"Damn!" He squeezed the sand through his fingers and felt the raindrops on his face. A bolt of lightning flashed over

Chappaquiddick. He clenched his fist and watched the sunbathers scramble for shelter.

"We better go." Anne had pulled off her sunglasses and was staring at him with concerned eyes.

"Yeah, we should talk." He stood up and looked down at the stack of books on the blanket. The rain was spattering off the leather bound covers. Watch that rain, idiot. Last thing you need is Columbia's medical library on your case.

He reached for the books and noticed a white envelope protruding from the stack. He remembered yanking it out of the mailbox when they left for the Cape. Nothing new. In the past two months, he'd gotten used to the "overdue" notices stuffed in their mailbox. He'd saved this one for a bookmark.

He started to lift the books and hesitated, his eyes staring at the envelope's return address.

"Come on, honey. I'm getting soaked."

He ignored her and ripped open the water-stained envelope. His trembling hand unfolded the crisp, one page letter.

"What's wrong?"

He stared at the letter while a bolt of lightning flashed across the sky, followed by a deafening clap of thunder.

"Dammit, Karl, we're going to get fried!" She tugged on his arm, but he didn't respond. "Honey?" She felt for a pulse, her eyes trained on his stunned face.

He heard her crying out to him, but he couldn't move. His eyes were fixed on the letter...

June 1, 2010

Mr. Frankton:

> We are impressed with your excellent scholastic record at Columbia-Presbyterian Cancer Center. Please consider this a formal offer to join our FDA research team in Bethesda, Maryland for three months of intensive work at our CDER research lab

(June 14 through September 10). While our salary offering is limited due to government restrictions, we can provide all living expenses during your residence. You will also be entitled to full tuition reimbursement at Columbia while you remain in our internship program.

We look forward to your joining us at FDA, both short and long-term.

Sincerely,

Zoltan Mermer
Director of Drug Evaluation and Review
Food and Drug Administration
United States of America

"God."
"Karl?"
The letter blurred and faded away...

. . .

Karl blinked at the sunlight flashing through the Plexiglas window. Beyond the wing, Mt. Rainier's snow-capped peak jutted through the haze. He stretched his stiff back and glanced at his watch. It was 8:40 a.m., Pacific Coast Time. They'd been airborne five hours and he'd slept every minute of them. He rested his head against the seat and rubbed the sleep out of his eyes.

The beach was gone and so was Anne, but he could still see the boldface type on that fateful letter. So many hopes and dreams were rekindled when he unfolded that white piece of paper three years ago. It was more than a financial blessing. A summer in FDA's Drug Evaluation and Review Program would give him the break he needed to reach the goal that had driven him since he first gazed into a microscope's eyepiece, a simple glance at a flagellating protozoa in a high school biology class. Until that moment, Karl Frankton's young life was aimless—purposeless.

Without that look into the eyepiece, he would have spent his useless existence earning a meager paycheck at a local food store, then blowing it in York's pool halls and bars chasing sweet young things while getting blind, staggering drunk.

Oh yeah, mustn't forget the inevitable back seat impregnation scene with some hot-blooded country gal. Followed of course by the ill-advised marriage, kids, money problems, drunken arguments, and backbreaking divorce.

But it didn't happen that way. Maybe it was the sun shining on the microscope through the high school lab's blinds. Or the unexpected rush of anticipation when he squeezed the medicine dropper and watched the bead of clouded water plop onto the glass slide. Maybe the sharpened image when he turned the focus knob and trained his blue eyes on the twisting, vibrating creature in the lens.

There was another world in that lens, an incredible, unseen world that would humble any astronomer. Why search for alien life on a far-off planet when it was at your fingertips in a simple drop of pond water?

This would be his dream, his passion. He would dedicate his life to exploring the churning, alien world inside that lens. It would be his world, a mysterious new world. And finally, after four years of college and six years at Columbia's prestigious medical school, a young man's fantasy was about to come true with a little help from the ol' FDA.

His face twisted in a frown. If he'd only ignored M-13...

"Awake?"

Karl glanced at the man seated across the aisle.

"Better lift that seatback. We're almost down."

Karl nodded and forced a smile. He barely knew Hampsted, but he already disliked him. He pressed the seat button and looked at Seattle's Space Needle and skyline.

Hampsted closed his attaché case and rested it on his lap. He leaned toward Karl and spoke in a subdued tone. "Good you got some rest. I'm not sure when you'll sleep again." "What's going on?" "You'll know soon enough." Hampsted leaned back in his seat and flinched as the plane rattled from the touchdown at Sea-Tac's international airport.

The *Gulfstream* taxied off the runway and rolled to a stop two hundred feet from the charter hangars. After shutting down the engines, the pilot stepped through the cockpit door, the same forced smile on his face. He grasped the exit door's handle and gave it a yank. The compartment flooded with sunlight as he pushed the door open and dropped the exit ramp into place.

Hampsted stood up and clutched his attaché case. He stretched his back and nodded at the opened door. "Ready?"

Karl pushed out of his seat and followed Hampsted through the exit door. When he stepped on the ramp, he noticed a brown-suited man with sandy hair staring at them from the security fence. The man flipped off his sunglasses and walked toward them, his green eyes trained on Hampsted.

"Mr. Hampsted?" The agent flashed his CDC card.

Hampsted raised his ID card and stared at the stern, young face. "Where's the chopper?"

"Coming in, sir." The agent glanced to his left where an olive-drab, Bell *Turbocopter* was descending on the tarmac, its blades flickering in the morning sun.

Hampsted glanced at Karl and gestured toward the chopper.

"We're taking that?"

Hampsted nodded and headed for the chopper. When Karl tried to follow him, the agent seized his arm.

"Your card, sir?" The agent's green eyes burned into him.

Karl reached into his shirt pocket and fumbled for his photo-ID card. He held it up and frowned at the agent.

"Thank you, Mr. Frankton." The agent released his grip and gestured toward the chopper.

"What about my bag?"

"We'll take care of it, Mr. Frankton. Please hurry."

Karl shook his head and followed his two favorite people toward the waiting chopper.

A quick hop up the chopper's foot ladder and Karl was strapping in beside Hampsted. The agent had taken the passenger seat in front of them, alongside the black-helmeted pilot.

Hampsted placed his attaché case on the floor and leaned toward the pilot. "How long will it take?"

"About thirty minutes, sir. We're cleared for takeoff."

Hampsted nodded and dropped back in his seat as the pilot squeezed the throttle, lifting the chopper into the haze above the tarmac. At a thousand feet, the pilot pressed the control stick to the left and trained his black visor on the tilted ground below his side window.

Karl stared at the swaying horizon while trying to control his churning gut. After thirty-three hours in the air, his stomach was in no mood for aerobatics. He gripped the armrests and prayed he wouldn't barf on his new supervisor.

The chopper veered to the left until the compass atop the console read 225 degrees. With the sun behind them, the pilot leveled off and pressed the control stick forward, dropping the helicopter's nose into an aggressive attitude. A powerful force pressed them back in their seats as the chopper accelerated to 175 mph. They were headed southwest toward the Pacific Ocean, ninety miles away.

Karl unlocked his white-knuckled hands from the armrests and looked at Mt. Rainier. "Where are we going?"

"Enough questions, Mr. Frankton." Hampsted leaned forward and tapped the agent's shoulder. "Everyone in place?"

"Yes, sir. Since fifteen hundred yesterday."

"Equipment?"

"Everything they requested."

Hampsted nodded and eased back in his seat.

The chopper cleared the city's haze and darted over the islets dotting Puget Sound. The cockpit flickered from the sunlight reflecting off the water. Quite a change from parched savannah grass and dead trees.

Twenty minutes out, they got an impressive view of Olympia, the state capital. Beyond it, Karl spotted Saint Helen's enormous cirque sitting atop the haze. The mountain looked so peaceful, yet thirty-three years ago it filled the sky with the biggest explosion of modern time, its pyroclastic cloud blasting a stern warning that man only rents space on this fragile planet.

With Olympia and the mountains fading behind them, Karl could see the Pacific Ocean converging from the west, its blue veneer glistening through the haze. A narrow peninsula lay to the south, its strip forming an elongated inlet that opened to the ocean at the peninsula's northern tip. They were headed straight at it.

Hampsted leaned forward and tapped the pilot's shoulder. "That's it?"

"Yes, sir. Dead ahead. We'll be down in five minutes."

Hampsted peered at the approaching peninsula, his hand fumbling with the handle of his attaché case.

Karl trained his eyes on the windshield and nearly jumped out of his seat when another chopper dropped in front of them, only a hundred feet off their nose. The pilot mumbled something through the mike on his helmet and pressed the stick forward.

They began an aggressive westward descent toward the peninsula's northern tip and were nearly over it when the lead chopper swerved left and darted south along the peninsula's interior shore.

Karl gripped his armrests and hung on while they veered left and followed the black chopper down the peninsula. Through his side window, he could see stretches of cranberry bogs and forests running the length of the peninsula. The rich green landscape was patched with sand dunes and beach towns. The tide was out and the inlet resembled a marsh. Add the pounding surf on the ocean side, and the thirty mile peninsula looked like the perfect vacation retreat.

They were nearing the inlet's southern shore when Karl noticed the lead chopper drop toward a cluster of fishing boats docked at a small pier. An uneasy feeling came over him as he stared at the descending chopper. It reminded him of the landing in Somalia.

The lead chopper faded into the haze. For a moment, Karl's chopper hovered above the haze while the pilot exchanged communications with what sounded like ground personnel. The pilot glanced back at Hampsted. "We're cleared to go in."

"What about suits?"

"No need, we'll be a quarter mile from the tape." The pilot eased the throttle and dropped into the haze.

The pilot's words echoed in Karl's ears. He looked out the window and spotted the lead chopper's blades gleaming through the sunlit haze. A cluster of shacks materialized about a quarter mile beyond the landed chopper.

They touched down beside the first chopper, only fifty feet from the water. As their blades slowed, six armed soldiers advanced toward them from the gravel shore. The soldiers were dressed in camouflage and carried automatic weapons. Their young faces were expressionless beneath their helmets.

Karl stiffened. Three men stood off to the side. They were dressed in white bio-suits with the plastic helmets cradled in their arms.

"Well, now you know."

Karl looked at Hampsted who was staring at him with slate-blue eyes. "You mean—" The words jammed in his throat.

Hampsted frowned and looked at the soldiers. "We're not sure. That's why you're here."

"Me? I don't know anything. We didn't find anything over there."

"You know more than we do, Mr. Frankton."

The brown-suited agent slid open the cockpit door and crawled out, followed by Karl and Hampsted. One of the bio-suited men stepped forward and extended an ungloved hand. "Herb Masters, Mr. Hampsted."

Hampsted nodded and shook his hand. "How's it going?"

Masters frowned. "Nothing yet."

Hampsted glanced at Karl. "This is Mr. Frankton. We brought him in from Mogadishu. Thought he might help."

Masters shook Karl's hand and forced a nervous smile. "Did you find anything over there?"

Karl shook his head.

"Well, come on. I have a tent ready for you. Port-a-shower and changing room are behind the Vickers. Sorry for the rush, but we need to work fast to take advantage of the haze. It's pretty crowded on the peninsula with all the vacationers. Too many wanderers."

Masters patted Karl's shoulder and led him toward a cluster of tents near the shore. They were almost there when Karl heard a roar and saw the twin choppers lift into the haze. Hampsted was seated inside the lead chopper. "Where's he going?"

"He'll be back in the morning."

Karl turned toward Masters who was staring at him with concerned eyes.

"We want to keep this quiet. We've shut off Highway 101 above the Bear River. We're telling everyone the black bears are acting up. It'll give us a few days." Masters waited for his words to sink in. "Better get started. From now on, you report to me."

Karl followed Masters into the cluster of tents. His legs felt like rubber. The nausea had returned. It was coming at him too fast. No time to think.

It only took a minute to unpack his duffel bag. His unwashed clothes stunk from Somalia. He stuffed them in a plastic bag and dropped it outside his tent. Maybe they had laundry service.

He plucked the empty flask out of his kit and stared at it while recalling Buckley's tirade. By now, Buckley's report had reached the bureaucrats in Atlanta. No danger there. The spineless wimps wouldn't do anything until they formed a committee, and that would take weeks. By then, this mess would be over and everything would be conveniently forgotten. He stuffed the flask in his kit and grabbed a folded towel off the cot.

The next fifteen minutes were automatic. A quick walk to the portable shower behind the Vickers where he stripped off his clothes and stuffed them in a plastic bag. Then came the soaking spray of disinfected water. No time to shave off the stubble. Just scrub down and ignore the medicinal smell. No need to remove any jewelry. His watch was in his tent and his wedding ring was long gone. No neck chains, bracelets, or pierced earrings. They were for the Maslow "Level Five" types. The secure, high achievers. Not a washed-up, med school reject.

He stepped into the small enclosure behind the shower and toweled down. A quick rub of alcohol and antibacterial powder, and he was slipping into green scrub pants and a matching top. Forget the underwear. It's *au naturale* in the CDC.

He tugged on the white socks and surgical gloves, then doubled them up with another pair before strapping the socks and pants with duct tape, an outdated precaution that was more a superstition in this modern era of one-piece suits and hermetic seals. His gloved hands trembled when he ripped the tape. A chopper roared overhead and faded into the haze.

The white bio-suit had been positioned on a standup rack for ease of entry. Some ease. He nearly fell over stepping into the legs and attached boots. He stuffed his arms into the suit's insulated sleeves and forced his gloved hands through the openings. The suit's tight elastic sleeves pressed against his gloved wrists, but he would still insist that someone tape the sleeves to the gloves. He grabbed the white-plastic helmet and stepped through the weighted curtain into the daylight. Masters was standing beside the van with his helmet on. A second helmeted agent stepped forward and yanked up the oiled zipper on Karl's suit front. He was about to step back when Karl held out the roll of tape. The grinning agent applied the tape to Karl's extended wrists. At thirty-one, Karl Frankton was a dinosaur.

Karl slipped on his helmet while a third suited-agent stepped behind him and strapped an oxygen pack on his back. The man plugged in the umbilical hose and stepped back while Karl's helmet filled with a welcome rush of oxygen.

"Okay?"

Karl nodded at Masters through his clear plastic visor.

"Karl, this is agent Thurmat." Masters gestured toward the helmeted man on his right.

"I'm Burns." The other helmeted agent gave Karl a mock salute.

Karl returned the salute. "How bad is it?"

Masters glanced at the large watch strapped to the right sleeve of his suit. "We have a half hour before the tanks run out." His brown eyes trained on Karl. "Don't bog down in there. I just want the big picture. Look for any pattern similar to Africa."

Karl forced out the words. "How many?"

"Twenty-three."

"Any surviv—"

"None."

Karl stared at him.

"Ready?" Masters waited for the three men to nod.

They walked toward the fishing shacks and approached a familiar stretch of yellow tape. Masters hesitated and pulled a HEPA detector out of his pack. He nodded at the three men and stepped through a break in the tape flanked with biohazard signs.

In his two years of field work, Karl had stepped between those signs two dozen times, but the feeling of anxiety was never greater than now. His gut churned while he recalled the ominous warning scrawled on the blackboard outside CDC's Level 4 Lab during his orientation two years ago. A simple play on words...

Viruses are planet earth's immune response to the human race...

He clenched his gloved fists. Maybe this would be his last walk through the signs. Maybe this time Karl Frankton wouldn't come out because a mutating killer found its way through the white plastic and rubber. Maybe this would be the way they finally got rid of him.

They walked down a dirt path that snaked between the fishing shacks, taking care not to scrape their boots against the rocks and rusted beer cans. The sun had broken through the haze and patches of blue sky flashed overhead. A thermometer on one of the gray shacks registered sixty-eight degrees. It was high noon on Long Beach Peninsula. They were twelve thousand miles from Somalia.

The path terminated at a weathered boathouse and dock. Three gray fishing boats were moored to the dock, their unattended bells clanging in the breeze. The tide had gone out, making Willapa Bay look more like a thirty-mile-long marsh than a brackish inlet of the Pacific Ocean. The fishing boats were tilted to one side, their curved bottoms resting in the mud beneath the shallow water.

Karl watched Masters flip up a latch and pull open the boathouse's creaking double doors. There were no barking dogs. No shouts of protest from irate villagers. No sounds except the creaking doors and gusting breeze.

Twin rows of silver body bags lay in the shadows, each carrying a tag numbered from "1" to "23". Masters edged beside bag "1" and gestured for Karl to come forward. He waited until Karl was standing beside him before bending down and unzipping the bag.

Karl stared in horror at the gray, fear-stricken face peering up at him. It was a woman's face, her glazed hazel eyes frozen in terror, her froth-covered lips parted in a desperate gasp for breath, her facial muscles taut beneath her skin. He convulsed from a surge of vomit and burst through the opened doors.

"Wait! Don't take that helmet off!" Masters charged after him, but it was too late. Karl flung his helmet on the ground and dropped on his knees. He clutched his wrenching stomach and puked his guts out for the third time in thirty-six hours. When he regained his senses, Masters and the others were staring at him.

"You okay?" Masters edged toward him.

Karl gasped for breath. "Same as Somalia. No trace of anything. Just those bulging eyes." He yanked a HEPA detector out of his pack and swept it through the air. The indicator light remained green.

Masters glared at him. "Put on that helmet and follow procedures. That green light means nothing. You could be dead in seconds."

Karl staggered to his feet and picked up the helmet. He slipped it on and groped for the umbilical, his eyes trained on the boathouse.

Masters stepped forward and re-attached Karl's umbilical. He backed away and peered at him through his plastic visor. "Well?"

"I'm okay."

"Sure?"

Karl took a deep breath and nodded at the opened doors.

"Then come on. We have twenty-two to go." Masters turned toward the opened doors while a chopper roared over their heads.

The next four hours were hell on earth, interrupted by brief escapes to replace their oxygen tanks. Each bag was unzipped while they extracted the required blood and tissue samples. First came the blood, each syringe carefully tagged and placed in dry ice. Then the urine, semen, and vaginal smears. When they got to the liver samples, Karl thanked God there were only two children in the bags, one a boy, the other a girl. He made small incisions and twisted the biopsy needle while saying a prayer for children too much like his own.

The hardest part was turning over the bodies for the spinal and cerebral samples. *Rigor* had begun and some of the bodies seemed to resist when turned over.

When they finally exited the boathouse with the samples, Karl noticed three other bio-suited agents collecting dirt, air, and water samples. They introduced themselves as Wiley, Promot, and Smith. All were exhausted.

Karl was about to follow the others through the signs when he spotted a dead heron lying on the shore. Two others floated in the water beside it, their heads bobbing below the surface. He opened a plastic bag and dragged the dead creature into it. The terrified, frozen eyes made him shudder when they disappeared into the bag.

After an anti-toxin shower and disgusting meal of dehydrated food, distilled water, and coffee, Karl took his turn at the lab table inside the Vickers. It was nearly nine p.m. when the van's door popped open and Masters stepped into the red-lit interior.

"How's it going?"

Karl pushed back from the scope and flexed his stiff neck. "I keep thinking I'm in Somalia. There was this doctor named Nihalla."

Masters smiled. "How about a break? Burns'll pick it up for the next couple hours."

They exited the van and stepped into the cool night air. The black sky was filled with stars and a full moon reflected off the bay's rippling waters. Quite a change from Somalia.

After showering and changing into their fatigues, they walked to Masters' pressurized tent and plunked down on two folding chairs. The temperature had dropped into the forties, making it uncomfortable for a man clothed in a shirt and khakis.

Masters switched on a portable heater and poured a cup of coffee. He extended the cup to Karl. "How are you holding up?"

"I'll make it."

Masters poured himself a cup. "I've been in the field six years and never saw anything like this."

Karl sipped his coffee and put the cup on Masters' work table. He glanced at the illuminated PC screen beside the cup. "Anything new on Mombassa?"

"Mombassa?" Masters shrugged. "First I've heard of it." He sipped his coffee and stared at Karl.

"We heard rumors of an outbreak."

Masters shook his head. "Hell with Mombassa. What about Willapa Bay?"

Karl rubbed his tired eyes. "Same as Somalia. Frozen faces. Deoxygenated blood. Symptoms of pulmonary arrest. They went really fast." He leaned forward and rested his elbows on his knees.

"That's it?"

"I thought the bug was airborne until today."

"You mean, that scene with the helmet?"

Karl nodded. "Something this lethal doesn't come and go. If it was airborne, I'd be history and so would you."

Masters took a nervous sip of coffee. "Maybe it's in the water?"

Karl shook his head. "So far, Willapa Bay looks pretty clean. Nothing but plankton, oyster waste, and a little oil from the fishing boats."

"Well, you better get some sleep."

Karl locked his blue eyes on him. "How long have you known Hampsted?"

"Hampsted? Just met him today."

"I'd watch him. I've seen his kind before. They smile at you, then stick a knife in your back."

"He's just under pressure like the rest of us."

"No, it's more than that." Karl stood up and stretched his back. "Thanks for the coffee." He started to push through the tent flap.

"Question?"

Karl hesitated and looked back at him.

"What happened at FDA?"

Karl recalled his attorney's warning. "Just a little misunderstanding. Guess I rubbed someone the wrong way."

"I heard it was more."

Karl shrugged and pushed through the flap. It was ten p.m. on Willapa Bay.

He tried to sleep, but the time changes had done him in. At midnight, he rolled off his cot and stumbled into the chilled night air. His head was spinning from the past forty-eight hours.

No, it was longer than that. The phone had rung five days ago. He'd just returned to Atlanta from a false alarm in upstate New York. A farmer had seen rats scurrying from his barn. Then his boy came down with fever and nearly died. They thought it was Hanta virus. It turned out to be measles.

Karl recalled the dead rats, half of them blown away by shotguns, the rest of them poisoned by the panicked farmers. Hell, all they wanted was some of that stored grain. Poor little guys. Get blamed for everything. Plague, rabies—everything. A few hundred years ago, we were hunting cats. They were supposed to be agents of the devil. People killed them and kept rats for pets. Now, it's the other way around. What a screwed up world. He cracked a smile. Maybe in a hundred years, the rats and cats will be in, and we'll be the hunted ones.

He flashed his ID at an army sentry and shuffled along the shore. From here, he could see the moonlit bay running north toward its outlet to the ocean. In front of him, tiny Long Island sat in the middle of the bay, its silhouette barely visible in the soft light.

He'd borrowed a guidebook from Thurmat and skimmed the local geography. Long Island was a wildlife refuge, its red cedars, spotted owls, and black bears protected from boaters and hunters by the National Park Service. It sounded like a nice place to escape from the rat race. He smiled and shook his head. There you go with the rats again.

In the morning, he'd suggest they boat over to the island for some samples. Easier to spot something in a protected area. Pristine, like a giant test tube.

He paused and looked at the full moon. The water lapped at his boots. A cool breeze brushed his face. Behind him, an owl hooted in the darkness. He took a breath of pine-scented air. Everything was so peaceful. So normal. He frowned and headed up the shore.

When Karl reached the yellow tape, he was challenged by a second sentry. Unlike the first, this sentry wore military-issue bio-gear and an oxygen mask. Karl flashed his ID card and forced a smile. "Just walking the perimeter."

The sentry shook his head and waved him back.

"The perimeter's okay. We've strung HEPA detectors and alarms along the tape."

"Sorry, Mr. Frankton. My orders are to let no one near the tape."

"Why?"

The sentry hesitated. "Nerves, I guess."

Karl peered at the shadows beyond the tape. A bell clanged in the darkness. Then another. The clangs were coming from the abandoned boats. Or was it the dead calling out to him. Trying to tell him what had happened on Willapa Bay. He turned and headed back to his tent.

Chapter 4

Bitter Memories

He rested his hands on the sink and glared at the shaken face in the mirror. *Snap out of it! You're hallucinating! Soak your head and get the hell out of here!* He twisted the knob and ducked his head under the faucet.

It was September 6, 2010 and the Bethesda facility was closed for Labor Day. No classes today. No tedious hours hunched over lab tables, PC screens, and electron microscopes. Time to be with family and friends at cookouts, volleyball games, and outdoor concerts. Time to relax, unless you were an obsessed medical student named Karl Frankton.

He was amazed when he flashed his ID at the guard and noticed the blank admittance list. Didn't the fools know they were blowing it? Because of a stupid holiday, they'd given him a chance to take the lead in the brutal thirteen week marathon. With Anne and Jeremy off to her mom's, he had the perfect opportunity to gain a day's edge on the competition. Performance reviews were only one week away, and every minute was precious.

The past twelve weeks had been the most exhilarating of his life. Through intensive lab sessions, he'd gotten a glimpse of the FDA's "code red" list of toxins and carcinogens, many of them lying around our workplaces and homes in brightly colored aerosol cans, bottles, and cartons. Well-intentioned chemicals formulated to make our lives easier. Only these chemicals were lethal.

It was more than rusted drums of hydrochloric acid near Lake Michigan, or occasional bursts of radiation from the world's decaying nuclear plants. Forget the cataclysmic reactor explosion or Bhopal chemical disaster. They were miniscule compared to man's daily ingestion of his own profit-driven poisons. Man-made toxins floating in our air, water, and soil like a trillion ticking time bombs. A growing, unseen menace that might someday snuff us out like the dinosaur.

Last week, they'd transferred him to the FDA's top-secret pharmaceutical testing lab, a powerful sign he was under consideration for retention in the program. Here, he would gain exposure to the newest miracle drugs before being promoted to the FDA's prestigious Drug Evaluation and Review team.

There was only one problem. Two others had been transferred with him, candidates Smith and Harrison, two wealthy preps from Harvard Medical School. Three men fighting for two slots in an exhausting game of musical chairs, with one out the door when it was over. No way would they crowd him out.

He gripped the sink and stared at the cold water dripping down his face. It had begun so innocently. A simple trip through the lab's computer database searching for "AV Agent M-13," the latest trial drug in the war against AIDS.

He'd noticed M-13 on last week's online list of "CANDIDATES FOR INVESTIGATION," new drug applicants chosen for the brutal first-stage gauntlet of tests aimed at eliminating hyped miracle drugs before they consumed the agency's strained resources.

His first surprise came when he noticed M-13 had received a "surrogate end point waiver," meaning accelerated review and possible approval within six months. When he checked the reason code, it indicated "HIGH SUCCESS PROBABILITY," a rating reserved for candidates passing the first stage tests. Unusual, given M-13 had just appeared on last week's candidate list. It took a month to conduct the first-stage tests. How could M-13 pass those tests in only a week? Could the first-stage tests be accelerated that much? Was it a computer posting error?

Better to accept the screen and forget M-13. There were other drugs out there waiting for his student evaluation. Any would do for the final exam. No sense bogging down on M-13's little puzzle. Click that "CLOSE" icon, Mr. Frankton. You're wasting valuable time.

But he'd come too far to stop now. He was about to become a doctor, and that meant finding answers. It would only take a few minutes to pinpoint the drug's test status. He clicked the "OPEN" icon and winced from a burst of flashing red letters...

YOU ARE UNAUTHORIZED!

He stared at the flashing screen. Access to the FDA's drug evaluation database was restricted to the highest officials, unless you happened to know the password.

It only took a minute to break through. When would Professor Sandersen learn to quit tipping his hand at lectures. Everyone knew Sandersen's favorite subject was nicotine, alias $C_{10}H_{14}N_2$. Easy enough to deduce the password from there.

He was surprised Sandersen used the word "nicotine" instead of the formula. Not very creative for the lab's top professor. He clicked the mouse and blew past the flashing red letters. Next stop, M-13's test status.

At first, he thought he'd looked up the wrong drug. It couldn't be M-13. The first stage result showed "PASSED" with all supporting tests indicating the same positive result.

A quick scan of the tests proved it was impossible to perform them in only a week. Four of the test cultures required two to three weeks gestation before conclusions could be drawn. Something wasn't kosher. It could be a computer system glitch or posting error, but this was one of the most important databases in the nation. Try another drug. Maybe they were all screwed up with the same computer bug.

He was about to exit M-13's test status screen when he noticed the drug's test initiation date...

"6 / 7 / 10"

Three months ago? Three months earlier than the "8/30/10" entry date on the first-stage candidate screen? What the hell was going on? It was too late to back off. He had broken into the FDA's most sensitive database. When they checked the audit logs in the morning, M-13's access would be recorded, and he was the only student in the lab today. He had opened Pandora's Box.

The final shock came when he penetrated the critical "T Cell Compatibility" test. For an immune system drug to work, it must be accepted by the body's lymphatic sentinel cells, much like another Trojan Horse, the deadly HI Virus. It was the only way the drug could enter the body's immune system to conduct its war against HIV and AIDS.

He rubbed a paper towel across his face and stared at the mirror while recalling the final screen display. AV Agent M-13 had failed the T Cell test miserably, killing seventy percent of the white rats tested, yet the result was marked "PASSED."

The hallucination occurred when he tried to print the result finding. As the paper flowed out of the LaserJet, the PC screen flashed red and the test result disappeared. A new result took its place, this one indicating a "LESS THAN 10%" fatality rate among the tested rats. It was more than a computer program error. Karl Frankton had entered a forbidden world and gotten an accidental glimpse of a disease more frightening than any carcinogen. A disease called greed.

"My God." The face in the mirror disappeared...

.   .   .

Karl's eyes snapped open to the roar of a descending chopper. He sat up on the cot and steadied himself while recalling the flashing red warning on the lab's computer screen.

God, if he could only relive that moment. A simple click of the mouse and M-13 would have been gone forever. Instead, an ambitious medical student's curiosity had destroyed his career and family, and left him with a nightmare that was just beginning. He tucked in his shirt and staggered through the tent flap into the sunlight.

"Put on your suit!"

Karl spun around and saw Masters rushing toward the landed chopper, his helmet dangling from his hand. Thurmat and Burns had donned their bio-suits and were walking beside him. The military personnel had taken positions just clear of the rotating blades, their eyes fixed on the chopper's exit door.

Karl glanced at his watch. Seven thirty and no one working? They'd all overslept. No wonder Masters looked so nervous. Not the best way to greet your boss.

The exit door slid open and Hampsted stepped out. His gray suit was badly wrinkled and he needed a shave. The black attaché case dangled from his left hand. He ducked the slowing blades and scurried clear of the chopper.

Hampsted trained his bloodshot eyes on Masters. "Well?"

Masters shook his head. "We've pretty much confirmed it's the same thing that hit Somalia."

"That's all you have?" Hampsted turned toward Wiley, Promot, and Smith who were gaping at him with frightened eyes. "Why aren't you in bio-suits?"

Promot was stupid enough to open his mouth. "We were just climbing into them when you landed."

"Were you now." Hampsted glared at Promot. "Listen, you idiot. We're in big trouble and you're all we have. Now get in that suit!" He clenched the attaché case and watched the three men scramble for the showers.

Hampsted turned toward Karl. "What about you? I'm surprised you're taking this so lightly. Think I don't know what happened in Somalia?"

Karl restrained himself and started toward the showers. "Wait a minute." Hampsted stepped toward him until they were nose-to-nose. "I don't think you get it, Mr. Frankton. Blow this one and you're finished."

Karl felt the blood rush to his face. He tried to turn away, but Hampsted jabbed a finger into his chest. "I don't care about back room deals or attorneys. You screw this up and you're out." Hampsted brushed past him and headed for the tents.

For two years, Karl had fought the urge to strike back, but this jerk was too much. He clenched his fists and felt the words spew out. "Sure about that?"

Hampsted wheeled around, his face twitching with anger. "What did you say?"

Karl forced a quivering smile. "Just making sure I heard you right."

Hampsted's glare became a sneer. "Careful, Mr. Frankton. I don't play games." He turned and walked away.

Karl glanced at Masters who was staring at him in shock. "Guess I better suit up." He walked past his shaken supervisor and headed for the showers.

That afternoon, Karl got the word from Masters. No explanation. No warning. Just a simple order to catch the morning plane to Atlanta and call CDC when he got in. When Karl asked the obvious question, Masters gave him the cold-shoulder and said it was out of his hands.

Karl spent the evening in his tent munching dehydrated cookies while going over his notes. He'd thought about having dinner with the others, but the note clipped to his tent flap was pretty clear...

Sorry Karl,
Probably best you eat alone tonight.
Good luck in Atlanta.
Herb

He tried to sleep, but Hampsted's glaring eyes kept snapping him awake. He lay in the dark, his face coated with sweat. If he only had a drink. Something to get him through the night.

His hand groped for the flask. He popped it open and spilled the last burning drops of scotch on his tongue while cursing himself for not picking up a fresh bottle. He flung the empty flask at the darkness.

What was happening? He couldn't breathe! He tugged at his soaked collar and recalled the incident at the boathouse. Maybe Masters was right. Maybe he had gotten a fatal dose of the invisible killer. Maybe it took time for the virus to overcome his immune system before penetrating his blood cells. That was it, dammit! His time was up! The damn thing had him!

He rolled off the cot and crouched on his knees, his fingers ripping at his collar. *Get hold of yourself, man! It's a panic attack! Ride it out!* He curled into a ball and prayed for the suffocating palpitations to end.

The attack subsided. He wiped the sweat off his face and stared at the darkness. A little dizzy, but things could be worse. He buried his face in his trembling hands and waited for his head to clear. Ten minutes later, he pushed off the tent floor and staggered into the chilled night air.

Snores reverberated from the darkened tents. Masters and the others were out cold from too many hours of exhaustive research. It didn't take a psychologist to know they were burned out from Hampsted's warning that heads would roll if they didn't have something when he returned in the morning.

He glared at the tents. The jerk was inhuman. How could a creep like that get into a position of power over good men like Nihalla and Masters? If anyone belonged in a body bag, it was Parker Hampsted. He fought a heart palp and took a calming breath. *Easy, old buddy. Save your hate for the bug.*

He shuffled along the shore toward the village. No one was in sight except the bio-suited military guard standing at the tape. The three fishing boats had righted themselves in the rising tide, their flat bottoms freed from the mud, their bells clanging a lonely tune. They looked like ghost ships swaying under the starlit sky.

He leaned against a tree and stared at the moonlit bay. After three years of struggle, Karl Frankton was ready to throw in the towel. Time to go back to York and a simpler life. Take some mindless job and chase the local chicks. Maybe help his sister with the farm. He rubbed his tired eyes and listened to the water lap at the gravel shore. Hell of an ending for a man who once peered through a microscope and dreamed great things.

It was more than a failed career. More than disgrace and harassment. How about the loss of a precious wife and son, torn away in a bitter divorce. How about that, Mr. Frankton? Enough to make you thirsty?

He glanced at his watch. In San Diego, his beautiful ex-wife was probably climbing into the sack with Ralph Moran, one filthy-rich entrepreneur. Can't blame her for remarrying so fast. Gotta think of Jeremy and the bright future she'd promised her son.

Can't blame ol' Anne. She'd given her ex-husband every chance to pull his shattered life together. And he might have made it if not for the self-pity and booze.

He dug his fingers into the tree and fought back the tears. What was he saying? He was human for God's sake. This wasn't his fault. He'd tried to do the right thing—the honorable thing. Didn't she know? Didn't she care? Did she hate him that much?

He ripped off a piece of bark and clenched it in his fist. Maybe that was it. Maybe she didn't care. Maybe she never cared. After all, he'd done his job. Put his wife through med school while struggling with the same burden. Now, she was a big shot doctor with a rich husband and cushy life in La Jolla.

And her ex was a drunken shell of what he might have been, yanked from assignment to assignment like that duffel bag in his tent. Yeah, Frankton. It made sense. Real good sense. She never cared. She'd used him, dammit! Damn her to hell!"

His eyes filled with tears. Last month was Jeremy's twelfth birthday. No cards allowed. No visitation. No phone calls. Hell, she'd probably shut off the e-mails too.

He'd sent his son a gift from upstate New York, a set of fly-fishing lures to try out the next time they were together. Yeah...next time. He flicked away a tear and retreated up the shore.

He was nearly to his tent when the uneasiness swept over him, the same eerie feeling he'd experienced in Somalia. He looked back at the moonlit dock. Everything was still except the rocking boats. He stared at the boats, their bells clanging in the darkness, their ropes creaking against the moorings.

What was it? What was missing from the painting? He shook his head and ducked into his tent.

.   .   .

Karl boarded the chopper at six a.m. His only contact with the team was a halfhearted wave from Herb when the chopper lifted into the fog-shrouded sky. The others weren't in sight.

The pilot dipped the chopper's nose and sped north along the peninsula while its passenger looked back at the disaster sight, its dock fading into the gray haze. So peaceful. So deadly.

The chopper landed at Sea-Tac's airport in time for Karl to catch the 7:30 flight to Atlanta. He tried to get some sleep, but the bitter memories kept bubbling up from the depths along with that uneasiness about the unfinished painting. He gazed at the passing clouds while recalling a better time.

The 767 touched down at Hartsfield International Airport at 3:45 p.m. Karl's first instinct was to call CDC, but he hadn't seen his apartment in a week, and he needed a decent shower and shave. The way things were going, they'd probably drag him straight in. Better take advantage of the slack time. Hell, he might even type up a summary of the past week. Not much to say, but at least it would make him feel better.

It was a beautiful summer afternoon in the historic city. Peachtree Plaza jutted into the blue sky, its seventy-three-story tower glistening in the sunlight. Below it, expansive Peachtree Center marked the hub of downtown Atlanta with its office towers, glass skyways, and massive Marriot Marquis Hotel.

WNN Center was nearby, as was Colony Square, and the enormous Georgia World Convention Center. Throw in Turner Field, the Georgia Dome, Atlanta Market Center, Apparel Mart, Underground District, and a wealth of Fortune 500 headquarters, and it was clear the South had risen again.

The taxi exited the Northeast Expressway at North Druid Hills Road. After a quick left at Roxboro, it turned onto Peachtree and drove past the Lennox Square Mall and *Tom Tom* Restaurant. The *Tom Tom* was only a stone's throw from Karl's one bedroom apartment, and a good place to catch a snack before going in.

His apartment building was on Lennox, a simple red-brick structure with aluminum awnings, sliding glass windows, and that disgusting pot of dead flowers beside the entrance. Hard to believe the owner hadn't replaced it with something more inviting. Then again, why bother with no vacancies and a mile-long waiting list.

Karl paid the driver and slung the duffel bag over his shoulder. His eyes were already on the weather-beaten '01 *Honda* sitting in the shaded portal at the rear of the driveway. Hell, start it later. Just get out of these smelly clothes and take a human shower. No disinfectant. No alcohol or bleach. Only hot sprayed water with a human toilet and shaving mirror nearby. Funny, how little things mean so much after a few days in the field.

The small, green-carpeted lobby had a familiar odor of cooked bacon and cigarette smoke. A baby's cry echoed off the walls. Karl was too tired to climb the four flights of stairs, so he punched the elevator button and rode it to three, and its dimly lit hallway.

He was within a few feet of his door when he spotted the note taped to the gray knob. He didn't have to open it to know what it said. He hadn't paid last month's rent and the landlord already hated his guts. He crumpled the note in his fist and jammed his key in the lock.

He scanned the austere living room and frowned. A black-vinyl couch and glass cocktail table faced a black-veneer credenza on the white wall opposite him. A portable TV sat atop the credenza, its dark screen covered with dust. On his left, a black-veneer desk was jammed beneath a green-curtained window, its bare surface coated with dust. A rattan chair and chrome floor lamp jutted out from the corner on his right, a pile of medical books stacked beside them on the faded brown carpet. A real *Shangri-la.* No pictures or mirrors. Only an empty glass frame nailed to the wall above the TV.

The place smelled from mildew and spoiled food. Forget the refrigerator in the closet-sized kitchenette on his right. By now, it probably resembled one of those cultures in the lab. Clean it later.

He stepped through the doorway beside the credenza and flung his duffel bag on the black-quilted bed. His clothes came next, underwear and all. A quick shuffle into the bathroom and he was groping for the light switch. Thank God, the power was still on. Now for the important part. He reached into the shower and twisted the handle until a stream of piping hot water splashed off the drain. He smiled and stepped into the steaming shower. Ah, paradise. Home, sweet home.

The car started too. Not bad, three for three. He grabbed a snack at the *Tom Tom* and headed back to his apartment for some fast word processing on the ol' laptop. First, a stop at apartment "1" where he slipped his delinquent rent check under the door while praying it wouldn't bounce. No matter, he'd probably get paid today. Most likely a severance check, or whatever they give contracted employees.

He was stepping off the elevator when his cell phone went off. He rushed to his door and unlocked it. The phone was on its ninth ring when he yanked it out of his pocket and popped it open.

"Mr. Frankton?"

"Yes?"

"This is John Wheatly at Executive Park. Just get in?"

"Yes."

"Don't unpack."

"What?"

"How fast can you catch a plane to Phoenix?"

"Phoenix?"

"We have an outbreak across the border in Nogales. Looks like Hantavirus. The Mexican authorities are asking for help. We have a team on the ground, but they need an extra person."

Karl felt the phone drop away from his ear. He stared at the sun shining on the faded brown carpet.

"Mr. Frankton?"

"What about Somalia and Willapa Bay?"

Wheatly hesitated. *"E-mail me a report from Nogales. We'll use it at tomorrow's meeting."*

"Meeting?"

Wheatly's voice grew impatient. *"Don't worry about it. You're needed in Nogales. Call us when you land in Phoenix. We'll give you instructions there."*

"But, I can help. I've seen both sites."

"An e-mail will be fine. Better get going, Mr. Frankton. They're expecting someone tonight. Sorry for the surprise. We'd send one of our own, but no one's available." The phone clicked and went dead.

He spent the next few minutes sitting on the couch, his eyes gazing at the phone on his lap. Were they mad? At least let him attend the meeting. Revenge was one thing, but this bug was serious. Twelve thousand miles for God's sake. Gotta overlook personal feelings. Fire him later, but let him finish the job.

His eyes focused on the bottle of scotch on the glass table. He'd bought it on the way back from the *Tom Tom*. Hadn't planned on opening it until tonight.

He glared at the bottle. Tonight? That's a laugh. By tonight, you'll be in Nogales waiting for the next crushing phone call. Damn them!

He twisted off the cap and took a long, deep swig. It burned going down, but it felt good. More dammit. He guzzled the scotch and slumped on the couch, his hand clutching the half-empty bottle. His eyes drifted to the pile of mail on the cocktail table. He swiped at it and noticed an envelope with an official seal. It only took a second to rip it open and unfold the letter...

Samuel H. Dobson
2113 Merchant Way
San Diego, CA 44122
Attorney for Defendant

SUPERIOR COURT OF CALIFORNIA
FAMILY DIVISION
SAN DIEGO COUNTY

PLAINTIFF: ANNE MORAN

vs.

DEFENDANT: KARL FRANKTON

ORDER

This order, having come before the court on the 1st day of July, 2013, upon notice of motion filed by the plaintiff, and the Court having read and studied all associated arguments from both the plaintiff and defendant, it is hereby ordered that the defendant be forbidden to visit his son, Jeremy, for a period of one year hence. At the completion of said term, the defendant may petition the Court for reconsideration provided he undergoes Court-specified medical and psychological screening to assure the Court, and plaintiff, that he is free and clear of all alcoholism.

Tobias Menken / Presiding Judge

The next few minutes were a blur. He remembered crumpling the letter in his fist while cursing the woman he once loved. He relived their last bitter encounter in the courtroom four weeks ago when she stood in front of the judge in that expensive, pin-stripe designer suit, her new husband smiling lovingly at her from the gallery. The unnerving silence, followed by a simple question from the bench, and equally simple answer from the plaintiff...

Mrs. Moran, before I render judgment in this matter, are you certain of the period requested?

Yes, Your Honor. One year should give Mr. Frankton the wake up call he needs. It's for my son's safety, Your Honor.

Safety? I'm his father for Christ's sake! I love him! And you too!

He remembered screaming at her while his attorney grappled with him. How could she do this to him? Jeremy was all he had left. Only a few hours on the weekends. Not much for a father who loves his son. He'd stay sober. Do anything. Even shake the scum's hand.

Please, Anne! For God's sake, I'm sorry!

He guzzled the scotch and looked up at the empty frame on the wall. She'd bought it for him three years ago to house his diploma from Columbia, a diploma that would never come because a medical student named Karl Frankton ignored a warning message on Labor Day, 2010.

He glared at the frame. It had hung on that wall for two years, an unsettling reminder of the price for bucking the system. In a few hours, he would land in some obscure town across the Mexican border. From there, back to Atlanta to be jerked somewhere else. Who knows, maybe next time they'd send him to hell.

He threw the bottle at the frame, shattering it to smithereens. One of the glass chards caught him on the forehead, but he didn't feel it. He was too busy throwing the cell phone at the wall. The last thing he remembered was flying memory chips and broken plastic...

Chapter 5

The Article

"Atlanta? You're still here?"

Karl rested his head against the pay phone. "Sorry, the jet lag got me."

"That's no excuse! What about our people in Nogales? What do I tell them?"

Karl ignored Wheatly's tirade. "I checked the flight schedules. With a little luck, I can be there by midnight."

"And I'm supposed to rely on that?"

"That's up to you, but if you want me in Nogales, you better send some cash. I just used my last quarter on this call."

"What about your cell phone?"

"Broken."

"Then buy a new one! You think this is a travel bureau? You just cost us three hundred bucks! That's the third time this year. This one comes out of your pay."

Karl pressed the mouthpiece against his lips. "Do you want me there or not?" He clenched the receiver and listened to Wheatly's strained breathing.

"Give me your number."

Karl gave him the phone number and hung up. He took a deep breath and closed his eyes.

The past three hours were a blur. He recalled staggering out of the chilled shower and throwing on some clothes. No need to pack. He'd never unpacked.

The living room was a mess. Phone fragments, broken glass, and scotch all over the place. Cracked plaster where

59

the frame had hung. Shreds of paper that were once a legal document.

Hell with it. His rent check would cover the damage. He wasn't coming back. Nothing in that rattrap but bad memories and cheap furniture. Let the landlord worry about it.

He looked down at the battered duffel bag. In two years, he and that bag had logged nearly two hundred thousand miles together. Dropped into some interesting places too. Barely made it out of a couple. Hell, that worn out bag was the only thing he owned besides the *Honda*, and the car wouldn't last much longer with his payments so far behind. He reached down and patted the scuffed leather. Not much to show for thirty-one years of struggle. Not much at all...

His thoughts were jarred by a loud ring. He straightened up and lifted the receiver off the hook. "Yeah?"

Wheatly's voice crackled though the earpiece. *"Go to the Air West counter. Your ticket will be there in ten minutes, along with a hundred bucks. I booked you on the seven-forty plane to Houston. Couldn't get anything to Phoenix. I'll arrange a charter to get you across the border. It'll be a little tricky with all the drug surveillance, but we'll manage."*

"What about my check?"

"Your what?"

"My pay check."

"Just get on the plane! We'll clear your account when the assignment's over."

"Clear?"

"You know what I mean." The phone went dead with a loud click.

The 737 took off a half hour late due to traffic, but Karl was unaware. He'd passed out the moment his head hit the seat. When he awoke, they were only twenty minutes from Bush Intercontinental Airport. The e-mail note clipped to his ticket instructed him to stop at the *Charters Southwest* counter where a cross-border flight had been arranged for the Nogales leg.

P.P.M.

How thrilling. A night flight through drug-infested air corridors with DEA fighters prowling overhead. He had to be nuts for not telling them to shove it. Then again, that hundred bucks felt good in his pocket, and he needed that final check to buy a few precious weeks until he figured out what to do with his screwed up life.

He yanked a crumpled *Houston Chronicle* out of the seat pocket and scanned the headlines. Nothing unusual, just some garbage about the latest DC sex scandal and its impact on the approaching congressional elections. Below it, an update on the recent rash of serial killings in Los Angeles. Heads in refrigerators. Cryptic notes from the killer. How tantalizing. Oh yeah, mustn't forget the latest car bombing in Haifa, and drug bust in Miami. Yup—same old, same old.

He slapped the paper shut. What was wrong with them? The jerks were writing about a senator's overactive libido while a hundred seven corpses decayed in body bags from an unknown killer. The finest technologies and minds were baffled by an angel of death that had wiped out two villages twelve thousand miles apart without warning or explanation. Didn't anyone know what was happening? Were they all that ignorant?

He looked at the darkening sky. In a few days, this mess would be over and he'd be on his way back to Atlanta. Who knows, he might even take a little side-trip to La Jolla. A belated social call to congratulate the Morans on their bright new life. Maybe reminisce about a husband's devotion and his wife's infidelity. About broken vows and unrequited love. About the vulture who moved in before the bed got cold. Yeah, time for a little sit down with his two favorite people.

He looked down at his clenched fists. Enough, dammit! Want to end up on death row? Two years is enough for self-pity. You can't change the past. It's over, Frankton. *Kaput — finis!* Time to quit the booze and salvage what's left of your life. Let it go before you kill someone.

He thought about Jeremy and the promises a father makes to his son. The fishing trips, baseball games, and vacations. The graduation he'd never see. The wedding he'd never attend. The grandchild he'd never hold. Promises made, but not kept. What about them, Frankton? Not easy to let them go...

"Ladies and gentlemen, I've turned on the seat belt sign. We'll be on the ground in ten minutes. Thank you for flying Air West."

He took a calming breath and released his death-grip on the newspaper. He was about to stuff it in the seat pocket when a small headline caught his eye. Only a few words at the bottom of the front page, but there was something about them that made him uneasy...

FLU OUTBREAK NEAR HOUSTON
MILITARY OFFERS NO EXPLANATION FOR ROADBLOCKS AT TRINITY RIVER

He unfolded the newspaper and read the article while his seat rattled from the 737's extended air brakes.

Quarantine? What were they talking about? Quarantines are useless for flu. It's going to spread no matter how many roadblocks you set up. It's airborne, dammit. Blow right through you. If an ocean can't stop it, what good is a quarantine?

His eyes lit up. Hell, this is July? It's too early for flu? The next bug is still bubbling up in the Third World? It won't hit the states for six months?

He recalled the roadblocks on Long Beach Peninsula. They'd told the vacationers it was because of the black bears. Anything to keep outsiders away while CDC searched frantically for an answer to the mysterious killer.

"Sir, please lift your seat back and fasten your belt."

"What?"

The stewardess patted his shoulder. "We're landing, sir."

"Oh, sorry." He pressed the seat button and smiled at her. "Say, maybe you can help me. I'm trying to get to the Trinity River. Do you know anything about the area?" She leaned toward him and smiled. "Born and raised. Can't you tell?"

"That's quite a drawl."

She nodded at the magazine in his seat pocket. "There's a local map in that magazine. Trinity's about forty-five minutes east of Houston. Not much to see. You ought to go a little further to Big Thicket National Park. It's a lot prettier." She patted his shoulder and hurried down the aisle.

He yanked out the flight magazine and flipped to the abbreviated map of Houston. According to the article, the roadblocks were set up along Route 90, thirty miles northeast of the city. Less than an hour's drive.

He glanced at his watch. Only nine p.m. He still had a few bucks left on his charge card. Enough for a rental car. Some risk, but he should make it through the roadblocks with his ID. If it was flu, he'd still have time to drive back to Houston and catch the Nogales charter. Tell them he got confused or something. Hell, worry about it later. He looked down at the map and felt a chill. What if it wasn't flu? What if—

The 737 shook from a hard touchdown. He stared at the blue and red runway lights flashing past his darkened window and listened to the voice ringing in his ears.

Snap out of it, man. Are you that desperate for self-worth? Think you're back at the FDA looking for the latest conspiracy? You're imagining all this. It's from the booze. You've turned paranoid. Come to your senses before you wipe out what's left of your life. You screw this up and they'll finish you. Make sure you never work again. You'll end up on the street. Never see your son again. Do you want that? Now forget this crap and get on that charter!

He felt the plane roll to a stop. The ramp locked into place as the passengers scrambled for their luggage. He'd have to go down to baggage claim to retrieve his duffel bag. Pass the car rental counters along the way. Time enough for a decision.

. . .

"Dr. Thala?"

Thala looked up from the microscope and smiled at the young man peering through the tent flap. "Yes, Samuel?"

The young man ducked into the tent and held out a walkie-talkie. "Just took a call from the guard post. Looks like we have a visitor."

"Visitor?"

"Someone named Frankton. Says he's with CDC. Wants to come in."

Thala grasped the walkie-talkie and pressed the transmit button. "This is Dr. Thala. You have someone from CDC?"

A voice crackled through the earpiece. *"Yes, Doctor. His name is Karl Frankton. His ID's intact. Contracted pathologist."*

Thala stroked his charcoal hair. "Put him on." He heard the guard mumble something in the background.

"Dr. Thala?"

"Yes?"

"Karl Frankton. Just flew in from Atlanta. They said you needed help."

Thala scratched his head and stared at the PC on the lab table, and at the red *"CDC"* scrolling across its screen. "Have you been briefed?" He released the transmit button and waited for an answer.

"I was in Somalia."

Thala's black eyes lit up. "On the Shabeelle?"

"Yes, and on Willapa Bay."

Thala gripped the PC's mouse and positioned the cursor over the screen's personnel search icon.

"Doctor?"

Thala pressed the talk button. "Let me speak to the guard, Mr. Frankton. He'll drive you in."

After clearing his visitor with the guard, Thala handed the walkie-talkie to the young man. "Thank you, Samuel. Better get some sleep. It'll be a long day."

The young man smiled and ducked through the tent flap.

Thala was well into his computer search when he heard the jeep approaching. He shut down the PC and stepped through the tent flap into the warm night air. A full moon had risen over the hills, its pale face shimmering on the Trinity River's black water. He could see the jeep coming toward him in the soft light, a plume of dust trailing behind it. Route 90 was two miles away...

Karl glanced at his watch. Nine-forty and things were still clouded. He clung to the bouncing jeep while focusing on the cluster of tents dead ahead. Two were darkened. The third glowed dull orange. He could see a man standing in front of it, his arms folded.

They were within a hundred yards of the man when Karl noticed another object on the right. A familiar vehicle that made his stomach churn. A Vickers Mobile Lab.

The jeep screeched to a stop. "We're here, Mr. Frankton." The uniformed driver nodded for Karl to get out.

Karl snatched his duffel bag off the rear seat and climbed out of the jeep.

"Mr. Frankton?" Thala stepped forward and extended his hand. "I'm Dr. Thala."

Karl smiled and grasped his hand.

"You're a physician?"

Karl shook his head. "Pathologist and budding microbiologist, depending on who you ask." He studied the black face looking down at him. "My lord, you're the tallest doctor I've ever seen."

Thala smiled. "You were in Somalia?"

Karl glanced at the Vickers. "This site reminds me of Somalia." He locked his blue eyes on Thala. "How many, Doctor?"

Thala hesitated.

"There were eighty-four in Somalia. Twenty-three on Willapa Bay."

"We have fourteen here."

"God."

Thala shook his head. "I'm afraid He's not here today. The devil maybe."

Karl scanned the moonlit river. "I don't see a village?"

"There isn't any. They were illegals. Probably headed cross-country from the Mexican border. The truck probably dumped them out here."

"They came a long way."

"Yes, until now."

Karl glanced at his watch. It was nearly ten and he was toast. He took a deep breath and dropped the duffel bag. "Well, I'm ready to work."

Thala looked at him in surprise. "Maybe you should get some rest. You can use the cot in the van. No need for a suit. Everything's secured."

"I'm fine. Slept on the plane." Karl picked up his duffel bag. "How many with you?"

"Only two. Agents Kremler and Dolstadt. They're from the area." Thala nodded toward the two darkened tents. "They're out cold. Been at it since yesterday."

"How much do they know?"

"Not as much as you. They think this is the first site."

Karl nodded. "No sense waking them. I'd like to see the bodies, if it's okay."

"If you insist, but a question first?"

"Sure."

"When did you leave Somalia?"

Karl hesitated. "Sunday, I think."

"Sure it wasn't Monday?"

"Why?"

Thala looked down. "The body count in Somalia isn't eighty-four. It's eighty-six. We lost two men on Monday."

Karl stared at him. "Two?"

"A Somali physician named Nihalla, and a young man named Powell. You knew them of course."

Karl couldn't speak. His mind drifted back to the confrontation with Buckley.

"Are you all right, Mr. Frankton?"

Karl looked at him with desperate eyes. "How did they..."

"We're not clear. It sounds like they died along the Shabeelle. Dr. Nihalla had gone off to take soil samples and didn't return. Powell went after him. Their bodies were discovered along the shore, a half mile from the village. They were stricken with the same symptoms as the others."

"Were they wearing suits?"

"That's classified."

"Classified?"

Thala nodded and glanced at the river. "Well, let's get on with it. You can drop your bag in the Vickers." He led his shaken visitor toward the van.

It only took a few minutes to go through the portable shower and dressing station. They helped each other with the umbilicals and took turns securing the other's suit. When Karl extended his gloved hands for taping, Thala smiled at him through his Plexiglas faceplate. "I thought I was the only one who still did that. You're a bit young for old habits."

Karl smiled inside his helmet. "Superstitious, Doctor. Superstitious..." He watched Thala tape his wrists and returned the favor.

Thala backed away and nodded toward the river. "They're down there. We've already taken samples." He switched on his flashlight and led Karl down a slope to a familiar yellow tape. Beyond it, fourteen body bags lay against a cluster of rocks, the river flowing past them.

Karl knelt beside the first bag and pulled down the plastic zipper. A pair of terrified eyes looked up at him. The man's gray face was twisted in agony, his frothed mouth opened in a final, desperate gasp for air. The others were the same. Nine men, three women, and two children. Karl stood up and stared at the bags.

"Enough?"

"Yeah."

"A chopper's coming in the morning. We'll fly them to Corpus Christi for preservation. Too many animals out here. The temperature reaches into the nineties by noon."

Karl nodded and started to turn away.

"One second, Mr. Frankton." Thala aimed the flashlight at the river bank. "Anything like that in Somalia?"

Karl stared at the two dead fish floating against the bank. He snatched the flashlight from Thala and stepped toward them. "You've taken samples?"

Thala nodded and eased beside him. "Same symptoms as the fourteen. No oxygen in the blood. They suffocated."

Karl looked at the river. "There were dead herons in Willapa Bay. Dead fish too. Nothing on the Shabeelle. Not enough water to sustain life."

Thala stepped closer to the shore. "I think it's in the water. I think we're all going to die." He glanced at Karl and headed back to the camp.

.   .   .

"Mr. Fletcher, you have a scrambled call."

Jonathan Fletcher sat up in the leather chair and rubbed the sleep out of his eyes. The illuminated clock on his desk read 12:20 a.m. He leaned forward and pressed the intercom button. "You're still here, Kate?"

"As long as you, Mr. Fletcher."

He sighed and shook his head. "I'm so sorry. Your husband's going to kill me. Tell him I owe you both a lunch at Sans Souci."

"Be careful, Mr. Fletcher. He'll bring the whole family."

Fletcher cracked a smile. "No problem. Put me through and go home. Sleep in if you want."

"I'll be here at eight sharp. Goodnight, sir."

"Sleep well, Kate."

Fletcher leaned back in the chair and studied the rain-smeared window facing his desk. The Capitol's amber dome glowed in the darkness, its flag obscured by the low-hanging haze. He glanced at the PC screen on his left, and the American Eagle displayed on its face. His eyes focused on the flashing intercom button.

He snatched the phone off the intercom and pressed it against his ear. It took a few seconds for the cryptic warbling to clear. "Go ahead."

"We've run into a little snag."

Fletcher sat up and rested his elbows on the desk. "Snag?"

"I just took a call from Executive Park in Atlanta. Frankton didn't show up in Houston."

Fletcher squeezed the phone while fumbling through the stack of folders on his desk. He yanked out the one marked "K.F." and flipped it open.

"Are you there?"

"Did he board in Atlanta?"

"Confirmed, and there's no record of him boarding another plane in Houston. We're checking the car rental agencies at Bush Intercontinental."

"Rental?" Fletcher listened to Hampsted's nervous breathing.

"It's just a hunch, but I think he might be at the Trinity site."

Fletcher felt a knot in his stomach. He rubbed his forehead and fought a rush of anger. "Listen to me, Parker. Under no circumstances is that maggot to be allowed on that site. I want him arrested. You clear on that?"

"*Understood.*"

"Now you get back to me with good news. I'll stay here all night if I have to, but I want him stopped." Fletcher slammed the receiver on the hook and glared at the photograph in the folder.

Two years had passed since he saw that face, but it seemed like yesterday. He leaned back in the chair and recalled his final contentious moments with Karl Frankton's attorney...

Well, Mr. Fletcher. Do we have a deal?

Let me be clear, Mr. Dobson. If your client breathes a word of this to anyone, he's toast.

He'll cooperate if treated with respect.

Mr. Frankton will be assigned to CDC as a contracted pathologist. He'll receive accelerated training in our EID program, coordinated with sufficient field work to keep him whole. No more, no less. He'll be under strict surveillance. Any insubordinate action will mean immediate dismissal. Understood?

Please remember that my client has been through a lot. He has some problems to work through. A little compassion is in order. Two years guaranteed employment should suffice.

Two years? That scum's a whistle-blower. He's lower than a worm, and you ask for compassion? Six months, no more.

Two years seems fair after what you've put him through.

That's unacceptable. Frankton's an alcoholic. A ticking bomb waiting to go off. One sign of trouble and we'll crush him like a bug.

Then, we have no deal?

I don't think you get it, Mr. Dobson. It's not just the government. Your client cost some powerful people a lot of money. *They won't rest until he's held accountable. Get my drift?*

I'll communicate your concern to my client. Remember, I'm just trying to work things out for all parties.

Cut the bs. Do you have the printout?

Right here.

This is a copy.

You'll be given the original when you sign the agreement.

How can I be sure there are no other copies?

You can't. That's what makes it a good deal. Each party must respect the other.

You threatening me?

Of course not. Just trying to cut a deal that will last. You know, one with teeth.

And you expect me to buy that?

It's your decision, Mr. Fletcher.

I need to talk to some people. You'll receive our answer in the morning. Now get out of here. This meeting never took place…

Fletcher lifted the photograph and stared at the signed agreement beneath it, a simple paragraph offering permanent silence for two year's guaranteed employment at CDC. An agreement signed by Karl Frankton, Jonathan Fletcher, and Samuel Dobson, Attorney for the Defendant.

He frowned and lifted the agreement, exposing an aging laser printout…

> United States of America
> Food & Drug Administration
> Candidates for Investigation
> First Stage Test Result:
> T-Cell Compatibility=29% success
> conclusion=FAILURE
> Date Tested: 6/07/10
> Date Evaluated: 7/06/10
> Candidate: AV AGENT M-13

Fletcher closed the folder and stared at the rain-smeared window.

Chapter 6

Dr. Jekyll

They dragged him across the stone floor toward the rusted door at the end of the corridor. The only light came from the flickering bulb on the corridor's ceiling. Through his stupor, he heard pleas for mercy echoing from the barred metal doors on his right and left. Some begged in *Fangalo*, others in *Zulu, Xhosa,* and *Sotho.* He understood them all.

His stomach wrenched from nausea, but there was no food left to vomit. The beatings had taken a hard toll on his ribs and kidneys, making it impossible to keep anything down. He dry-heaved and felt one of the guards jerk his arm.

"You blow off on me and I'll slit your throat. Hear me, monkey?"

The guard's rasping voice rang in his ears. He couldn't control the agonizing convulsions. Each dry heave brought knifing pain from his broken ribs. He tried to steady himself, but his knees buckled under him. Everything was spinning. The blood rushed from his head.

No, dammit! Can't black out now. It's your trial, man. Your last chance to speak out before they kill you. Don't let your wife and daughters see you like this. You've got to hang on for Nelson, Desmond, and the others. The people must know the truth. The Afrikäners are using Buthelezi and his Inkatha to drive a wedge between us. We're killing each other while the fat pigs smile and count their gold. They've turned brother against brother. Sister against sister. We've got to stop the madness before it's too late. Zulu, Xhosa, Sotho—it doesn't matter. We're one people! The Afrikäners can't stop us if we stand together. It's your time, man. Stand and speak the words. They'll listen to a dying man. They'll listen to Mandu Thala. On your feet, warrior. On your feet!

One of the guards unlocked the rusted door and pushed it open, flooding the corridor with blinding light. He tried to look away, but the light was everywhere. The guards jammed a metal bar under his armpits and yanked it upward, making him cry out in agony. They lifted him off his feet and carried him into the light.

Where were they taking him? This wasn't the way to the prison bus? Had they changed the location of the trial? Moved it to another day? Why hadn't they told him? Yasmin would be waiting for him at the justice center with Correla and Xolisile? Who would tell them? Where was his counsel?

He tried to speak, but the pain was too great. With his last ounce of strength, he forced his head up and squinted at the bright sunlight through his swollen eyes.

They were dragging him across a gravel courtyard toward a concrete building at the far end of the prison. He could see the gray metal door leading inside, its rivets gleaming with reflected sunlight. As his head slumped forward, he caught a glimpse of the Afrikäner words stamped on the plaque above the door, and his heart broke…

Women's Prison

"No!"

"What's wrong, monkey. Isn't this what you wanted? A little reunion with the wife and kids? This is your lucky day, kafir. Get to spend some time with the family, or what's left of them."

The guards unlocked the door and dragged him into the darkness…

.   .   .

Thala looked up at the darkness and fought the panic surging through him. The screams had faded, along with the horrible sight of loved ones being tortured. His sadistic prison guards were gone, as were Botha and his apartheid nightmare. A great war had been won against the evil in men's hearts, but at a tragic cost.

His trembling hand grasped the miniature gold bible dangling from his neck. A tear rolled down his glistening face. Twenty-five years had passed since that black day in Pretoria. Twenty-five years fighting another war. Lonely years. Sad years. He squeezed the tiny bible and said a prayer for his wife and daughters.

His heart slowed and his breathing eased a bit. He sat up on his elbows and squinted at the illuminated PC screen on the lab table, and its brilliant sun rising from a slate-blue sea.

He'd created the screen saver from a photograph taken on a beach near Durbin many years ago. A magnificent sunrise over the Indian Ocean on the last day they were together.

A soft smile crept across his face. Oh, how the girls loved to play on that beach, the sunlit surf washing over their bare bodies when they scampered into the warm, churning waters. He could still feel Yasmin's warmth against him when they watched their children splash in the waves. They'd spent that last night beneath the stars, their bodies intertwined, their hearts joined as one. A happy time. A loving time.

His fingers toyed with the bible. Yasmin had given him the necklace when he returned triumphantly to his homeland with a hard-earned medical degree from America, his eyes aflame with freedom, his heart bursting with pride.

The bible and gold chain were more than a gift for her proud husband. They were a tribute to the man who had overcome impossible odds to become a physician, a dangerous precedent for a non-white in apartheid South Africa.

He slipped his hand under his soaked shirt and rested it on his ribs. The knifing pain was gone, but the dull ache in his side would be a lasting reminder of the terrible day in Pretoria Prison when a man's dreams were crushed by the wrenching screams of his dying wife and daughters.

Enough! He rolled off the cot and staggered through the tent flap into the warm night air. It was one a.m. on the Trinity River. The full moon shined down on him from the starlit sky. He frowned and looked toward the river.

Impossible to sleep now. Too many demons lurking in the shadows. Might as well check the site. With only a few hours remaining to the pickup, don't want any hungry animals disturbing the bodies.

He was nearly past the Vickers when he noticed the pale glow coming from the small window on the rear door. An uneasy feeling swept through him. He'd planned to wait until morning to confront his guest, but important questions needed answers.

He stepped to the rear of the van and eased up the foot ladder. Polarized light flooded his eyes when he opened the door. His guest was asleep at the lab table.

"Mr. Frankton?"

Karl sat up and squinted at the dark face peering down at him. "Must've dozed off."

Thala glanced at the metal box beside the electron microscope. "Better put those blood samples back on ice."

"Sorry." Karl slipped on a glove and reached for the ice chest. "Hope you don't mind. Just wanted to take a look."

"I prefer you wear a suit if you're going to handle the samples. We don't know what we're up against."

"Sure, Doc. No problem." Karl opened the chest and lowered the samples into the dry ice.

"I was checking the site when I saw the light in the van. If you're going to sleep, you should use the cot. It's easier on the back."

Karl nodded and closed the ice chest.

Thala locked his black eyes on his guest. "You said you were assigned from Atlanta?"

"Right."

"Your supervisor?"

Karl looked up at him. "Something wrong?"

"Just curious. I might know him."

"Sounds like you've been with CDC a long time."

"Twenty-five years."

"That accent sounds South African."

Thala nodded. "Born and raised."

"One of their independent states?"

Thala's eyes flashed. "The Kwa Zulu state, Mr. Frankton. Non-independent. Too rebellious to become one of their slave states. Apartheid at its finest."

"You had a rough time?"

"I prefer not to discuss it. Your supervisor?"

Karl forced a smile. "I have a feeling you've been checking on me."

"Maybe."

Karl's smile faded. He sank in the chair and gazed at the ice chest. "I was supposed to catch a plane to Nogales. Something about Hantavirus. There was an article in the paper. It didn't sound right, so I came here instead."

Thala folded his arms. "What do you mean, didn't sound right?"

Karl slipped off the insulated glove. "Come on, Doc. Roadblock? Quarantine? Flu in mid-summer? You guys can do better than that."

"It's possible."

"So's snow in Somalia."

Thala unfolded his arms and snatched the vacant stool beside Karl. He sat down and stared at his guest. "I checked your history on the computer. Interesting record." He watched Karl's face redden.

"That's supposed to be classified."

"It is."

"Then, how did you—"

"Never mind that. By now, they're looking for you."

Karl shrugged. "I sort of guessed that. A little awkward for both of us."

Thala glared at him. "You have an interesting way of putting things, Mr. Frankton. CDC's flying in some heavies at ten hundred hours. Best let them deal with you."

"Then, I can stay?"

Thala shrugged. "If I were you, I'd drive back to Houston and plead ignorance. From your record, they'll probably think you got drunk and went off looking for trouble. Then had second thoughts and headed back to the airport. Actually, it's quite believable."

"Is it now."

Thala scratched his head. "It's not my business, but you really messed up. Best in your class. Uncanny analytical mind. Hard-earned success at your fingertips. Great family. Great future. What happened?"

"Like you said, it's not your business." Karl glanced at the ice chest. "If it's okay, I'd rather keep at it tonight."

"Here?"

Karl nodded. "I feel lucky."

"You sound desperate, Mr. Frankton."

"Let's just say I'm trying to go out in style."

Thala looked down. "You know I'm going to plead ignorance when they land. Don't expect any good words from me."

"Didn't ask for any."

"You won't have tonight if the guards get the word. They'll be on you like those Texas horseflies."

"C'est la vie."

Thala stood up and pushed the stool under the table. "Then know this, Mr. Frankton. We're in trouble. Big trouble. Since you got here, three more outbreaks have been reported. One is in Pretoria."

Karl stared at him. "South Africa?"

Thala's eyes flickered with anger. "Ironic, isn't it? Blacks and whites struck down by the same invisible hand. I guess the devil is color-blind."

"How many?"

"Classified." Thala looked down at the electron microscope. "It's growing geometrically. First Somalia, then Mombassa and Willapa Bay."

"Mombassa?"

"Yes, Mombassa. Now Trinity, Buenos Aires, Pretoria, and Santo Domingo. I've never seen anything like it. Global presence. Strikes without warning. No pattern or residue. Nothing but dead blood cells and frozen faces. Makes one want to pick up their bible."

Karl glanced at the ice chest. "We'll find it."

"Maybe, but we're in a race against time, and it's running out." Thala rested his hand on the electron microscope's monitor. "We're up against something better than us. The creature I've feared for twenty-five years. The perfect mutation." He patted the monitor. "We need everyone on the battlefield, even the desperate ones. Good night, Mr. Frankton. I'm suddenly very tired." He turned and pushed through the van's metal door.

Karl felt his ears pop as the door slammed shut. For the second time in a week, he'd found someone to respect. A six-foot-six-inch Zulu with penetrating black eyes and charcoal hair. A powerful man whose face showed the scars of bitter times.

It was more than Thala's strong words. There was a clarity to him. A resolve like Nihalla's. Two men that might make a difference, and one of them was dead.

He recalled Nihalla leaning against the van in the moonlight, his face worn from exhaustion. God, if he'd only made him that cup of chamomile tea. A man should have his tea before he dies.

He stared at the ice chest. What about you, Mr. Frankton? Anything left in the ol' tank? There's a bottle of scotch in your bag. Lots of bad memories too. Tomorrow, you'll be out of work with a few dollars in your pocket and a one-way ticket to York. Is that the way to close the book on seventeen years of struggle? Your call, old chum. You still have a few hours.

He slipped on the insulated glove and opened the ice chest. He'd been through the box of blood samples twice since entering the van, each time with the same futile result. Dead blood cells floating on the electron microscope's white screen, each one starved for oxygen, a microcosm of their suffocated host.

He lifted out the frosted box and unzipped its tape seal. His gloved hand reached through the vapor and grasped the first slide. He inserted it in the electron microscope's viewing chamber and activated the vacuum pump. It would be his third look. He clicked on the camera and adjusted the focus knob until the dead blood cells sharpened on the screen.

Nothing. Just dead blood cells floating on a white screen. The other thirteen slides would show the same result. Of all the tests, the blood test was most important. In the end, whatever gets you ends up in the blood.

He leaned forward and grasped the magnification knob. Full power, dammit! It's there all right. You're just too dumb to see it! He twisted the knob and waited for the refreshed screen to come into focus.

Zero. He ripped off the glove and threw it on the floor. Somalia, Mombassa, Willapa Bay, and four other sites across the globe. One, two, four. Know what comes next, Frankton? Eight, dammit. Then sixteen, thirty-two, sixty-four!

He clenched his fist and shook it at the screen. Think, for Christ's sake! Be the doctor you never were. The answer is on that screen. It's in that blood. Now get creative and find the damn thing!

He slumped on the stool while recalling Dr. Jekyll staring at the vapor-covered flask in his London laboratory. He'd read the novel many years ago. Took a liking to it, maybe because he was a lot like Jekyll, and Jekyll's not so pleasant friend.

His eyes focused on the black medical bag beside the stool. He lifted it on his lap and popped it open. His hand grasped a cellophane packet containing a fresh syringe and needle. He placed them on the lab table, along with a small bottle of alcohol and wad of gauze.

He ripped off the cellophane and gripped the syringe while recalling Thala's words. It would only take a few seconds to inject one of the blood samples into his vein. Then a few more to draw a sample of his own blood for the electron scope—if he was still alive. He'd activate the CD and voice recorders before injecting the sample. Then, he'd know.

He pulled blood sample tube "3" out of the ice chest and stuck the needle into its plastic cap. His trembling hand switched on the recorders. It was two a.m. on the Trinity River.

"You were right, Doc. Desperate men do desperate things."

Chapter 7

The Devil's Face

Fletcher slammed the receiver on the hook and glared at the phone. *Idiot! Are you nuts! That's a public line!*

He collapsed in the leather chair and looked down at his clenched fists. *Better call Parker. He'll know what to do. Just take it easy. Don't let Estelle see you like this. That's the last thing you need.* He rested his head against the leather and stared at the portrait above the stone fireplace.

The morning sunlight had reached the portrait, illuminating the four faces smiling down at him. He took a calming breath while recalling how Estelle kept poking him and the two boys when they posed for the portrait last year. Hard to stay awake when you're forced to sit long hours with an artist peering at you. He must have dozed off a dozen times during that two month ordeal.

He studied the two young men flanking him and his wife, their hands resting affectionately on their parent's shoulders. Hard to believe Franklin and Robert were nearing graduation. Seems like yesterday they were playing in the yard behind him.

God, how the years had flown. Nineteen of them since he took the oath at the Lincoln Memorial. So clean and uplifting on that sunlit, autumn day. How things had changed.

Nineteen years, dammit. Nineteen years dodging arrows and bullshit. Night sweats and ominous phone calls. Crisis meetings and frantic trips. Purges and regime changes. Egomaniacs and bureaucrats. Media scum digging for their big story. Dirty politics and unsavory deals. Two-faced bosses and their friends. All of it crammed into a cesspool called Washington, DC. An unflushed toilet clogged with its own waste.

He shook his head. Patience, old man. In a few months you'll be out of this zoo. You're still young. Estelle too. Lots of good years ahead. You owe her that. Yourself too.

He glanced at the opened folder on the desk. He'd jammed the folder into his briefcase before leaving the office at two a.m. A soft phone call had assured his wife nothing was wrong. Home before sunrise. Nothing new. He remembered climbing in beside her and holding her close until she dropped off to sleep. Then staggering down to the study to await Hampsted's phone call. A call that never came.

He glared at the photograph of Karl Frankton. Five hours had passed since he talked to Hampsted. What was taking him so long? Get on with it, dammit. Can't let things unravel now.

He pressed a finger against his lip and rubbed it back and forth in a nervous motion. Better clean up and head back to the office. Gotta be there when they introduce the new top dog. A real idealist from the scuttlebutt. Just what we need, another do-gooder.

He started to get up and froze when the cell phone went off. He snatched the buzzing phone off the desk and pressed the cold plastic against his ear. It took a few seconds for the warbling to clear.

"We've got him. I'm in a chopper closing on the site. Should land within the hour."

Fletcher stiffened. "He's at Trinity?"

"Since last night."

"In custody?"

"Not yet. I told the guards to wait for me."

"You what?"

"I'm not sure about the team leader. Some guy named Thala. Won't respond to calls or e-mail. We're going to surprise him, just in case."

Fletcher pressed his mouth against the phone. "Don't blow it, Parker. That scum could finish us."

"*Understood.*" Hampsted hesitated. "*Have you heard about the other sites?*"

"Never mind that. Just get this over with. We have another problem."

"*Another?*"

"What's this?"

Fletcher's head snapped up. Estelle was standing between the study doors, her hands grasping the handles. She was wearing the yellow robe he loved so much.

"*What's wrong?*"

"Gotta go. Get back to me at nine." Fletcher pressed the off button and placed the phone on the desk. He closed the folder and smiled at his wife.

"Oh, honey, look at you." She shuffled beside him and plopped down on his lap. "You need to take it easy. You know what the doc said."

Fletcher slipped his hand under her robe and probed the soft flesh. "I'm fine. Just the usual garbage. It'll all work out."

She rested her head on his chest. "Want to come up?"

Fletcher felt his member harden. He could smell the perfume in her blond hair. She was so warm. So soft. He squeezed her against him and forced out the words. "Can I take a rain check?"

She slapped his chest and looked down at him with concerned eyes. "You said that yesterday. Then you worked all night."

"I'm sorry."

"The boys will be home in a few weeks. Then a whole month before they go back. We should make the most of our free time."

"Please, honey. I feel bad enough."

She smiled and kissed him with a warm tongue. "Tonight then, but that's my final offer. Blow this one and you better buy some porno magazines." She stood up and looked down at him with those baby blues. "What's going on? It's only six?"

"A lot of crap. I have to go back in."

"Looking like that?"

"I'll grab a shower."

She bent down and kissed him on the forehead. "Want me in there too?"

Fletcher broke into a grin. "Be up in ten minutes." He watched her sashay through the twin doors while thanking God for life's little pleasures. At forty-five, his beautiful wife had the body of a twenty-year-old. And him sitting on his ass with the world ready to blow up.

He snatched the cell phone off the desk and started dialing an international code. The first digits were 011-43-662. He hadn't dialed the number in years, but it was burned into his brain like a brand.

.   .   .

"You have a phone call, Herr Menchen."

Gunthar Menchen blinked at the silver-haired man looking down at him in the bright sunlight. "Frau Menchen?"

"No, Herr Menchen. He sounds American. He won't give his name, but he said you would want to talk with him."

Menchen shaded his eyes. "No name?"

"No, Herr Menchen. I could barely understand him. Very bad connection."

"Bad?"

"A strange warbling and echo. I asked him to call back, but he refused. He said it was important he talk with you." The servant extended a small cell phone.

Menchen sat up in the lounge chair and squinted at the sweeping view of Salzburg and the Salzach River. He rubbed his face and glanced at his watch. Just past noon. His wife and daughter would be back from Innsbruck soon, their faces blushed from hiking in the summer sun. He breathed a frustrated sigh and looked at the sunlit Festung Hohensalzburg fortress on Mönchsberg hill above the city.

It was a beautiful summer day in Salzburg, and Gunthar Menchen had enjoyed every moment of it—until now. He snatched the phone from his servant's hand. "Thank you, Alfred. That will be all."

"Yes, Herr Menchen."

Menchen waited until his servant disappeared through the opened patio doors before pressing the phone's talk button. He placed the phone against his ear and spoke softly. "Yes?"

For a moment, the only sound was a distant echo. The line cleared and a voice crackled in his ear. *"I turned on the scrambler. Best to play it safe."*

The Austrian stiffened. "Who is this?"

"Star—"

"What?"

"Star—"

He lowered the phone and stared at it in shock. He hadn't heard that voice in a decade. He raised the phone to his mouth and forced out the second syllable. "—burst."

"It's been a long time."

"Why are you calling me?"

"I thought we'd better talk. I think we have a burn."

"A what?"

"Sixteen sites and growing. You're not the only one I'm contacting. There are two others."

Menchen shook his head. "This is lunacy. We agreed never to talk unless something was confirmed. You have no right to call me with meaningless speculation."

"I'm sorry, but things could break any minute. So far, the media's been out of it. That won't last long. It might be a coincidence, but I don't like what I see."

Menchen groped for the pen in his silk robe. He yanked it out and snatched the newspaper off the lounge table. "Give me locations, counts, and symptoms." He scowled while jotting notes on the folded newspaper. His breathing elevated. A bead of sweat trickled down his forehead. When he was done, he stared at his notes in disbelief.

"Are you there?"

Menchen gripped the newspaper. "No need for you to make the other calls. I'll contact the necessary parties. Just a precaution, you understand?"

"Of course."

Menchen lowered the newspaper. "Who on your side is working the sites?"

"CDC for now. They've uncovered nothing, but you never know. I'll keep things tight on this end, but I need your help."

Menchen hesitated. "Give me a day to check with my associates. I'll phone you tomorrow. Four p.m., your time. Please confirm your number." Menchen jotted down the number. "Tomorrow then." He pressed the off button and fell back on the lounge, his eyes locked on Festung Hohensalzburg.

. . .

"Papa!"

Xolisile ran toward him across the sand, her lithe young body glistening in the morning sun. He stood up and brushed off his pants. "What's wrong, little one?"

She jumped into his arms and wrapped herself around him. "Who are they, Papa?"

"Who?"

"Those men." She pointed toward the dunes.

He squinted at the sand swirling into the blue sky above the dunes. The wind had picked up from the sea, creating sand devils along the beach. In his daughter's imaginative mind, those wisps of sand were ghosts. He smiled and whispered in her ear. "Playing games with your father?"

She sat up in his arms and gave him the evil look he adored. "I'm not playing. Who are they?"

He smiled and stroked her wet hair. It was time to leave, but there was always room for a little game. "Hmmm, I don't know. Maybe we should take a closer look."

She hugged his neck. "I don't like them, Papa. Make them go away."

"Ah, I see them now. They're ghosts coming up from the sand. Let's chase them away." He forced back a grin and shuffled toward the dunes, his daughter clinging to his neck. Oh, how she loved to play games with him. This time, it was sand phantoms swirling across the dunes.

"Where are you going?"

He stopped and looked back at Yasmin standing beside the van, her black hair blowing in the wind. Correla stood beside her mother, gaping at her father and sister.

"Only a minute. We have to chase some ghosts." He turned away and ran toward the dunes while Yasmin shouted at him, but the crashing waves drowned out her voice.

He was within a few feet of the sand swirls when he saw the jeep roll over the crest and grind to a halt above him. Three men were seated inside, two in the front, one in the back. He stared at the jeep and listened to the waves, and he felt a sudden chill.

The three men climbed out of the jeep and marched down the dune toward him. They wore khaki uniforms and were armed with batons and pistols. At ten feet, they halted and peered at him. The center man wore an officer's cap.

"You're Mandu Thala?"

The policeman's Afrikäner accent cut through him like a knife. He nodded and eased Xolisile down on the sand.

The officer stepped forward. "You're to come with us."

He looked at the officer with stunned eyes. "What have I done?"

"Never mind that." The officer looked down at Xolisile. "Let's not disturb the child. Better you come peacefully."

He heard Yasmin shuffling through the sand. She grabbed his arm and pressed against him.

"What is it, Mandu?"

"I don't know."

"Let's go then." The officer stepped forward and seized his arm while Yasmin stared at the scene in shock.

"But why? What has my husband done?"

"That's our business." The officer glared at her. "Get along home with your family. You shouldn't be here. Go back to Kwa Zululand before I arrest you."

They grabbed his arms and led him up the dune to the jeep. As they drove away, he managed to look back at his wife and daughters. Yasmin was holding them close, her black eyes locked on the jeep, her face wet with tears. He watched them disappear behind the dune, the Indian Ocean at their back, the sun rising over them. It was the last time he saw them before that horrible day in the women's prison. The dune faded away...

. . .

"You okay, Doc?"

Thala's eyes snapped open. He sat up and glared at the man standing beside his cot. "What are you doing in here?"

Karl backed away, his face glistening with sweat. A used syringe dangled from his left hand. "Better come with me."

Thala stared at Karl's strained face—and it hit him. He'd seen that face before. In Zaire and Uganda. In Mexico and Honduras. In countless crisis sites across the globe. The fatigue and bloodshot eyes. The matted hair and sweat-covered brow. His own mirrored face at the moment of discovery. He crawled off the cot and followed Karl through the tent flap.

It was 5:10 at Trinity site. The moon had dropped into the western sky and the first traces of daylight flickered on the eastern horizon. A coyote's howl cut the darkness. The only other sound was the river sloshing against its banks.

Thala shuffled past the darkened tents, his eyes glancing nervously toward the rocks where the bodies lay. He followed his guest into the van and closed the metal door behind them.

Nothing unusual. The electron microscope's screen hissed with gray static. The polarized lamps were set to their lowest level, tinting the compartment with soft, pale light. The cot hadn't been used. The ice chest was closed and all was in order on the lab table.

Karl sat down and gestured toward the vacant stool. He rested his elbow on the lab table and watched Thala sit beside him.

"Well?"

Karl looked down at the syringe. "I pulled sample three and drew its blood. Same blood type as mine. Worth a try, don't you think?

Thala's eyes widened. "You shot that dead blood into your vein?"

Karl placed the syringe on the table. "Came mighty close. Turned on the recorders. Activated the scope. The whole nine yards. Only take a second to inject it. Then a few more for the ol' ticker to pump it through my body. Time enough to stick in a fresh needle and suck out a few drops."

"For God's sake, are you mad!" Thala jumped off the stool, his eyes filled with anger.

"Easy, Doc. We're working on vapor here."

Thala's black eyes locked on the syringe. Had the man beside him snapped? Had the alcohol and personal loss finally taken their toll? Fine line between despair and insanity. Doesn't take much to cross it. If anyone knew that line, it was Mandu Thala. He leaned forward and spoke softly. "What happened, Mr. Frankton?"

Karl looked down at the syringe. "I chickened out. Can't explain why. Guess I'm not ready to die."

"You didn't inject the blood?"

Karl shook his head.

Thala leaned closer. "Then why are we here?"

"I was ready to shut things down when an idea hit me."

"Idea?"

Karl placed his finger on the CD's play button. "I drew my blood and injected it into sample three." He pressed the button. "Guess it worked."

Thala looked at the flickering screen. The static gave way to blurred spots on a field of white, which quickly sharpened to sample three's dead blood cells. He watched Karl's injected blood surge across the screen, its red cells rich with oxygen. The two samples collided, dead cells mixing with live.

Thala noticed his guest's hand trembling. "Are you okay, Mr. Frankton?"

"Not really." Karl nodded at the screen.

What was it? What was happening? Thala stared at the screen in disbelief. A bright flash. Then another. The healthy cells withered, their membranes drained of life-giving oxygen.

Karl pressed the pause button, freezing a third white flash before it disappeared. He stared at the bright screen while sharpening the focus. "See it?"

Thala reached out and touched the screen, his fingertips resting on the blurred structure barely visible in the flash. "What is it?"

"I don't know, but it isn't a virus."

Thala squinted at the screen. "It looks like—"

"Right on, Doc. A chemical compound. Manmade, all the way. And it's invisible."

Thala backed away from the screen. "I better wake the others."

"No."

Thala looked down at the trembling pathologist. "We need clear heads. You can barely keep your eyes open."

"This is my show, remember? I still have five hours."

Thala shook his head. "If you're right about this, we should notify CDC."

Karl glared at him. "We are CDC! Now give me my five hours and get the hell out of here." He turned away and snatched sample #7.

Chapter 8

Decision

The chopper landed at 0610, its blades kicking up the sand. The roar awakened Dolstadt and Kremler who staggered out of their tents in shock.

Dolstadt swiped at the flying sand. "What the hell's going on?"

"Beats me. Looks like an invasion." Kremler started toward Thala's tent and froze when he saw him burst through the Vickers' rear door.

Thala rushed down the steps and shuffled beside his two colleagues. He gripped Kremler's arm and stared at the chopper. "Let me handle this."

The chopper's passenger door slid open and two military police jumped out, followed by a gray-suited man. They ducked the slowing blades and walked toward the stunned team.

The gray-suited man pulled off his sunglasses. "You're Thala?"

Thala nodded.

The man flashed an ID. "Parker Hampsted, Doctor. Where's Frankton?"

Thala glanced at the van. "I'll get him."

"Never mind." Hampsted pointed to the van and watched the two MP's climb the rear steps, their hands grasping drawn pistols.

"What's wrong?"

Hampsted glared at Thala. "I've been trying to contact you since midnight. Nothing but static and out-of-service messages."

Thala frowned. "We're pretty tired here. I turned off my electronics so I could get some sleep. Why didn't you call the guards?"

"That's not the point. It's protocol, dammit. You never break communications in the field. Don't they teach you guys anything?"

Thala's frown deepened. "This isn't the military, Mr. Hampsted."

"Never mind that. What do you know about Frankton?"

Thala shrugged. "He arrived last night. Said he was assigned from Atlanta."

"You didn't confirm?"

Thala glanced at his two colleagues who were standing off to the side. He leaned forward and lowered his voice to a whisper. "He knew about Somalia and Willapa Bay. Even the body count."

"That's not enough. You're supposed to check all entrants. This is serious business, Doctor. Another slip like that and you're through." Hampsted brushed past him, leaving the stunned Zulu trembling with anger.

Thala watched the MP's lead Karl out of the van, his hands cuffed in front of him. Their eyes met briefly. The message was clear. Sorry, Mr. Frankton. No help promised. None given.

The MP's escorted Karl to the chopper. They were climbing aboard when Hampsted shouted for them to wait. He stepped beside his prisoner, his eyes filled with rage. "I warned you. Always trying to make trouble. This time you went too far."

Karl scowled at him through bloodshot eyes. "Cut the crap and get on with it."

Hampsted backed away and watched them push Karl into the chopper. He turned toward Kremler and Dolstadt who were shaking in their boots. "What do you know about this?"

Kremler fumbled for words. "We took a call from the guard post last night. They said we had a visitor. We turned it over to Dr. Thala."

Hampsted edged closer. "You lying to me?"

Kremler's voice broke. He looked at Hampsted with pleading eyes. "We're just trying to do our jobs. We don't know anything about this."

"That's enough!"

Hampsted spun around and saw the six-foot-six Zulu glaring down at him. "Easy, Doctor. Your visitor's a security risk."

"A what?"

"Get on with your work, Doctor. We'll check the van and be on our way."

Thala's glare softened. "What about the bodies?"

"The transport team should be here by noon. Now get to work. We don't need any more distractions." Hampsted slipped on his sunglasses and retreated to the Vickers.

Thala watched the MP's jam their exhausted prisoner into the chopper's rear seat. First came the leg irons. Then the wrist manacles. He saw Frankton grimace when they tightened the metal cuffs—and something stirred inside him.

He rested a hand on his ribs while recalling the nightmarish day in Pretoria. The pain. The screams. The clinking chains. Yes, these men were too much like the Afrikäners.

Hampsted spent ten minutes in the van before heading for the chopper. He was climbing aboard when he noticed Thala staring at him, his black eyes seething with anger. He leaned toward the Zulu and shouted above the whine. "Was Mr. Frankton helpful?"

"Helpful?"

Hampsted's eyes burned into him. "You know what I mean. Are you hiding something?"

Thala backed away and nodded at the chopper. "You're taking up valuable time. We don't need any more distractions."

95

Hampsted's eyes flashed. "You have me worried, Doctor. I'll be watching you." He climbed into the passenger seat and slammed the cockpit door.

Thala swiped at the blowing sand and caught a glimpse of Frankton's face through the plastic bubble. Their eyes met briefly. Thala raised his hand and nodded farewell...

. . .

The second chopper landed at 1214. It was larger than the first, capable of transporting a substantial payload in its stripped cargo compartment. In this case, the cargo would be fourteen body bags.

Thala stepped out of the Vickers and watched the black hulk descend on the campsite. He'd spent the morning secluded in the van while Kremler and Dolstadt drew backup samples from the bodies. His two colleagues watched from the rocks, their bio-suits smeared with dirt and mud.

The chopper dropped beside the tents, its blades churning up the sand. The cargo door slid open, exposing three khaki-clad personnel with medical bags. One was a woman. She appeared rather attractive beneath the military-issue sunglasses.

The young woman shuffled toward him and extended her hand. "Dr. Thala?"

"Yes?" He clasped her hand.

"Susan Cayman. We're here to relieve you."

"Relieve?"

She nodded. "We'll take the bodies to Corpus Christi and pick up where your team left off. You're cleared to shut things down and head back to Atlanta. You can release your men."

Thala stared at her in shock. "Are you quoting an order?"

"Yes, from Mr. Hampsted." She pulled an e-mail out of her pocket and handed it to him.

Thala scanned the e-mail until he spotted the sentence regarding "excessive fatigue." He frowned and handed it back to her. "We've made good progress here. It doesn't make sense to pull us out."

"Not my idea, Doctor. I checked with Atlanta for confirmation. It seems Mr. Hampsted carries a lot of weight."

Thala shook his head. "That message is dated yesterday. Mr. Hampsted didn't get here until today. How could he know our condition beforehand?"

"Not my business. I've been traveling since yesterday. All the way from Somalia."

Thala's eyes lit up. "You were on the Shabeelle?"

"Yes, Doctor. A real paradise."

"You know about—"

She nodded. "Haven't gotten over it."

"How did they—"

She sighed and looked at the river. "Nihalla went into the jungle and Jim followed him. We found their bodies at sunset. The samples revealed deoxygenated blood. Same as the others. The tests showed nothing. Cause of death... unknown."

"I'm sorry."

"How about here?"

"Same thing. Dead blood and dead hosts. No explanation." Thala hesitated. "You know Mr. Frankton?"

Her face reddened. "A real troublemaker. I was stunned when they told me he was here. How long was he with you?"

Thala hesitated. Call it experience—instinct—whatever. There was something about her that bothered him. Naïve—innocent—yet coldly persistent. And that e-mail putting her in charge. He recalled Hampsted's final words...

I'll be watching you.

"Doctor?"

"Oh, sorry. Maybe Mr. Hampsted was right about the fatigue. You were asking about Mr. Frankton?"

"Yes."

"Good worker. Jumped right in. Not very bright though. Couldn't trust him with anything too involved. I think he has a drinking problem."

She nodded and looked at the van. "We should get moving. I'll have my men help with the bodies and samples. Maybe we can spend a few minutes going over your findings."

Thala nodded and watched her give instructions to her men. He glanced down at the medical bag in his hand.

There was still time to back out. He could do it during the briefing. Charge it off to excessive fatigue. Give her the CD and samples, and be on his way. A simple exchange and all would be forgotten. Or would it?

He tightened his grip on the bag. Why were they so worried about Mr. Frankton? He might be a boozer, but the man was special. He'd seen it in others. A sixth sense that digs out the truth, regardless of the obstacles. An uncanny recklessness that ignores the rules to find the answer. Frankton was a renegade, but he was the perfect warrior to fight the killer in that flashing light.

And who was Parker Hampsted? In his twenty-five years at CDC, Mandu Thala had grown quite proficient at cracking the government's "secured" computer databases.

After searching CDC's human resource banks, his only finding was a cryptic reference to "PH" within the government's "transferred" file. Maybe nothing, but he recalled a similar result for a colleague he'd worked with some years ago, a CDC pathologist who disappeared one night in the Middle East, never to be heard from again, except for the same cryptic reference.

Thala stiffened. Time for a difficult decision. Hiding the truth could end his career at CDC, the only thing left in his shattered life.

For twenty-five years, he'd fought an enemy greater than the pain of Pretoria and the Afrikäners. An enemy that transcended national borders, corrupt governments, and human slavery. An enemy that didn't have an atom of prejudice in its plasma body.

But he never expected this. A microscopic creation that sucked the life out of a person's blood like an invisible vampire.

Thala turned toward his tent. He didn't know it, but his decision would determine the fate of the species known as *homo sapiens.*

. . .

Karl knew something was wrong when the Gulf of Mexico flashed through the haze on his left. They were headed southwest toward the Mexican border. Atlanta was two thousand miles behind them. Things were getting a little tense in southwest Texas.

"So, where are we going this time?" Karl grimaced from a sharp nudge in the ribs.

"No talking."

Karl raised his manacled wrists and glared at the MP. "Isn't this a bit much? These damn things hurt."

"Don't move and they won't hurt." The MP folded his arms and leaned back in the seat.

Karl lowered his hands and stared at the blue sky above the plastic bubble. He was sandwiched in the rear seat between the two MP's. Hampsted sat in front of him beside the pilot, his eyes trained on his laptop PC. From the tapping of the keys, his favorite person was exchanging e-mails with headquarters.

Karl closed his eyes and felt the chopper veer to the right. The Gulf of Mexico faded into the haze as they headed inland.

They touched down in the desert an hour later. Through the swirling sand, Karl noticed three wooden shacks surrounded by a chain link fence. Add the barbed wire strung along the top, and the place resembled a deserted government installation in one of those cheap sci-fi's. A second chopper rested on the sand beside the shacks. It was empty.

They led him out of the chopper toward the first shack. It was hot as hell and the sun was at ten o'clock. He squinted at the blue sky and streaked cirrus clouds while shuffling toward the two blue-suited men standing at the opened door.

One of the men stepped forward and removed his sunglasses. "Mr. Hampsted?"

Hampsted nodded and gestured for the MP's to take Karl inside.

They led him down a dark hallway to a door that opened to a small room with a cot, chair, table, and battery-powered lamp. A small fan had been placed on the table to keep the air circulating. It was hot as an oven. They removed his manacles, gave him a bottle of water, and locked him in. There were no windows. He took a swig of water and was asleep in seconds.

Chapter 9

Extreme Prejudice

"Let's call him Bernie."

Karl nodded and rested his chin on his hands. They were sprawled on the ugly brown carpet in Karl's apartment, their eyes trained on the horny lizard peering at them from the oversized cage.

Karl placed his finger on the cage's door latch. "Ready?"

Jeremy slid the jar of freshly caught flies beside the cage door and unscrewed the jar's plastic cap.

"Here you go, Bern. Your favorite, flies under glass." Karl opened the cage door and listened to his son's laughter as the iguana lurched backward, its amber eyes glaring at them. "Let 'em go, Jerry. Your lizard's famished." He watched Jeremy stick the opened jar into the cage.

Bernie didn't need prodding. His darting tongue flicked two of the escaping flies out of the air. The others never made it out of the jar.

"Cool! Did you see that!"

Karl rested a hand on his son's shoulder. "Remember to use live ones. Ol' Bern likes 'em nice and fresh. Right, Bern?" He watched the lizard crawl to its water basin at the far-end of the cage.

Jeremy looked down at the empty jar. "Hey, I got an idea."

"Yeah?"

"Let's feed him you!"

Before Karl could react, his son sprang onto him and began a wrestling match filled with slobbering laughter and screams. The two lunatics got so loud, Bernie charged across the cage to get a better look. Probably trying to figure out who eats who.

"Gottcha!" Jeremy pressed his dad's shoulders into the brown carpet and leaned forward with all his might. "One! Two! No!" He let out a shriek as his dad's fingers dug into his highly ticklish ribs. Jeremy pushed away the probing fingers, but his dad wouldn't quit. His fingers broke through Jeremy's defenses and dug into his ribs.

Jeremy laughed hysterically while pressing on his dad's shoulders. "So, you wanna play rough!" He slipped his hands under his dad's armpits and tickled with all his might. The laughter was deafening. Karl would hear about it for sure, especially with the landlord's rent past due.

Hell with it. This was his son, dammit. In two days, Jeremy would be back on a plane with his mom, and the loneliness would return.

Karl broke out laughing and returned his fingers to their tickling position. Jeremy nearly had him when the cell phone went off.

Karl glanced at his watch while trying to keep his eleven-year-old assailant at bay. He snatched the cell phone off the cocktail table and popped it open.

"Karl?"

Karl gave his giggling son a pat on the back and felt him relax against his ol' dad.

"Having a good time?"

"Yeah. Wait till you see his birthday present."

"I can imagine." Anne sighed nervously. *"We'll be coming by to pick him up in an hour. Hope that's okay."*

Karl's smile faded. "We?"

"There's someone I want you to meet. He'd like to buy you a coffee, if that's okay."

Karl patted Jeremy on the back and sat up while his son crawled beside the caged iguana. "I'm not dressed for going out."

"We'll keep it casual. It won't take long. I have an eight o'clock plane back to New York."
"Tonight? I thought you weren't going back until Tuesday?"
"Change in plans. Sorry."
"I bought tickets to the basketball game. Jeremy's really looking forward to it...and so am I."
"Sorry. See you soon."
Karl listened to the click and stared at his son...

. . .

"How are you feeling, Mr. Frankton?"
Karl squinted at the shadow peering down at him. He tried to focus, but the image kept doubling up.
"Sorry about the grogginess. It'll wear off in a bit." Hampsted eased into the wooden chair beside the cot. His white shirt was soaked with perspiration and his tie hung loose from his opened collar.
Karl sat up on his elbow and gripped his throbbing head. "What did you give me?"
"Just a mild sedative. Makes it easier for both of us."
"Easier?"
"We need answers, Mr. Frankton, and we don't have much time." Hampsted leaned toward him. "Why did you go to Trinity?"
Karl forced a smile. "Flu epidemics don't happen in summer."
Hampsted's face reddened. "What about the syringe?"
"Syringe?"
"The one we found in the disposal unit."
Karl felt the hairs prick up on the back of his neck. "How the hell should I know? Ask Thala and his boys. They're the ones that took the samples. Must be dozens of used syringes in that unit."

Hampsted leaned toward him. "We found a print on the syringe that matches yours. We checked the residue. It's your DNA, Mr. Frankton. Why did you draw your own blood?"

Karl shrugged. "Standard safety procedures. Just like Somalia and Willapa Bay."

Hampsted pointed a trembling finger at him. "You're lying, Mr. Frankton. What did you find in that van?"

"Find?"

"In the dead blood."

Karl grimaced. Was he bluffing? No time to figure it out. Just take your best shot. He sighed and blurted out the words. "I think it's a mutant virus. Probably a Marburg derivative. I was close to something when your storm troopers dragged me out of there. If you're smart, you'll fly me back to Trinity so I can finish the job."

"That's it?"

"Pretty much."

The door creaked and one of the blue-suited men popped his head through the opening. "You have a call, sir."

Hampsted nodded, his eyes fixed on Karl. "Nice try, Mr. Frankton. You have five minutes to tell me what you saw on that screen. You know...inside the flashing light." He stood up and stepped through the opened door. The door closed behind him.

Karl collapsed on the cot and stared at the spinning ceiling. They'd used pentothal, dammit. Got him to spill his guts about the blurred image on the screen—maybe with a little help from Thala.

He shook his head. No sense going on with this. Tell Hampsted what you saw, get out of this heat, and head back to York. Stacking shelves looks pretty good right now.

He closed his eyes and thought of Jeremy. A year had passed since that day in the apartment. Odds were, ol' Bern was dead or abandoned. Anne never liked Bernie, and the iguana didn't care much for her. No surprise. Animals sense two-timers better than husbands.

104

He rubbed his sweating face and visualized a chilled martini. God, what he'd give for a double. Surprising they hadn't tried that on him. Cheaper than pentothal, and a lot more effective. His bloodshot eyes locked on the creaking door.

Hampsted stepped into the room, followed by the blue-suited man. He folded his arms and looked down at Karl. "You're going back to Atlanta."

"What?"

Hampsted frowned. "Looks like you have friends in high places, Mr. Frankton. I just got reamed for dragging you away from the site."

Karl stared at him in shock. "Why send me to Atlanta? Get me back to Trinity."

"Trinity's closed down." Hampsted unfolded his arms. "Guess I owe you an apology. Things are pretty tense right now. I shouldn't have overreacted. Can you walk?"

Karl glared at him. "I'll walk."

They gave him a canteen of fresh water and helped him out of the shack into the bright sunlight. He remembered Hampsted patting him on the shoulder when they led him across the compound to the black automobile. A hot, dry breeze brushed his face. He tasted the grit between his teeth. The sun stung his eyes. From the shortness of his shadow, it was early afternoon in the desert.

He paused at the rear passenger door and looked back at Hampsted who was standing in front of the shack, his hand clutching the wrinkled gray jacket. "We're not taking a chopper?"

Hampsted shrugged. "We need the choppers. It's twenty minutes to a dirt strip near here. We'll have a Gulfstream waiting for you. You'll be in Atlanta before midnight. Sorry for the trouble, Mr. Frankton." Hampsted turned and disappeared into the shack.

Karl felt one of the agents press him toward the opened door. He frowned and ducked into the sweltering back seat.

The agent slid beside him while the other took the driver's seat and started the engine. A rush of cool air swept through the car's interior as they accelerated through the opened barbed wire gate. Behind them, the compound faded into the drifting sand.

Karl leaned back in the seat and felt the agent's shoulder jostling against him from the rough road. The cool air felt good against his face. Maybe he'd catch a nap before they shoved him into the *Gulfstream.*

He took a breath of cool air. Friends in high places? What a laugh. Just a damn good deal cut by a damn good attorney two years ago. Someone upstairs must have gotten wind of Hampsted's little maneuver and pushed the panic button. Last thing the wimps needed was a three-year-old FDA scandal dumped in the media's lap.

He felt his eyes closing. Wonder who was waiting for him in Atlanta? Probably that jerk Wheatly with a fat severance check. The deal was for two years, and time was up. Then again, if they knew what he saw on that screen, they might keep him a little longer. They must know he was close to something. All he needed was another day. He'd nail the damn thing in another day.

His body relaxed against the seat, and he recalled his attorney's warning...

They won't rest until Karl Frankton is a name on a tombstone...

His eyes snapped open. Something was wrong. In the heat of interrogation, the wolves had suddenly backed off because of a phone call from "friends in high places."

He'd seen Hampsted in action. The bastard was too paranoid to commit himself without clearing things first. It didn't compute. Too sudden. Too contrived. He sat up and felt the agent press against him.

"Easy, Mr. Frankton. Almost there."

Karl looked into the agent's gray eyes and felt a sudden chill. He dropped back in the seat and stared at the windshield. They were driving straight at the mountains. The terrain had become more rugged. Certainly no place for an airstrip. The driver veered onto a gravel road that wound up a grade toward a butte overlooking the desert. Karl felt his heart pounding against his ribs. The dizziness was gone. He sat up and felt the agent press against him.

"Relax, Mr. Frankton. The plane should be down in a few minutes. Hope you don't mind. Just protocol."

Before Karl could react, the agent snapped a handcuff on Karl's right wrist. The agent reached for Karl's left wrist, but Karl jerked it away. "This isn't necessary. I haven't done anything."

"Protocol, remember?" The agent lunged across the seat and snared Karl's left wrist. The cuffs were engaged before Karl could react.

Karl felt a bead of sweat roll down his cheek. He glanced at the agent's parted jacket and spotted a nine millimeter protruding from a shoulder holster. The car accelerated up the gravel road as it closed on the butte's boulder-strewn summit.

Karl clenched his fists and felt the cuffs squeeze his wrists. He looked beyond the driver's head at the windshield. They were nearly to the summit. To his left, a rugged slope dropped toward the desert floor.

He heard a zipping sound and looked down. The agent had opened a small black case, exposing a silver syringe. The agent lifted the syringe out of the case with his right hand and grasped Karl's handcuffed wrists with his left.

Karl's eyes filled with horror. *Seconds man! You've got seconds! The bastard's gonna kill you!* He let out a primordial yell and slammed his clenched fists into the agent's face, driving the agent's head backward against the seat. *The needle! Get the needle!*

GARY NAIMAN

Karl snatched the agent's right wrist as the needle squirted black fluid in the air. The stunned agent jabbed Karl in the ribs with his left elbow, but Karl clung to the agent's trembling right hand, and its deadly syringe.

"Pull over and give me a hand with this jerk!" The agent hit Karl in the face with a vicious left backhand, but his prisoner refused to let go. "Damn you!" The enraged agent slipped his left hand inside his jacket and whipped out the nine millimeter.

Karl fought the blackness sweeping over him. *One chance! The gun! Get the gun!* He jammed his shoulder against the agent's left arm.

The air echoed with a loud bang from the discharging nine millimeter, followed by a gasp from the front seat. Blood spurted from a gaping hole in the driver's head.

The car swerved out of control, throwing Karl to the floor. The agent raised up on his knee and pointed the nine millimeter at Karl's head, but a terrific impact propelled him over the front seat into the windshield. Karl felt the seat give way as the car flipped over, flinging him at the ceiling. He gripped a safety strap, but the car's centrifugal force was too great as it careened down the slope. He slammed against the passenger door, then against the floor and ceiling. Glass exploded around him. The passenger compartment was collapsing. No chance. Say a prayer and grab onto something.

The passenger door ripped away and bright sunlight struck his face. He felt the gravel and sand tear at his clothes. Then came the explosion and pieces of flying metal. The last thing he remembered were the two corpses sprawled on the slope below him, and below them the flaming car rolling toward the desert floor. A blast of hot wind struck his face, and everything went black...

Chapter 10

Starburst

"Good night, Papa."

"Güter nachtschlaf mein leibchen." Menchen embraced his young daughter and watched her scamper out of the dining room. He breathed a father's sigh and smiled at the beautiful woman seated across from him. "Gretta is so happy. It must have been beautiful up there."

Nicole lowered her coffee cup and rested her hand on the table. "It would have been better with you there." She leaned forward and stroked his hand. "She missed you, Gunthar. I missed you."

Menchen's smile faded. "When I feel better, we'll take a long vacation in the Alps. No phones. No pagers. Just the three of us and the mountains." He tried to avoid his wife's concerned stare, but Nicole was persistent. She gripped his hand, her brown eyes burning into him.

"You should see Dr. Braun in the morning. You look so tired. It's only three months since the attack. You are working too hard, Gunthar."

Menchen forced a smile and placed his napkin on the table. He pushed out of his chair and eased beside her.

His gnarled hand caressed her blond hair. He leaned over and kissed her softly on the cheek. "Do you know how much I love you?"

"Yes, and that's why I am so concerned. You're my life, Gunthar. Our life."

He felt her warm, moist lips press against his, and for a moment, he was young again.

"Herr Menchen?"

Menchen straightened up and glared at the dining room's mirrored wall. Alfred was standing behind him at the opened door, obviously uncomfortable for the intrusion. "I'm sorry, sir. You have two calls in the conference room." Menchen frowned while clutching his wife's shoulder. He waited for Alfred to withdraw before kissing her a second time. He straightened up and tugged at his blazer. "These infernal overseas calls. Don't they know I have a life? They should be more considerate. I told them six p.m."

She smiled and patted his hand. "They have lives too. The world is too large for all this technology. Too much pressure." She kissed his hand. "Remember what Dr. Braun said about your temper. Stay calm, my darling. I'll be in the living room."

He patted her shoulder. "I won't be long."

"Better not. I have pictures of your daughter's first rappel."

Menchen's eyes brightened. "Yes?"

"Oh, yes. The instructor said Gretta is a natural climber. He wants her to join the youth club."

Menchen smiled with a father's pride. "She must have looked magnificent in that red anorak. A natural, he said?"

Nicole nodded. "Like her father."

Menchen's smile faded. "You mean, like her father was."

She watched him disappear through the mirrored door. When he was gone, she wiped away a tear. It was nine p.m. in Salzburg.

The conference room resembled a small screening room with its four-by-six-foot viewing screen, console, and polished black table. A snakelike mini-cam projected from the console, its filament lens aimed at the black leather chair at the head of the table. The cool air smelled from pine spray.

Menchen entered the conference room from the rear of his study. He closed the acoustic door and dropped into the black leather chair while staring at the two yellow lights flashing on the console. He pressed the activate button and watched the lights change to solid green as two faces materialized on the viewing screen.

The stern face on the left appeared Germanic, like his own. The face on the right was a handsome oriental with piercing black eyes and black hair. The man's white turtleneck clashed with the dark background.

"Good evening, Menchen-san. It has been too long."

Menchen leaned back in the chair and nodded at the oriental. "I wish it were under better circumstances, Nakashima-san." Menchen turned to the face on the left. "Good evening, Herr Schoenfeld."

The hardened, Germanic face peered at him. *"It better be important, old friend. I left a party because of this."*

"I'm afraid it is." Menchen took a deep breath and placed a map under a second video cam. He flipped the cam's activate switch and watched the map's image appear below the two faces on the screen. He adjusted the focus and waited for their reaction.

Magnus Schoenfeld's face twisted in a frown. He leaned toward the screen, his gray eyes trained on the map's sixteen red circles. *"What is this?"*

"Today, I received a call from our contact in America. It appears we have a problem, gentlemen." Menchen leaned forward and rested his elbows on the table. "Each circle displays the same killing pattern. Death by rapid suffocation. Nearly a thousand victims."

Schoenfeld's head snapped up. *"It's a mistake. Your friend in America is smoking something."*

Menchen ignored the German's tirade and turned his eyes toward the oriental. "Your thoughts, Yoshio?"

Nakashima stared at the map. *"Do you have the times of the outbreaks?"*

Menchen nodded. "I'll transmit them to you within the hour. They're only estimates, mind you. When CDC personnel arrived at the sites, no one was alive to tell them anything."

"It was that sudden?"

Menchen nodded.

"When was the first outbreak?"

"Last Tuesday in Somalia."

Schoenfeld interrupted. *"Impossible. We were meticulous. The follow-up tests revealed nothing."*

The oriental shrugged. *"Send me the times. I'll pull the dispersion charts and take a fresh look. Hard to believe it has been seventeen years. I thought we would never talk again."*

Menchen nodded and leaned back in the chair. "You know I would never contact you unless it was absolutely necessary." He waited for their nods. "There is something else."

Schoenfeld glared at him. *"Yes?"*

"My American contact advised me that Herr Adams has come unglued. He ignored my advice." Menchen watched them lean forward, their eyes filled with shock.

"He's still alive?" Schoenfeld leaned closer, distorting the focus momentarily.

"Barely. The last heart attack nearly finished him, but his madness sustains him."

"I thought you had him under control?"

Menchen frowned. "The media has gotten word of the outbreak in Quebec. He saw the television coverage. It must have set him loose."

Schoenfeld dropped back from the screen. *"Then, it's out?"*

"I'm afraid so."

Schoenfeld's face twisted in anger. *"I warned you about him. We should have taken care of that lunatic a long time ago."*

Nakashima's head snapped to the right. *"Please, Schoenfeld-san. I will not be part of such talk. We are honorable men."*

Menchen nodded approvingly. "Well said, Yoshio. I just wanted you to know the gravity of things. My American contact will take care of Herr Adams. We have more

112

'honorable' matters before us." He waited for Yoshio's nod. "When should we meet again?"

Nakashima sighed and looked down at the map. *"Give me twenty-four hours to review the models. I'll contact you tomorrow at nine p.m., your time."*

Schoenfeld shook his head. *"I don't like it. We should stay out of touch until this blows over. Let your American operatives silence Adams. Pretend this never happened. That's the smart play. The safe play."*

Menchen's patience had run out. For the first time since his heart attack, he felt a deep throbbing in his ears. Not a good sign for a man well into his sixties. He took a calming breath and leaned toward the screen. "You're outvoted, Magnus. I suggest you start reviewing those dispersion models."

Schoenfeld's face reddened. *"Are you threatening me?"*

"No, my friend. I'm ordering you. We're in this together, Magnus. That's the way it began, and that's the way it will end. Everything you are is due to Starburst. You're no different than the two faces on your screen. Like it or not, we're brothers in this matter." He watched the shocked German back away from the screen. "We'll conference tomorrow at nine p.m. I'll expect conclusive findings, Yoshio."

Menchen waited for a confirming nod before locking his blue eyes on Schoenfeld. "And from you, old friend, a complete re-test of the seventeen year samples using Herr Adams' procedure."

Schoenfeld trembled with anger. *"You expect me to put on my chemist's hat and sit in a lab for twenty-four hours? Do you know who you're talking to?"*

"I do, and you will. Auf Weidersehen, gentlemen." Menchen pressed the disconnect button and watched the two faces disappear. He slumped in the chair and rested a hand on his chest.

His eyes focused on the map beneath the viewing cam. He didn't know it, but the sixteen circles were now forty-two.

.   .   .

"Good luck, Doctor."

Thala grasped Susan Cayman's extended hand and forced a smile. "Sure you don't want my help in Corpus Christi?"

"You've done your job, Doctor. Get some rest. We'll take it from here." She nodded toward the waiting jeep. "You better get going. Your plane leaves at seven."

Thala glanced at the two men standing beside the tents. "Give me a minute. This was their first crisis assignment."

It was hard saying goodbye to Doldstadt and Kremler. It had been an exciting three days for the young pathologists, a chance to make a difference.

He shook their hands and thanked them for their efforts. No questions were asked, except for the pained look in their eyes.

They'd gotten a taste of the hunt and had it snatched away by an unexpected reassignment. Instead of following the bodies to Corpus Christi, they were going back to Houston for a night of tedious lab work. No explanation or briefing. No pat on the back. It was as if the three days never happened. If they only knew how lucky they were.

Thala gripped his medical bag and walked to the jeep.

After transferring to a sedan, Thala made himself comfortable working his laptop in the car's back seat. No words were exchanged with the two dark-suited men seated forward. He scanned CDC's e-mail database, looking for some reference to Trinity or Mr. Frankton, but saw nothing. His thoughts were interrupted by a flicker of lightning.

"Looks like a storm's coming in from the Gulf."

Thala glanced out the darkened window and nodded at the young man smiling at him from the front seat. "They'll probably delay the takeoff with all that turbulence."

The young man glanced nervously at his watch. "No chance of that. We're taking a charter."

114

"Charter?"

"Better for you, Doctor. No interruptions or hassle. Take a sleeping pill on the plane and you'll wake up in Atlanta."

Thala looked down at the message alert flashing on his laptop's screen. "I must be important to earn a charter."

The young man nodded. "You have friends in high places, Doctor."

Thala didn't respond. His eyes were focused on the screen...

> You're all I've got, Doc. You were right about desperate men doing desperate things. Hampsted's goons tried to terminate me with a shot of curaré. Car accident saved my life. This thing's out of control. If we don't stop it, we're all gonna die. Need you, Doc. Call me at 210-487-9821, at 10 p.m. If I'm wrong about you, I'm a dead man—and so are you—and everyone else.
>
> KF

"You okay, Doctor?"

Thala's head snapped up. "Sorry, I must be more tired than I thought. I'd like a few minutes to freshen up, if that's alright. My stomach's acting up."

"Sure, but please hurry. We want to make Hartsfield before midnight."

They drove through the charter gate after flashing their badges at the security guard. The terminal was packed with business travelers trying to get out before the storm broke over Houston.

One of the agents carried Thala's suitcase while the other eyed the medical bag dangling from Thala's hand. They were passing the men's room when the Zulu bolted through the entrance portal. "Just be a minute."

"Wait, Doctor."

Thala pretended not to hear the agent above the noise of the concourse, but he knew what would come next. Too many close calls in South Africa had prepared him for this moment.

He stepped into the first open toilet and locked the door. Frankton's message flashed in his mind. If his young friend wasn't hallucinating, the next five minutes would be the most important in Mandu Thala's life. He sat on the toilet seat and wiped the sweat off his face.

He heard a rap on the toilet door. "You in there, Doctor?"

"Yes."

"You okay?"

"Just a little stomach problem. I'll be fine."

The agent hesitated. "Want to give me the bag so you don't have to worry about it?"

Thala froze. "I'm fine...really."

"Okay, I'll be at the exit."

Thala watched the agent's shoes slip away from the toilet door. He leaned forward and eased back the latch. Through the bank of mirrors, he spotted a man guiding his wheelchair toward the handicapped toilet. Another man placed his raincoat and hat on a hook beside the sinks and began splashing water on his face. Now or never, Doctor. Now or never...

Five minutes later, the agent knocked on the toilet door. "Everything okay, Doctor?"

"Huh?"

The agent ripped open the door, his eyes glued on the baldheaded man gawking at him from the toilet seat.

"What the hell are you doing? You some kind of pervert?"

The stunned agent slammed the door and stepped to the next occupied toilet.

"Hey! Watch it, buddy!"

The agent backed away from the opened toilet and scanned the men at the sinks and urinals. A chill shot through him. He started for the exit and froze.

"My chair! The pig lifted my chair!"

The agent spun around and glared at the handicapped toilet. He rushed toward the swinging door and saw a crippled man seated on the toilet seat, his eyes filled with anger.

"My chair, dammit! What kind of scum does a thing like that? He helps me in here, then he steals my chair. What the hell am I gonna do?"

"Hey, where's my coat and hat?"

The agent turned toward the stunned man standing at the sinks. The man looked at him with pleading eyes. "I just looked away for a second to wash my face. Can you believe it? That raincoat's worth five hundred bucks!"

The agent burst through the exit into the crowd. His eyes locked on the other agent leaning against the wall.

"What's wrong?"

"He's gone. In a fucking wheelchair."

The other agent stared at the rushing crowd. "That was him?"

"Go!" The first agent charged into the crowd, followed by his stunned comrade. They found the abandoned chair a minute later, but Mandu Thala was nowhere in sight.

Chapter 11

Wildfire

Fletcher rested his arms on the conference table and stared at the blank viewing screen. It was eight p.m. in Washington, DC. The videoconference had taken only six minutes, just long enough to drive his blood pressure into the danger zone.

After introducing himself with the usual formalities, Samuel Tarver had cut to the chase with his first order as CDC's new chief…

"I'm asking all directors and their deputies to report to Corporate Square for a meeting at midnight. If you can't attend due to geographics or illness, please contact my office for alternate arrangements. I assure you this is a matter of gravest importance. For those of you already involved, I'll expect no leaks to the media like the one we just had in Quebec. I look forward to seeing you tonight at our Corporate Square conference facility. Thank you."

Fletcher leaned back in his chair and eyed the four men seated around him. "Well, how about that."

Stan Harris looked down at the table. "Today's my wife's birthday. We were going to have an early dinner and catch a play at the JFK Center. She's been trying to reach me for three hours. I better call her."

The reactions ranged from anger to fear. The five men seated at the table knew the unexpected meeting concerned the reports coming in from across the globe. The press had it now, and there was still no answer. And that shocking introduction from Tarver...

"Good evening. I'm sorry for the delay, but I've been preoccupied with the news coming in from the field. I wish my first communication weren't so melodramatic. It's always best the new boss have a chance to settle in with his staff before something breaks. Guess that's not in the cards. We have a wildfire, people."

Fletcher glanced at his watch. "I'll have Kate make the travel arrangements. I assume you're all coming with me?" He waited for their painful nods. "See you on the plane." He stood up and watched them leave the conference room. When they were gone, he snatched the cell phone out of his pocket and pressed Hampsted's calling code. It took a few seconds for the scrambler to kick in.

"Yes?"

"You lost them?"

"Temporarily, but we're on it."

Fletcher's face reddened. "On it? Do you know what this means? If they have that CD, we're toast."

"We think Thala rented a car. Once we catch the GPS signal from its beeper, we'll nail him."

"The hell with him. What about Frankton? How could you blow it?"

Hampsted's voice sharpened. *"You think this is easy? We lost two good men because of that scum. I'll get him, and when I do, you and I are gonna settle up."*

Fletcher stiffened. "Are you threatening me?"

"You're damn right. I've had it with your crap. It's time to settle up. I'll deal with those two jerks, but when I'm through, it's over between us."

Fletcher slumped in the chair, his eyes gazing at the blank screen. He'd dealt with some rugged characters in the past nineteen years, but none tougher than Parker Hampsted.

Easy, old man. Last thing you need is Parker jumping ship. Time for a little diplomacy.

He took a calming breath and lowered his voice. "Look, Parker. We're all uptight. I'll be glad to settle things when this is over. Hell, I'm getting out too."

"You're what?"

Fletcher sat up and rested his elbows on the table. "I was going to tell you in a few weeks. I'm fed up too. Time to cash out. Don't worry about money. I'll work out a good package for you."

Hampsted's voice softened. *"We never talked about that."*

"How about two million, tax free?"

"We'll see."

Fletcher sighed. "Just get it done, Parker. And remember, it's three targets, not two."

"Understood."

Fletcher squeezed the phone. "Don't fail us, Parker. We're betting on you."

"Yeah...one big, happy family." The phone clicked and went dead.

.   .   .

The cattle truck pulled into *Sarah's Truck Haven & Motel* at 6:45 p.m. after a three hour run down Interstate 10. *Sarah's* was just outside Kerrville, Texas, fifty miles northwest of San Antonio.

Karl had waved down the trucker after stumbling onto Interstate 10 from the desert. At first, the trucker was reluctant because of Karl's cuts, bruises, and torn clothes, but that quickly faded when Karl made up the story about being carjacked while flashing a wad of twenties in front of the trucker's face—to pay for all the gas and food. The money came from the wallets Karl lifted off the two dead agents when he probed their pockets for the handcuff keys.

After gassing up, the trucker offered to take Karl into San Antonio for medical help, but *Sarah's* looked a lot safer just now. Karl wished the driver well and watched him accelerate onto I-10 while clutching the laptop he'd dragged from the wreckage. Amazing it worked after the impact and explosion. It only took a minute to break the laptop's password. A quick check of the wallets provided the necessary birth-date. A bit morbid, but this was no time for compassion. Then came the hard part. Thala had warned him not to expect any help, but the South African was all he had. Karl took a painful breath and sent the e-mail.

The next three hours were the longest in Karl Frankton's life. He plunked down on a log near the pay phone and shooed horseflies while his watch closed on ten p.m. Things looked pretty bleak in southwest Texas.

He was stunned when the pay phone rang at 9:58. He lifted it off the hook and pressed it against his ear. A trickle of sweat stung the cut on his forehead. "Yeah?"

"What's going on?"

Karl's eyes brightened. "That you, Doc?"

"I wish it weren't."

"Where are you?"

"In a rented car west of Houston."

"Hang on, Doc." Karl ripped open a map and held it up to the glow coming from the red neon sign above his head. "Take Interstate Ten past San Antonio until you see a sign for Kerrville. I'm at Sarah's Truck Stop. Room seven. Knock once and wait."

"Are you crazy? That's over two hundred miles?"

"Hurry, Doc. This thing's out of control."

"Thanks a lot, Mr. Frankton."

"For what?"

"Sharing your grave with me." The phone clicked and went dead.

Three hours later, Karl was awakened by a sharp rap on the motel room door. He staggered off the bed into the darkness. The digital clock on the nightstand read 1:30 a.m.

"That you, Doc?"

"Open the door."

Karl unlocked the door and stared at the tired face looking down at him. He stepped back and watched Thala slip past him. The exhausted Zulu collapsed in the chair beside the bed, the black medical bag dangling from his hand.

Karl locked the door and checked the drapes before turning on the lamp above the table. He squinted at the man sprawled in the chair. "Is that your car outside the door?"

Thala nodded.

Karl glared at him. "Those cars have GPS beepers. It'll lead them straight to us."

"I disabled the beeper two hours ago."

"You what?"

"Never mind that. What the hell's going on?"

Karl eased into the chair beside the table and rubbed his aching forehead. He slumped in the chair and gazed into space.

"You look like you've been in a war."

Karl touched the ugly bruise on his cheek and winced. "A couple years ago, my attorney warned me about this."

"Warned?"

"He said they wouldn't rest until I was a name on a tombstone."

Thala leaned toward him. "What happened out there?"

Karl looked down at his trembling hand. "When they messed up the curaré injection, they tried to blow my head off with a nine millimeter. I still see the needle in the bastard's hand when the gun went off."

"Are you okay?"

"Don't know. My side aches pretty bad. Must be broken ribs."

"How did you get away?"

"Car flipped over. A real mess. I was lucky. The others weren't."

Thala stared at him.

"I hitched a ride, e-mailed you, and here we are." Karl took a painful breath and stared at the Zulu. "It wasn't easy sending that e-mail. I figured you tipped them off about the CD."

Thala stiffened. "They know about the recording?"

"They know."

Thala fell back in the chair, his black eyes staring at the medical bag.

"Well...did you?"

Thala's eyes flared with anger. He unzipped the bag and yanked out the CD. "You have a lot of nerve. I see why you're in so much trouble. No one has seen this except you and me."

Karl looked down. "Then, it *was* the pentothal."

"They drugged you?"

"Big time."

Thala glared at the CD. "Then Hampsted knew I was lying. Those agents weren't taking me to Atlanta. They were taking me to hell. If I hadn't read your e-mail..."

Karl pushed out of the chair and staggered to the bed. He collapsed on the mattress, his eyes staring at the stained ceiling.

Nothing was said for a few moments. The two exhausted scientists gazed into space while the odds sank in. The only sound was a truck pulling into the parking lot, its tires biting into the gravel.

Karl sat up on the bed and peered at the exhausted man stretched out in the chair. "Give me the disk."

"What?"

"The disk. You know, the thing that brought us together."

Thala frowned and flipped the disk at him.

"Watch it, Doc. This is all we have."

Thala's frown deepened. "We have nothing, Mr. Frankton. To put it in your vernacular, we're screwed."

Karl ignored him and inserted the CD into the player above the TV. He pressed the play button and watched the recording advance to the instant the blood cells failed. He pressed the pause button and stared at the blurred mass inside the flash.

Thala squinted at the light coming from the screen. "I stared at that flash for an hour in the van. It's like getting a glimpse of hell. There just isn't enough to work with."

Karl reached out and touched the screen. "There was something missing in Somalia and Willapa Bay. I can't explain it, but I have that same feeling now. Like it all comes together inside that flash."

Thala lifted his laptop out of the medical bag. "I'm going to do some work. I suggest you do the same." He nodded at the scorched laptop lying against the wall.

Karl shook his head. "I already tried. Can't get beyond an e-mail. Those government data banks are rock solid."

"Use this." Thala snatched a pencil and note pad off the nightstand and scribbled something down. He tore off the sheet and handed it to Karl.

"What is it?"

"Key to the kingdom."

"Looks like a password."

"THE password, Mr. Frankton."

Karl stared at the cryptic symbols. "How did you pull that off?"

Thala shrugged. "Don't know. I've always had a knack for that sort of thing. Used to drive them crazy at Columbia."

Karl's head snapped up. "You went to Columbia Med School?"

"Magna Cum Laude. Now please get to work."

Karl sighed and looked down at the note. "What are we looking for?"

"Don't know. I'll concentrate on e-mail traffic. From your history, you're good at interrogating medical databases."

Karl frowned. "Not funny."

"Not meant to be."

"Columbia, eh? How about that." Karl reached for the CD player's eject button.

"No, leave it on. Maybe something will click."

Karl nodded and forced a weak smile. "Sorry about dragging you into this mess."

"It's a little late for apologies. Our lives aren't very important just now." Thala looked down at the laptop screen. "Somalia just became a wildfire. We have seventy-two hot sites across the globe."

"Seventy-two? That's not geometric."

"No, we're beyond that." Thala rested his feet on the bed and began pounding the keys.

.   .   .

Samuel Tarver was a lean, six footer with auburn hair and penetrating brown eyes. His stellar record as a microbiologist in CDC's famed Special Pathogen's Branch had led to rapid advancement within the organization. In his nine year climb to the top, Tarver had developed strong relationships with key contacts at the National Security Agency, Environmental Protection Agency, Food & Drug Administration, Department of Health, *Institute de Medicine Tropical* in Belgium, and United Nation's World Health Organization. He would need them all in the harsh days ahead, for he must mobilize the world's finest pathologists in a war of survival against an invisible enemy that struck without warning or pattern. With crisis sites accelerating across the globe, time was short, and the agency's field teams were stretched to the breaking point.

Tarver waited until his administrative assistant closed the conference room's paneled doors before rising from his chair and stepping to the podium beneath the gold CDC emblem. He straightened his blue tie while scanning the semicircular table in front of him. Thirty men and women glared at him, their faces strained with hostility and fatigue. They had been yanked from their families and loved ones to attend the unexpected midnight meeting. There were no smiles of welcome for their new boss...no hint of applause.

Tarver rested his elbows on the lectern and spoke deliberately. "I'm sorry for dragging you in like this, but I'm sure you're aware that we have a crisis." He let his words sink in. "I thought it would be a good idea to open with an update from two of our field teams. That should give us a clearer picture of what we're up against."

Tarver nodded at the projection room window behind the seated attendees. The lights dimmed while a large viewing screen descended on the navy blue wall to his right. He turned toward the two faces materializing on the split screen. "Agents Schimmer and Marley, I believe?"

The young lady on the left forced a smile through her glistening face. The blond-haired man on the right raised his hand in a half-hearted greeting. Both appeared fatigued.

Tarver studied the two faces. "Can you see us?"

"Yes, sir."

"Agent Schimmer, maybe you can fill us in on the current conditions at site fifty-nine." Tarver glanced at the seated members. "That's the outbreak in Mumbai."

The young lady stepped aside while her minicam panned a sunlit park framed with tropical plants and trees. Beyond it, the towers of Mumbai rose into the powder blue sky. A clock tower was visible in the distance, its hands frozen on 10:50.

"We're using the park for a quarantine area. I've asked the Indian authorities to section it off from the rest of the city. They've been cooperative so far, but I'm afraid things are getting out of hand. We've heard gunfire in the past hour. There are reports of people dying in the streets."

"From the gunfire?"

"No, sir."

"The virus?"

"We think so."

Tarver's face twisted in a frown. "How many so far?"

Schimmer directed the remote cam toward a concrete fountain at the center of the park. Six concentric circles of silver body bags spiraled outward from the fountain, each circle larger than the one inside. A bio-suited agent stepped between the circles, spraying the bags with detox solution.

Tarver stared at the scene. "How many, Agent Schimmer?"

"One hundred fifty-eight at current count. They're coming in at ten per hour." Schimmer stared at the body bags. *"I'm afraid for the city, Mr. Tarver."*

Tarver felt the room come alive with shocked whispers. He clutched the lectern while trying to cope with his agent's words. On the screen, two bio-suited agents placed a fresh body bag in the outermost circle.

Fletcher stood up from his seat, his eyes trained on the screen. "May I ask something?"

Tarver looked at his east coast district director with grateful eyes. "Go ahead, Mr. Fletcher."

"I notice you're not wearing a helmet, Agent Schimmer. Is that wise?"

Schimmer brushed back her cropped black hair. *"We're short of oxygen. They're flying in fresh tanks from New Delhi. I gave my helmet to Jerry. He needs it more than me."* She nodded toward one of the bio-suited stretcher bearers.

Fletcher glared at Tarver. "Sir, we should get her a helmet."

Tarver nodded while the room broke into whispers of, "Well said, dammit," and, "For God's sake, someone get her a helmet."

Tarver raised his hand for silence and forced a painful smile. "Get yourself some shelter, Agent Schimmer. You're too important to be standing out there unprotected."

"Yes, sir. I have a pressurized tent. I'll be okay."

Tarver nodded, "Any problem with that oxygen delivery, and you get back to me."

"Yes, sir."

"And that pressure's no good if you're not in the tent."

She smiled and stepped back from the cam. *"Signing off then."*

Tarver watched Schimmer's half of the screen go black while focusing on the blond-haired man to the right. "Well, Agent Marley. How goes it in Belém?"

The Englishman frowned. *"Not well, sir. We've lost two hundred in two villages outside the city. We're using the latest technology and procedures, but all our tests are negative."*

Tarver struggled for words. "Any theories? Hunches?"

Marley rubbed his neck and scanned the spotlighted area behind him. *"It's bloody strange. When we landed yesterday morning, there were forty dead in the first village. Wiped out, like a nerve gas attack. Another fifty died yesterday afternoon. Then the bloody thing struck the second village at 0110 this morning."* He turned to face the camera, his blue eyes filled with tears. *"They were dropping in the fields like someone had turned a machine gun on them. Convulsing, like they couldn't breathe."*

Marley swiped his forehead with the back of his hand. *"By the time we climbed into our gear and moved in, they were gone."* He stared at the camera. *"A hundred dead in ten minutes. I've never seen anything like it. It seems to come in waves. No warning. No symptoms. One minute they're alive—the next minute they're dead. I'm beginning to think—"*

"Yes?"

Marley shook his head. *"I'm not a religious man, but maybe we've gone too far. You know…Revelations and all that."* He dabbed his forehead with the back of his hand. *"The natives say it's because we've angered the gods. They say the Amazon's turned against us. That we're all going to die."*

Tarver leaned closer to the screen. He could see the anguish on the young man's face. The trembling hand. The terrified eyes. "You okay, Agent Marley?"

"I don't know, sir. I don't—"

Tarver watched his team leader break down. Someone grabbed Marley's arm and pulled him aside. A young Hispanic stepped into view, his face strained with fear. He took a deep breath and peered at the screen. *"Sorry about that. I'm agent Sanchez. I'll spell Dr. Marley for a bit."*

Tarver stepped toward the screen. "Is he okay?"

Sanchez frowned. *"It's been pretty rough. We see them falling and hear reports of the latest outbreak. Then we run the tests and find nothing."* He glanced to the side. *"Kinda gets to you. All those bodies and we don't have a clue. What good are we for God's sake?"*

Tarver clenched his fists. "You're the best we have, Agent Sanchez. You'll find it. I know you will."

Sanchez lowered his head and sobbed.

A young woman in a navy blue suit stood up, her eyes trained on the screen. "Agent Sanchez?"

Sanchez squinted at the screen. *"That you, boss?"*

She nodded and smiled through her tears. "I'll catch a plane tonight and be there in a few hours. Sounds like you need a good cup of coffee."

Sanchez broke into a smile and started to say something, but the words didn't come out. His hands clutched his throat and he staggered back into the darkness while the stunned woman stared at the screen in shock. "My God, what's happening? What is it, Julio? What's wrong?" She stepped around the table and froze, her eyes locked on the nightmare."

Tarver rushed at the screen. "Your helmet, Sanchez! Put on your helmet!"

Sanchez collapsed on the ground while two helmeted agents rushed toward him. Tarver watched the agents kneel beside Sanchez' convulsing body. Screams were coming from the site. Someone ran into the minicam and knocked it over. The screen flashed and went black.

Tarver stared at the blank screen, waiting for the connection to resume. When he turned around, he saw two men helping the shaken woman toward the exit door. The others were standing, their faces white with fear.

One of the men lowered his head. "Sanchez is under Joyce's command. They're very close."

Tarver glanced at her name plate. "I'm sorry, Deputy Director Phillips. We'll do everything we can." He watched them help her through the exit door, and cursed the day he accepted this job.

Tarver looked down and felt their eyes burning into him, and he suddenly knew the awesome burden he'd assumed when he rested his hand on the bible and took the oath of office. "Let's take a break." He watched his shaken management team shuffle out of the room.

Chapter 12

Prophecy

Tarver's exhausted staff returned to the conference room at 0112. By now, word had reached Atlanta that agents Marley, Sanchez, Royston, and Meeks were dead, victims of the same mysterious killer that wiped out the two villages near Belém, Brazil. With the media pouring into the area, news of the deaths would soon reach the international wires where it would join the growing list of fatalities coming in from across the globe.

Tarver stepped to the podium while groping for the words to rally his shaken staff. He stared at the worn faces and quickly concluded that the closed-circuit disaster in Belém had taken too great a toll. Best to call it a night and let everyone get some sleep.

He rested his hands on the podium and spoke softly. "Before we adjourn, I'd like Dr. Carson to give a perspective of the situation. Then I'll ask each of you to maintain close contact with your field teams and this office. Please remember that any theories coming in from the field must be explored, no matter how far-fetched they may seem. We're dealing with an unknown virus and our best weapon is communication." Tarver stepped back from the podium. "Doctor Carson?"

Raquel Carson was the nation's most revered biologist, pathologist, and ecologist. At sixty-three, Ms. Carson still radiated the energy, determination, and political savvy that had guided her from an activist existence within Green Peace to the number two slot at CDC. If not for her radical roots, Carson would have easily beaten Tarver for the top position.

131

Carson rose from a chair in the shadows and stepped to the podium. For a moment, she shuffled her notes while mustering the strength to give her colleagues the hard, bitter truth.

She brushed back a strand of graying hair and rested her elbows on the podium. Her pale green eyes focused on the tired faces. "I didn't expect it to hit us this way. Invisible too. A bit dramatic, if you ask me."

She hesitated and looked down at Deputy Director Phillips. "I'm sorry about Sanchez, and Marley, and the others. They gave their lives without reservation. Let's remember them and beat this thing."

Tarver had taken a seat beside the podium. He could feel Carson's words inspiring the thirty exhausted people at the table. The defeat faded from their faces. Their tired eyes glistened with emotion, and in that moment, Samuel Tarver knew CDC's true leader was standing at the podium.

Carson straightened up and nodded at the projection booth. To her right, a global map appeared on the viewing screen. She glanced at the screen. "That white dot in Somalia was the first outbreak last Tuesday." She nodded at the booth and watched the screen come alive with flashing white dots. "Here's what we have now. Over seventy sites throughout the world, cropping up at one per hour. I'm afraid that will accelerate."

Carson hesitated while studying the map. "I've noted an interesting pattern. The outbreaks have occurred at, or near, bodies of water. In some cases, streams and rivers. In others, lakes and ponds. There has to be a link between the outbreaks and the water."

Deputy Director Fredericks raised his hand.

"Go ahead, Mervyn."

Fredericks stood up, his eyes trained on the map. "What about temperature? I went over the incident list. The outbreaks seem to boil up during the daylight hours when the sun is hottest."

132

Carson nodded. "Well done, Mervyn. I've noticed that too. There's a definite correlation between the outbreaks, water, and temperature...but it's not perfect. Seventeen of the outbreaks have occurred in cool climates in the evening, or overnight."

Carson rested her elbows on the lectern. "Let me throw a new one at you. Until now, we've assumed it's a new strain of killer virus. Perhaps, but the invisibility seems a bit much. Frankly, I'm beginning to question whether we're dealing with something other than a virus."

She watched the room come alive with whispers. "We can't rule out germ or chemical warfare. So far, our tests have focused on viral or bacterial detection. Maybe we should broaden our thinking." She glanced at Tarver who had risen from his chair and stepped beside her.

Tarver forced out the words. "I've contacted the army's germ warfare institute at Fort Detrick, Maryland. This isn't easy, but you should know that we've issued a terrorist alert for two of our own."

He watched the room fall silent. "We have reason to believe that a contracted pathologist and a twenty five year employee may be linked to a neo-nazi terrorist organization operating out of Berlin. Mr. Fletcher's team picked it up during a routine security check."

Tarver nodded at Fletcher who stared at him in shock. "The geographic correlations are too close to ignore. The contracted pathologist was assigned to the first sight in Somalia. The employee was case leader at the Trinity site near Houston. In the past year, both men have had extensive access to our Level Four Lab. We have to consider the possibility that something was concocted there and smuggled out. I'm sorry, but it's better you know. We just can't take any chances. When you walk out of here, you'll be under FBI surveillance."

Tarver lowered his head and walked back to his chair. He didn't realize it, but his final sentence had crushed his organization's morale.

Carson waited for the whispers to subside while struggling for the words to undo the damage done by her new boss. She knew the importance of the thirty people seated in front of her. If they gave up, precious time would be lost to apathy, and that could be fatal.

She raised her hand for silence and spoke the words she'd prayed would never be spoken. "I spent the day feeding Pandora every parameter I could fathom."

Carson didn't need to explain the expert system to her colleagues. They knew *Pandora's* sole purpose was to evaluate runaway viruses, better known as wildfires. Carson had developed the computer model over many years, using compiled knowledge and rules-of-thumb from the field's leading scientists.

Carson slipped on her reading glasses and scanned her notes. "It doesn't matter what we're up against. Terrorism, germ warfare, viral or bacterial strain. Pandora's proliferation model can deal with them all. In the end, it's a simple equation of incidence, kill intensity, and lead-time to respond."

She glanced at her notes. "I plugged in the past week's outbreak intensity and acceleration. The conclusion was obvious, but I wanted to hear it from Pandora." She hesitated. "Non-linear, non-geometric, non-logarithmic progression. It's growing in random bursts, much like a fire burning through kindling. That makes it harder to project, but I gave it a shot using an aggressive dispersion model."

She looked up to ensure their attention, but it wasn't necessary. Thirty pairs of eyes were glued on her. She glanced at Tarver. "Do you want me to continue?"

Tarver nodded, his face strained with concern.

"It's hard to extrapolate from so many unknowns, so I stayed with the week-old incidence and intensity pattern." She hesitated and flipped to her second page of notes. "Assuming we're able to fully commit our global resources, I'm confident we'll unmask the killer within three months. I can't assume anything more favorable unless we get lucky. On that score, keep this in mind. Whether it's terrorist, accidental, or a quirk of nature, it has already spread beyond our control. In other words, it can't be isolated. It's a wildfire, pure and simple. We've reached the next level. Our only chance is to uncover it, develop an antidote, overcome it, and live with the damage. I have to assume another six months for that scenario to play out."

Deputy Director Phillips leaned forward. "Nine months?"

Carson nodded. "Sorry, Joyce. That's the most likely scenario. It's the invisibility factor that does us in."

"Go on, Dr. Carson." Tarver stood up, his eyes locked on her.

Carson flipped to her last page of notes. "At the current rate of proliferation, the death count will easily double by next week. If we assume a similar doubling over each of the following thirteen weeks, and a trailing off as our presumed vaccine takes hold—"

Tarver leaned toward her. "How many, Doctor?"

Carson folded her notes, her eyes filled with tears. She leaned toward the microphone and forced out the words. "I'm sorry. We've squandered so much time with budget cuts." She lowered her head. "I'm so sorry."

"How many?"

Carson's voice was barely audible. "Armageddon."

.　　.　　.

The first traces of daylight flickered on the eastern horizon, accompanied by yelps of coyotes retreating to their caves in the escarpment above San Antonio. The sun wouldn't rise for another hour, but the last trucker had already pulled out of *Sarah's Truck Haven & Motel*, leaving only the two occupants in room seven.

Thala sprinkled the last packet of coffee into the automatic brewer and glanced at the man sprawled on the bed. "Cup?"

Karl shook his head and flipped the laptop's recharger switch. It would take fifteen minutes for the battery to re-energize. Just enough time for a nap. He rolled on his back and rested his head on the pillow, his tired eyes gazing at the ceiling.

"Mr. Frankton?"

Karl ignored him and closed his eyes. A sweet numbness ebbed through his limbs. The pain in his ribs eased. His breathing slowed. The room drifted away. He was nearly asleep when a strong hand gripped his shoulder.

"Wake up, Mr. Frankton."

"Go away."

"I just checked CDC's morning broadcast. They've brought in the FBI. They're telling everyone we're terrorists."

Karl's eyes snapped open.

"They've linked us to a neo-nazi group responsible for the outbreaks. Even provided evidence we smuggled mutant viral strains from Level Four. In a few hours, our pictures will be smeared on every newspaper across the globe."

"They're nuts. They'll start a panic."

Thala shrugged. "They don't seem to care."

Karl sat up and clutched his throbbing head. "I need a drink."

"Not just now, Mr. Frankton." Thala sat down at the table, his eyes focused on the PC screen. "Turn on your laptop and get back to work."

"Work? Hell, I just spent three hours searching three government databases and came up with zero. Cryptic code names. Military jargon. Alias this, alias that. It's useless, dammit. Can of worms."

Thala peered at the screen. "Forget all that. Start looking for a reference to Ringley Adams?"

"Who?"

"Ringley Adams."

Karl rubbed his neck. "Where did you come up with that?"
Thala sipped his coffee and leaned back in the chair. "An
hour ago, I broke into CDC's telecom data base. Quite an
encryption scheme, but once I deciphered the first two
characters, my Monte Carlo software did the rest."
Thala took another sip and studied the screen. "They keep
an online record of phone calls. I spotted a scrambled call
made at zero-six-hundred yesterday, Eastern Standard Time.
The source was a cell phone near Houston. The destination
was a cell phone in Georgetown, DC. It took awhile to
decipher the numbers, but once I cracked the three digit
exchange, the last four digits dropped into place rather quickly.
The Georgetown cell belongs to Jonathan Fletcher. The
Houston cell belongs to someone with the initials, PH."
Karl's eyes widened. "Go on."
"I checked out Mr. Fletcher in the government directory. It
seems he's a district director at CDC, only I've never heard of
him. I checked a little further and found his name in prior
positions at FDA and DOA. Before that, he was associated
with two environmental SIG's."
"SIG's?"
"Special interest groups. Lobbyists."
"Any names?"
Thala shrugged. "Green Earth and Terra Verde. Makes
you feel warm and fuzzy."
Karl felt the blood rush to his face. "You said his name is
Jonathan Fletcher?"
"You've heard of him?"
Karl frowned. "His name was on the agreement I signed
two years ago. He represented the FDA in my lawsuit."
Thala stared at the stunned man seated on the edge of the
bed. "I was wondering when we'd get to that."
"Leave it alone."
Thala sipped his coffee. "The press said you violated FDA
security for profit. Industrial espionage, and all that. Pretty

strong stuff. Next thing I know, you're working at CDC like nothing happened. How did you pull that off?"

Karl's eyes flashed. "It's not important."

Thala leaned toward him. "It's important to me, Mr. Frankton."

Karl glared at him. "I threatened to blow the whistle on a drug cover-up, so they cut me a deal. My silence for two years at CDC, and no drug release."

"Drug?"

"The bastards falsified testing records to fast-track an experimental drug that killed seventy percent of the mice tested. They were going to release it to late-stage AID's patients. I guess they figured the poor souls would die anyhow."

Thala stared at him in disbelief. "Sounds a little thin."

"Maybe, but my two years are up and they just made me a terrorist. If you listen good, you'll hear them carving my name on a tombstone."

"What about your attorney? If all this is true, he should be able to cover you?"

Karl looked down. "He's dead. Killed two weeks ago in a robbery. They stripped his office clean. Even broke into his safe. Guess they found what they were looking for."

Thala sighed and dropped back in the chair. "Let's forget the Houston call for now. It's the call Fletcher received from California that's got me. Placed at zero-five-fifty yesterday from an unlisted residence in San Clemente. That's three in the morning, Pacific Coast Time. It took awhile to identify the caller. I had to do some illegal searches."

"Adams?"

"Yes, but there's something else." Thala rubbed his eyes. "I've heard that name before. I just can't place it." He glanced at the laptop on the bed. "I could use some help, Mr. Frankton. I'm sorry for the crack about FDA. Maybe we'll have some time to talk when this is over."

"Yeah, nothing like a little chat between graves." Karl unplugged the recharger and placed the laptop on the table. They spent the next two hours searching for anything linked to Ringley Adams. Thala focused on CDC's archives while his exhausted companion probed the worldwide web. With his battery warning light flashing, Karl was about to give up when he noticed an obscure reference to a thesis done eighteen years ago by a biophysicist named Adams. He clicked the hypertext and stared at the screen. "I might have something."

Thala staggered beside him and looked down at the screen. "Download it, your battery's going." Thala snatched the pad of paper off the nightstand and scribbled down the URL while Karl saved the text to his hard drive. Ten seconds later, the laptop screen went black.

It only took a minute for Thala to access the web page on his PC. He pressed the scroll button and studied the script unfolding on the screen. Karl stood beside him, his tired eyes trying to focus on the screen.

The script reached page three when Thala released the scroll button. "I'll be damned."

"What?"

"I was there. University of California, Berkeley. June twelfth, Nineteen ninety-five. Their annual biotech convention. A bunch of bleeding-edge biophysicists reaching for angels and project funding." He stared at the screen. "I remember Adams. A real eccentric. Claimed to have discovered the magic bullet that alters matter."

"Too much weed."

Thala ignored him. "Adams presented a theorem for a radioactive burst that could change matter. Claimed he'd discovered it from nuclear research on subatomic particles called quarks, leptons, and bosons."

Karl shook his head. "You're way beyond me, Doc."

Thala scrolled to a diagram at the end of the article. "That's the schematic Adams presented with his theorem. The double helix on the left is a living organism. The latticework on the right is an organic compound. The atoms at the top are an inorganic compound. Adams unites them inside that blurred mass at the center, a burst of radioactive energy that mutates them into something new."

Karl shrugged. "You said it yourself. A real eccentric."

Thala stared at the diagram. "Maybe, but what if he pulled it off?"

"You're serious?"

"I remember the laughter when Adams walked off the stage. Everyone thought he was nuts. The classic mad scientist with electric white hair and crazed, bloodshot eyes." Thala hesitated. "I wonder if they'd be laughing now."

Karl stared at the screen. "I'm trying, Doc, but you have to give me more than that."

"Eighteen years later, Adams phones a ranking bureaucrat in the nation's capital. A few minutes later, the bureaucrat receives a call from Hampsted in Houston." Thala stared at the screen. "There has to be a connection."

Karl glanced at the TV. "Holy shit."

"What?"

Karl stepped to the TV and tapped the screen. Take a good look, Doc. Inside the blurred stew. See it?"

Thala stood up and edged beside the screen. He reached out and touched the starburst inside the blurred flash. He could feel the static electricity crackling on his fingertips. "God."

"Yeah, and then some."

Thala rushed to the PC and clicked "save. He snatched his medical bag off the floor and yanked the CD out of the player. "Come on, Mr. Frankton. We have a long way to go."

"Where are we going?"

"San Clemente." Thala unlocked the motel room door and squinted at the bright sunlight.

With the sun rising over Kerrville, the last two occupants skidded out of *Sarah's* headed for California. A careless phone call had opened the door to the one man who might make a difference, but he was fifteen hours away, and helicopters were closing from the east...

. . .

Fletcher rested his head against the cushioned seat. In another hour, his charter jet would land at Dulles International Airport. Then a half hour ride to Georgetown and he'd be in Estelle's arms.

His thoughts were interrupted by a beeping cell phone. He snatched the red phone out of his jacket pocket and flipped it open. The familiar warbling told him who it was. "Go ahead."

"We found them. A truck stop outside San Antonio. I need disposition instructions."

Fletcher lowered the cell phone and glanced at his watch. Seven a.m. He looked at the clouds and lifted the cell phone to his mouth. "Where are you?"

"Boarding a chopper in Corpus Christi. I should reach the truck stop within two hours. I've instructed Jordan to move in with FBI agents."

Fletcher rubbed his tired eyes. "How did you find them?"

"Got lucky. A trucker noticed one of the photos on a news show and called Jordan at the FBI office in San Antonio. Sounds like he picked up Frankton in the desert and dropped him at the truck stop. Jordan called me, and here we are."

"What about the other one?"

"He rented a car outside the airport and took off. We got a trace of his direction before he disabled the car's GPS. Interstate Ten toward San Antonio." Hampsted hesitated. *"I need disposition instructions."*

Fletcher frowned. "I just left Tarver's all-nighter in Atlanta. Everyone's pretty shook-up. Sounds like your terrorism story worked, except for one problem."

"Problem?"

Fletcher pressed the phone to his lips. "What the hell are you up to? How did Tarver get word of that terrorist crap before me?"

Hampsted hesitated. *"Hell, it sounded like a good idea. This way, you're not involved. I thought you preferred the arm's length approach. Sorry, it won't happen again."*

Fletcher squeezed the phone. "It better not or all bets are off."

"Understood."

Fletcher took a calming breath. "It *was* a good idea."

"I already said that."

"So, you're telling me we have two terrorists holed up in a truck stop outside San Antonio. One's a contracted drunkard and the other's a disillusioned leftover from apartheid." He hesitated and looked at the clouds. "We try to take them alive, but they open up with small arms fire and we're forced to bring them down. We find the usual papers linking them to the neo-nazi group, and that's it. No need to dispose of the bodies. Bring in the media, and we're heroes."

"I advise interrogation first. We have to be sure they don't have a poison pill."

Fletcher sat up." The recording?"

"We have to be sure."

"Okay, but only if you can keep it under wraps. If the media or FBI gets wind of what's going on—"

"I understand. If there are any complications, I'll blow them away."

"Call me when it's over, and keep that chopper fueled. Your next stop will be San Clemente."

"Adams?"

"The fool's out of control. He called me yesterday, threatening to go to the media."

"Shit."

"It's time to cut our losses. When you're done with Texas, you get to San Clemente and give that lunatic the heart attack he deserves."

"Clear."

"Call me at noon." Fletcher pressed the off button and stared at the clouds.

. . .

Hampsted's team swarmed *Sarah's Truck Haven* two hours later, but room seven was empty. It was only eight a.m. in Kerrville, Texas. Still time to track them down before Hampsted had to place that call to his boss. And while he procrastinated, a rented Ford with stolen license plates raced across the desert at ninety miles an hour, it's destination a beach house in beautiful San Clemente.

Chapter 13

Revelations

"Jonathan?"

Fletcher blinked at the beautiful face looking down at him.

"You have a call." Estelle nodded toward the beeping cell phone on the nightstand. She frowned and walked out of the bedroom. It didn't take a rocket scientist to know she was plenty mad.

He sat up and squinted at the sunlight beaming through the parted drapes. Birds chirped in the garden. The air smelled sweet from the perfume bottles on his wife's vanity. He glanced at the digital clock on the nightstand. Twelve fifteen. He'd slept two hours.

He dragged the cell phone off the nightstand and pressed it against his ear. It took a few seconds for the static to clear. "Go ahead."

"Bad news."

Fletcher dug his fingers into the mattress.

"They pulled out before we got here. The coffee's still fresh. I have six cars patrolling Interstate Ten and the side roads. We've put out an APB. They won't go far."

"What about choppers?"

"One's up and the other's waiting for me. My guess is they're headed for Mexico."

Fletcher fell back on the pillow, his eyes gazing at the ceiling.

"They won't get away."

"They've done pretty well so far."

"They're smart, but so are we. It's just a matter of time."

Fletcher fought the anger churning in his gut. Blowing up at Hampsted was the last thing he needed. Like it or not, the jerk was all he had.

"What about Adams?"

Fletcher took a calming breath. "Stay on the current targets. They're priority. Get back to me when you have them."

"Let's get Adams out of the way. I've already set it up."

Fletcher gripped the phone, his eyes flashing with anger. "Negative. Stay on the current targets. We can't afford any more mistakes. The media's all over this thing."

Hampsted's voice sharpened. *"I'll nail the targets. Then we'll talk about that money."* The phone went dead.

Fletcher splashed some cold water on his face before heading downstairs. His wife was seated on the leather couch in the family room, her eyes glued to the large television screen on the wall. The caption at the bottom of the screen read "New Orleans under attack." Above the caption, a reporter walked through a crowd of shaken onlookers. Behind him, a barricade had been erected along North Front Street and Woldenberg Riverfront Park. All access to the Riverwalk and Mississippi had been shut down by the police. Sirens blared in the background. A National Guard truck raced by, carrying armed troops. A helicopter's shadow flashed across the reporter's face, followed by the sound of swishing blades. The frustrated reporter tried to collar a National Guard officer clad in camouflage green, but he was pushed aside by two armed guardsmen.

Fletcher sat beside her and spoke softly. "Are you okay?"

She looked down at her clenched fists. "I spent the night watching this thing. They're saying it's a killer virus released by terrorists. No known identity. No known cure. Hundreds dead. Panic setting in. They've called out the National Guard in seven states. People are being warned to stay in their homes. Businesses are shutting down. Hospitals are flooded." She glared at him. "Then it hit me. All this is going on while my husband flies off to secret meetings."

Fletcher patted her hand. "It'll be okay. Just a couple of crazies trying to end the world. Hell, we've seen that before. We'll overcome it."

Her blue eyes burned into him. "The world's blowing up and you expect me to believe it's because some lunatics released a tube of virus? You expect me to believe that? I've been with you too long to fall for a story like that. It's breaking out everywhere. No virus can do that." She gripped his hand. "How bad is it, Johnny? I need to know the truth."

Fletcher's neck reddened. "Sorry, our orders are to say nothing until it's under control. There's nothing to worry about. Just stay calm and turn off that damned TV." He grabbed the remote and pressed the off button.

She brushed away a tear. "Franklin called this morning."

"Franklin?"

"They've discontinued summer classes until further notice. All students have been advised to return to their homes."

"Yale's closed?"

"Harvard too. Robert called an hour ago. He'll be home on the three o'clock train. Franklin's coming in at seven." Her head snapped up, her eyes filled with anger. "What's going on, Johnny? I'm your wife for God's sake."

Fletcher lowered his head. "I'm going to clean up. I need to go back in. I'll pick up Robert at the station."

She stood up and glared at him. "I'll take care of our sons. Don't want to mess up their father's priorities."

"Estelle, please—" He watched her storm out of the room. Their little argument had taken only five minutes, but in that time another twenty people had died across the globe, their lungs gasping for air, their blood starved for oxygen.

.   .   .

146

Fletcher's cell phone went off at 1:23 p.m., just as his chauffeured sedan pulled up to the Department of Health and Human Service's security gate. He was surprised when the "CALLER ID" revealed an extension within the same building. He pressed the "on" button and held the phone against his ear.

"Mr. Fletcher?"

"Yes?"

"Please wait, Mr. Fletcher."

Fletcher glanced nervously at his watch. Where the hell was Parker?

"Jonathan, this is Samuel Tarver. I need you to attend a two o'clock meeting."

Fletcher glanced at the security guard peering at him through the car window. "Yes, sir. Where?"

"The Pentagon. Just give them your name and show them your CDC card. You'll be directed to our conference room."

Fletcher fumbled for his identification card and handed it to the stern-faced guard.

"Jonathan?"

"I'll be there."

"Thank you." The phone went dead.

The guard scanned the identification card and flashed a light pen in Fletcher's right eye. It only took a second for the retinal scan to register on the guard's handheld computer. "Cleared to enter, Mr. Fletcher."

Fletcher took his card from the guard's outstretched hand. "Change in plans. I just took a phone call from my boss. I'm ordered to the Pentagon."

"No problem, sir." The guard stepped back while Fletcher's driver did a U-turn and accelerated down Independence Avenue to the 12th Street Expressway where he headed south across the Potomac toward the heart of the nation's military complex.

Fletcher closed his eyes and rested his head against the seat. It was coming at him too fast. Frankton, Hampsted, Menchen, Adams, Tarver, and now, Estelle. *Oh God, please*

make her understand. She's my life. I'm nothing without her.
He felt a tear trickle down his cheek. In the distance, sirens blared from the latest emergency test.

Fletcher stepped into the dimly lit conference room at 1:59 p.m. From the popping in his ears when he exited the elevator, he was several hundred feet below street level. A marine lead him to a vacant chair at the black semicircular table in the center of the room. The wall facing the table was covered with television monitors and a projection screen. The screen was spattered with 108 points of light, each one a crisis site on the screen's nine foot Mercator projection.

Fletcher sat down and placed his briefcase on the floor while staring at the imposing faces seated around him. In his nineteen years of service, Jonathan Fletcher had never felt the presence of so much power. On his left sat Clayton Morehead, Director of National Security; Langston Friedman, Director of the FDA; Bernadette Helsing, Director of the EPA; Colling Tors, Director of the CIA; Corey Whitman, Director of the FBI; and General David Stoyer, chairman of the Joint Chiefs of staff.

The seven people seated to his right seemed out of place for a Pentagon briefing. They appeared to be members of the nation's major newspaper and television conglomerates, as indicated by the identification cards in front of them. Fletcher's eyes caught Clarise Hilton, Editor-in-Chief of the *New York Times*. She acknowledged Fletcher's nervous smile and looked down at her notes.

A door opened below the screen and a naval officer stepped into the room. He paused and eyed the small gathering. "Ladies and gentlemen, the President of the United States."

Fletcher felt everyone rise to their feet. He pushed up from the table and stood on shaky knees, his eyes focused on the white-haired man standing at the door.

Harold Manis was a tall, slightly overweight man with striking white hair and a robust stride that echoed back to the days of Reagan and Johnson. Known for his infectious smile and piercing brown eyes, he walked to the small table below the projection screen and paused to survey his audience. The piercing eyes were there, but the infectious smile was absent, replaced by a troubled frown. "Please, be seated." He waited until everyone resumed their seat before taking his own.

Fletcher was so engrossed with the President that he didn't notice Samuel Tarver slip through the door at the rear of the conference room. He flinched when Tarver rested a hand on his shoulder. "I'm sorry, I didn't see—"

Tarver squeezed Fletcher's shoulder and leaned close to his ear. "I'm only staying for the President's words. Can you hang in for me?"

Fletcher nodded.

Tarver patted his shoulder. "Let's have an early dinner in my office. I need to talk over something."

Fletcher's face flushed. *Dinner? How about The Last Supper? They know, dammit! I'm toast!* He looked up at Tarver and managed a weak smile. "Looking forward to it."

"See you at four." Tarver stepped back into the shadows.

Manis folded his hands and stared at his audience. "We're in trouble, folks. Big trouble." He paused to let his words sink in. "We've spent sixty years worrying about nuclear exchanges and asteroids, and it turns out to be a damn bug. And the damn thing's invisible." He dropped back in his chair. "Well, how about that. The best minds and technology can't find a goddamn little bug." His face reddened. "Unacceptable."

Manis placed a red folder on the table and glared at the seven media executives. "I'm asking you to put a lid on this. I know that's difficult, but panic is the last thing we need. I'm going to give you everything we have, but I expect restraint." He waited for their stunned nods. "Good, we can proceed."

Manis opened the folder and scanned its contents. He frowned and spoke deliberately. "Over a thousand dead in eighteen countries." He glanced at the shaken executives. "And it's accelerating. If we don't unmask it and perfect a vaccine, that thousand will be two thousand by next week, eight thousand by month's end, and four million in three months." He closed the folder and leaned back in his chair.

Garth Minion, WNN's Chief Executive Officer rose to his feet, his green eyes locked on the President. "Are you saying what I think you're saying?"

Manis nodded. "If we don't have a vaccine by winter, the human race will cease to exist by next summer." He watched Minion collapse in the chair. The room was dead silent.

Fletcher looked down at his clenched fists. For the second time in twenty-four hours, he'd heard the doomsday prophecy. It wasn't possible. The idiots couldn't have screwed up that badly. They'd assured him everything was under control. The half life decay had worked perfectly. There were no anomalies. No trace detections. He glanced at his watch. Menchen said he would call today. But when? Four? Six? What if he called during the Tarver meeting? And what about Parker? Where the hell was he? Gotta tighten the reins, dammit. Can't let this go on. He wiped a bead of sweat off his forehead and listened to the President's words.

"At six o'clock this evening, I'm going to address the nation. We're trying to coordinate our action with other governments, but our Middle East foes aren't cooperating. The fundamentalists believe it's some kind of curse from above." Manis shook his head. "When are those fools going to realize that we all share this screwed-up planet. We're up against something that doesn't care about sacred causes, religious hatred, or racial prejudice. Something so powerful, it's going to kill us all regardless of race, color, or creed."

Manis rose to his feet and eyed the stunned faces at the table. "Forget about petty squabbles and turf battles. We're all on the same ship, and it's sinking. So get to work and pull out all the stops. We don't have much time." He snatched the red folder off the table and strode out of the room, followed by the seven media representatives.

The next hour was spent going over findings from the crisis sites. Useless speculation led to arguments and threats. When the President returned to the roomful of chaos, it was clear his appeal for unity had failed. These bureaucratic fools would fight for their turf to their last breath—which wasn't far off.

After tearing into the stunned attendees with words like "incompetent" and "suicidal," Manis shook them when he announced his decision to place all government resources under the one agency that offered our best hope for survival—the Centers for Disease Control and Prevention, and its new director, Samuel Tarver.

Fletcher was stunned when the President asked him to say a few words. With Tarver gone, Fletcher was the sole representative of the suddenly most powerful agency in the world. He stood up and managed to blurt out a few canned lines about teamwork and urgency, then quickly sat down while trying to digest the past hour. When he came to his senses, the room had emptied and the screen had gone black.

He collected himself and followed the marine guard to the elevator. When he reached street level, a limo was waiting to take him to Tarver's office in the Department of Health and Human Service's Building. It was 3:30 in Washington, DC, and 9:30 in Salzburg.

.　　.　　.

Menchen stared at the shaken face on the screen. "Are you certain?"

"I don't know how it could happen. It's impossible."

Menchen leaned forward, his eyes filled with concern. "But the models showed nothing?"

"Forget the models. They're useless, Gunthar. Everything was based on a half-life decay of three months. We were well within the safety limit for each target perimeter." Schoenfeld shook his head. *"Something went wrong."*

"Schoenfeld-san, please review the blood test again."

Schoenfeld glanced at the oriental on his left. *"My findings are irrefutable."*

Nakashima sighed. *"There must be something you overlooked."*

Schoenfeld glared at him. *"I've performed the test eight times with the same result, each time with a fresh sample from separate sprayings. The procedure was always the same. A drop from each sample was placed in a curing dish containing a drop of my own blood. Oxygen depletion took only twenty seconds. That's a lethality increase of six magnitudes above the original result."*

Nakashima shook his head in disbelief. *"That cannot be. Those are seventeen-year-old samples. They have been corrupted in some way. Perhaps a temperature anomaly, or contamination of the storage vault."*

Schoenfeld shook his head. *"Don't you understand? After seventeen years, the samples should be harmless. Instead, they're lethal."*

Menchen ignored the twinge of pain in his chest. "What about the more recent samples?"

Schoenfeld looked down at his notes.

"Magnus?"

Schoenfeld shook his head. *"That's the frightening part. The last sample is from a spraying eleven years ago. The lethality increase isn't as great—only two magnitudes."*

Menchen stared at the screen. "You're saying it's grown stronger with each passing year."

"I'm afraid so, with accelerating intensity."

For a moment, nothing was said as the three men pondered Schoenfeld's findings. Nakashima was first to speak. *"We must talk with Adams. There must be an antidote. A vaccine."*

Schoenfeld nodded. *"Yes, we'd better get hold of that idiot before he drops dead. Do it, Gunthar. Do it now."*

Menchen raised his hand for silence. "What about the dispersion models?"

Nakashima looked down at his computer printouts. *"I can only extrapolate because everything was based on a three month half-life duration."* He hesitated while unfolding a global map. It took a few seconds to position it under his scanner. Menchen and Schoenfeld stared at the Mercator projection on the screen beneath Nakashima's face.

Nakashima activated a red dot on the map using a laser pointer. He positioned the dot in the South Atlantic, off Africa's western coastline. *"Without half-life decay, the runoff would have spilled into the South Atlantic where the Benguela Current carried it north to the African Panhandle. From there, it would have swept west across the Atlantic to be picked up by the Brazil Current for a partial sweep along South America's east coast. The other half would have swept north toward Cuba via the South Equatorial Current. Then, into the Gulf of Mexico via the North Equatorial Current and upward toward the United State's eastern coast via the Gulfstream."*

"Enough!" Schoenfeld glared at Nakashima.

"I am sorry, Schoenfeld San. That is just one of the global flows. There are many others."

Menchen leaned back in his leather chair, his eyes fixed on the map. "It seems we have a problem that must be handled with great care. I'll arrange a meeting with Herr Adams and get back to you. Until then, it's imperative this matter stay between us and our American contact."

Schoenfeld glared at the screen. *"I don't like it. He's not one of us. How can we trust a man with two faces?"*

Menchen looked down at his clasped hands. "We can't, but we need him to deal with Adams and the others. When things calm down, we'll arrange for his silence."

Schoenfeld's glare softened. *"Don't wait too long, old friend. I've studied Mr. Fletcher's dossier. His kind will do anything to survive."*

Menchen nodded. "I'll get back to you tomorrow at nine p.m., Salzburg time. I warn you, it will cost a great sum to deal with Herr Adams. Without a deterrent, the outbreaks may go on for some time. Once we have what we need, we'll let our American contact handle the unpleasantries. Then we can get on with our lives and the world will be back to its usual chaos." Menchen hesitated. "Agreed?"

Nakashima forced a nervous smile. *"I'll say a prayer for the innocents who have died."*

Menchen returned his smile. "Don't be too hard on yourself, Yoshio. A few thousand will die, but remember how many we saved." He placed his finger on the disconnect button. "Tomorrow then." He pressed the button and stared at the blank screen.

The digital clock beside his hand read 10:20. Still enough time to kiss his daughter goodnight. Then a few moments with his beloved wife before placing that call to America. He nodded to himself. Yes...it would all work out and things would be normal again.

Menchen reached for the glass of brandy on the table. He sniffed the pungent bouquet and sipped it down, and while he savored its aftertaste, another thirty died.

·   ·   ·

Fletcher stepped into Samuel Tarver's office at 3:59, accompanied by an aide who gestured toward a small table beneath a bay window overlooking the Mall. The table was covered with a white linen cloth and two silver place settings.

"Mr. Tarver will be with you shortly. Please, have a seat." The aide led Fletcher to the table and pulled out one of the opposing leather chairs. He waited for Fletcher to sit down before lifting a napkin off the table and placing it on Fletcher's lap. "Care for a drink?"

"I'm fine, thank you." Fletcher took a deep breath and watched the aide leave the room. *How did Tarver find out? It was Adams, dammit. The scum sold me out. I'll kill that worm with my bare hands!*

"Ah, right on time."

Fletcher snatched the napkin off his lap and stood up. Samuel Tarver had stepped through a paneled door behind the walnut desk, a smile on his face.

Tarver closed the door and walked around the desk, his right hand extended. "Hope you don't mind. I'm sure you'd rather spend the time with that beautiful wife." He shook Fletcher's hand and eased into the chair across from him.

Tarver draped a napkin on his lap and lifted his covered platter, exposing a "blt" and some chips. "Go ahead, no formalities." He nodded at Fletcher's platter and watched his guest sit down and lift off the silver cover.

Tarver took a large bite of his sandwich and washed it down with some iced tea. He leaned back in his chair and eyed his guest. "Not hungry?"

Fletcher shook his head. "Just tired. I've been at it forty-eight hours."

Tarver nodded and sipped more iced tea. He placed his glass on the table and folded his hands. "Quite a mess."

"Yes, sir."

"I liked the way you spoke up at the meeting. It shows you care."

After nineteen years under fire, Jonathan Fletcher knew how to sense an opening. Forget the paranoia. Go with the flow. Things might not be what they seem. He lowered his head and put on his best show. "I'm not a physician or pathologist, but I've given nineteen years of my life to government service. I don't want it to end like this."

Tarver's smile faded. "You sound like someone ready to resign."

Fletcher stuck out his chin and looked his new boss in the eye. "Not until we beat this damn thing."

"And then?"

Fletcher sighed. "I've promised my wife some years of peace and tranquility. Nineteen years of struggle is enough. Let someone else stand the gaff. It's time for me to step aside."

Tarver nodded and sipped his tea. "Can't blame you for that. I'm glad you've decided to stay on until this mess is over."

Fletcher nodded. "Whatever you need."

Tarver put down his glass and looked at the Capitol. "We'll conquer it. I spent twelve years fighting microbes, and this one's no different than the rest." He picked up his glass and sipped more tea. "It'll burn itself out."

"Sir?"

"You know—like Ebola. Oh, it's more powerful, but that's the point. The mortality rate will soon exceed the dispersion rate. That's one of the convoluted things about viruses. The faster they kill, the faster they die off. They can't survive without living hosts."

Fletcher nodded. *I'll be damned. The idiot thinks it's a virus. He doesn't suspect a thing. No sweat, old buddy. You just dodged another arrow.* He snatched his sandwich and took a bite.

Tarver's smile returned. "Ah, the old appetite's back."

"Yes, sir."

"Well, I won't hold you up." Tarver placed his glass on the table. "Can I ask you something?"

"Of course."

"Just for the record, don't you want my job?"

Fletcher swallowed hard and snatched his tea. Tarver's words rang in his ears. He gulped down the tea and stared at his host in disbelief.

"Sorry about that. Please, hear me out."

Fletcher put down his glass and stared at the fourth-most powerful man in the United States behind the President, Vice-President, and Director of National Security.

"I just came from a meeting with the President. It's pretty simple. When this mess is over, I'll be promoted to National Security Director. The President thinks we need a change." Tarver looked at the Capitol. "The security job should be numero uno, except for the presidency. Instead, that jerk

Morehead—" He caught himself and smiled at his guest. "I need someone I can trust." He leaned closer. "Can I trust you?"

"Of course, sir." Fletcher snatched his buzzing cell phone.

"Do you want to take that call?"

Fletcher glanced at the international number on the phone's tiny screen. "They can wait."

"Well?"

Fletcher's head was spinning. Ten minutes ago, he'd stepped into Tarver's office ready to accept a death sentence. Now, he was being offered the kingdom. He took a deep breath and struggled for words.

Tarver stood up and placed his napkin on the table. "I need to know by tomorrow morning. I have a three o'clock meeting with the President. I want to recommend you to replace Zargon as CDC's Director of Operations. It's the perfect position for a man with your logistics experience. When we overcome the bug, I'll be promoted and you can move up behind me."

"To . . . Director?"

Tarver nodded.

"What about Carson?"

Tarver smirked. "Don't worry about her. She's lucky to have a job with her track record." He walked around the table and stood beside Fletcher. "Try to get some sleep. You should have a clear head for this sort of thing."

Fletcher looked down and felt Tarver's hand on his shoulder.

"Give me this and you can have your paradise. You have my word on that. All I'll ask is a year to put things in order. Then you can have anything you want, all expenses paid."

"Yes, sir." Fletcher stood up and stuffed the cell phone in his pocket. He shook Tarver's hand and started out of the room.

"Oh, one other thing."

Fletcher stopped and turned toward his boss.

"I've spent my life reaching for this moment. I can't fail, Jonathan. You understand what I'm saying?"

"Yes, sir."

Tarver glared at him. "Then don't say no."

Fletcher couldn't move. He watched Tarver walk to his desk and sit down. The first rays of late afternoon sun were striking the carpet.

Tarver picked up a pen and started writing. "Tomorrow then." He listened to the door open and close.

Chapter 14

Marianne

Thala shook the man sleeping beside him.
"Yeah?"
"We need to talk."
Karl sat up and winced from his sore ribs. He squinted at the late afternoon sun and sea of red tail-lights on the road in front of him. The clock on the dashboard read 5:40. An "I-10" sign drifted by on his right.
"We just cleared Phoenix, but this traffic is really bad. I'm barely making forty."
Karl rubbed his aching side. "Accident?"
Thala shook his head. "The first outbreak hit Prescott two hours ago. Now something's bubbled up in Phoenix near the Hayden Rhodes Aqueduct. There's talk of fatalities. The city's ready to blow up and we just drove into it."
Karl sank in the seat, his eyes gazing at the windshield.
"The government's clamped down on the media. It's breaking out everywhere."
"What about roadblocks?"
"The California border's sealed like a tomb. National Guard and state police everywhere. Helicopters patrolling the desert." Thala squeezed the steering wheel. "Our photos are flickering on every police terminal in the United States." He hesitated and stared at the traffic. "It's only a matter of time."
"Thanks for the uplifting news."
"Maybe we should give up."
Karl glared at him. "Are you nuts? We might as well commit suicide."

"Maybe we can get the media involved. You know, to give us a shield."

"You're dreaming, Doc." Karl popped open the glove compartment and shuffled through the car's papers.

"There are no maps, if that's what you're looking for."

Karl shut the glove compartment and snatched the laptop off the floor. "I'll find us another route. Something through the mountains."

Thala sighed. "Give it up, Mr. Frankton. They've shut off everything. We've had it."

Karl's face flushed. "What the hell's wrong with you? You saw what they tried to do to us. There's no way they'll let us live. I was dead meat when I detoured to Trinity site, and you were finished when you didn't turn me in."

"If we play our cards right and use the media—"

"Forget the media. There's a killer on the loose and the feds are desperate. No one's gonna stop Hampsted. No one!" Karl gripped Thala's shirt. "What happened to you? Or was that little speech about South Africa a bunch of crap?"

"That has nothing to do with it."

"Doesn't it? A man who stood up against apartheid is ready to throw in the towel to a bunch of vermin? Or doesn't that matter anymore? The beatings? The torture? Your wife? Your daughters? Did they die for nothing? Is that what you're telling me?"

Thala's eyes flared with anger. The man clutching his shirt had gone too far. "You better shut up."

"Pull over!" Karl seized the wheel and yanked it to the right, nearly sideswiping another car. The air erupted with squealing tires, blaring horns, and curses from the passing cars.

"Are you crazy? What the—" Before Thala could finish his sentence, they'd spun off the interstate in a cloud of dust.

Karl gripped Thala's collar and gave it a hard twist. "I may be a loser, but you're not gonna quit on me."

"Damn you!" Thala seized Karl's wrist and ripped his hand away. Before his stunned passenger could react, Thala

160

clenched Karl's collar in a death grip and wound up for a lethal right to the head.

Karl slumped against the seat, his blue eyes staring at the Zulu. "Go ahead, Doc. Whatever it takes."

"Fool!" Thala drove his fist into the dashboard, splitting the leather. He pushed Karl away and collapsed in the driver's seat, his eyes flashing with bitter memories.

Neither of them spoke. The only sounds were car horns from the frustrated drivers trapped on Interstate 10.

Karl finally broke the silence. "We should get moving before the highway patrol checks us out. We must look pretty weird sitting on the shoulder with our hood pointed the wrong way." He pushed open the passenger door and climbed out of the car.

Thala looked at him with tired eyes. "You are insane."

Karl ignored him and reached for the laptop. "Come on, Doc. We're wasting time."

Thala shook his head. "Why does a man who destroyed his life suddenly want to stand and fight?"

Karl gripped the laptop's carrying strap. "Good question. I'll have to think about it."

"No!" Thala seized Karl's wrist. "If you want me out of this car, you give me a reason now."

Karl tried to yank his hand away, but Thala's grip was like iron. He lowered his head and spoke softly. "Probably the same reason that made a kafir stand up and say no. Something that boils up in your gut when you can't take any more. When you want to feel good about yourself again. Maybe feel like a man again. Something like that." Karl pulled his hand away and snatched the laptop off the seat. "Now come on. I feel lucky."

They headed up the 51st Avenue exit ramp. When they reached the intersection, Karl gestured toward the row of weathered storefronts on the right, and the blistered sign hanging over the last one...

Marianne's Desert Flights
See nature from God's view

Marianne Finklestein had run the flight school for eighteen years. Between an occasional lesson and crop dusting job, she'd managed to enjoy a carefree existence flying over the Arizona desert. All that ended twelve years ago when the government clamped down on flight schools and crop dusters because of the terrorist attacks on New York and Washington. Marianne didn't have a seditious bone in her fifty-four-year-old body, but she got caught up in the national paranoia along with everyone else. And of course, she was one of the little people who always get screwed while the bigger fish survive.

After losing her crop-dusting contracts to a powerful agricultural conglomerate "for security reasons," Marianne barely had enough savings to maintain the thirty-year-old bi-wing sitting in the desert. With her business in debt up to its eyeballs, Marianne Finkelstein had thrown in the towel. Needless to say, she was stunned when two unlikely customers strolled up to the counter in her one-room rented office.

"You're the owner?"

Marianne put down her beer and squinted at the bruised face. She pushed up from the counter and straightened her distressed leather jacket. "Marianne Finkelstein, at your service."

Karl nodded at the tall man standing beside him. "Our car broke down in that damn traffic. We need to get to an important meeting in San Clemente. Can you help us?"

Marianne chugged her beer and swiped the suds off her upper lip. "San Clemente? That's pretty far. I hear the feds really shut down the air space." She nodded to herself. "Damn suicidal."

Karl reached into his pocket and dragged out the three hundred dollars he'd pooled with Thala. He placed the stack of twenties on the counter and fanned it. "Will this do?"

Marianne stared at the spread currency. "Hell, that's half of what you need."

"Half? Now wait a minute—"

Karl restrained Thala. "Sorry about that. He's just uptight. We've worked on this deal for six months and can't get to the most important meeting of our lives."

Marianne squinted at him. "Sounds pretty dramatic. What do you guys do?"

"We're land developers. We came up with a low-cost plan to restore some expensive property along the San Clemente coastline. It'll stop the erosion and protect the homes." Karl looked into her brown eyes. "You know how important that is?"

Marianne nodded. "Oh yeah, real important. So tell me, Mr.—"

"Schumman. Peter Schumman." Karl reached out and shook her hand.

"So tell me, Mr. Schumman. If it's so important, why can't you give me the six hundred bucks it's gonna cost to fly you there?"

Karl shrugged. "That's all the cash we have."

"I take credit cards."

Thala reached into his wallet and dragged out his American Express card. He snatched the money and placed the card on the counter. "Use this instead of the cash. Six hundred—no more."

Marianne pulled out an antiquated credit card zipper and placed the card in the slot. She positioned the carboned receipt and slid the zipper across the card. She was about to pull out the card when she hesitated and glanced at the small television set in the corner. "That's you, right?"

Karl turned and stared at the two faces on the screen. It was like looking in a mirror.

"I take it you're the two guys they're after."

Karl spun toward her, his eyes locked on the sawed-off shotgun she'd pulled from under the counter.

Marianne stepped around the counter and squinted at her two stunned customers. "So tell me, fellas. You causing all this?"

Thala stepped toward her and stopped cold when she waved the shotgun at him. He raised his hands and spoke softly. "We're with CDC. Do you know who they are?"

"Who doesn't these days. You're the one called Thala, right? Same as on the card?"

Thala nodded. "Please listen to me. You're all we have."

She shrugged. "Then you don't have much, big guy."

"Please. We're scientists—pathologists. We found something and we're trying to take it a step further. If you help us, it could save thousands of lives."

Marianne shook her head and leaned against the counter. "Cut the bull and show me your ID's."

Thala reached into his shirt pocket and pulled out his ID card. He placed it on the counter and backed away. "They don't want us to find the answer. If you turn us in, we're dead men."

Marianne looked at Karl. "So what's in San Clemente?"

"We're not sure. The computer came up with someone who might be linked to the outbreaks."

She cracked a wry smile. "Nice try, but you guys are trained to lie. Don't get me wrong. I don't care for the government, but I do care about innocent families dying. And I could use that reward money."

Thala locked his black eyes on her. "They'll kill you for sure. The only thing you'll collect is a grave." He glanced at his bag. "Can I show you something?"

She shrugged.

"Do you have a CD player?"

"There's one in the TV." She watched him open the bag. "I'd be real careful if I was you."

Thala eased out the disk and inserted it into the television's CD player. He turned on the player and froze the recording at the blurred flash."

"What the hell's that?"

"Human blood being drained of life by something inside that blur. If we can identify it, we can stop it. The guy in San Clemente is our best shot."

She squinted at the TV screen. "What is he, some kinda vampire?"

"You could call him that, but this vampire is going to wipe out the human race if we don't stop him." Thala stepped toward her. "So go ahead and shoot, Ms. Finkelstein. I'd rather take a bullet in the chest from a tough old lady than a lethal injection from a government agent."

"Watch it, big guy." She stepped back and waved the shotgun at him, but he kept coming."

"Sorry, Ms. Finkelstein. I don't have a choice."

She aimed the shotgun at his chest. "You're crazy, Mr. Thala."

"No, just scared."

She placed her finger on the trigger. "You gonna kill me?"

He forced a smile. "Looks like you're the one doing the killing."

She sighed and placed the shotgun on the counter. "Hell, it don't shoot. The firing pin's been broke for six years."

Thala stared at her, unable to speak.

"Gonna kill me now?" She folded her arms and leaned against the counter.

Thala shook his head. "We're trying to save lives, Ms. Finkelstein. Thousands of them, and we need your help."

She glanced at the ID card. "Sounds good, but you terrorists are damned good liars. I saw it in a movie."

Thala stepped back from her. "Like I said, you're all we have."

"Oh yeah? We'll see about that." She pulled Thala's Amex receipt out of the zipper and slid the card across the counter. "Forget the plastic and give me the three hundred bucks."

She watched Thala dig the money out of his pocket and place it on the counter. "Come on gents, my jeep's out back. We've got lots of miles to cover." She snatched the cash off the counter and brushed past the two stunned men.

It took forty minutes to reach the dilapidated hangar northwest of town, and its sole occupant, a rust-colored bi-winger with "*Marianne*" painted on the engine cowling.

They watched Marianne give the plane a loving pat before stepping on the wing and climbing into the pilot's cockpit. She jammed a leather helmet over her flaming red hair and nodded toward the rear cockpit. "Hope you guys aren't gay cause it'll be pretty tight for the next few hours. You'll have to share the seat and belt. There's a spare helmet and goggles on the floor. Now get in, cause we're outta here." She flipped the magneto and watched the propeller roar to life, sending dust into the faces of the two men standing beside the plane.

Thala shook his head and climbed into the rear cockpit. "Well, Mr. Frankton?" He nodded at his lap. "Or do you want me to sit on you?"

Marianne watched her second passenger climb into the rear cockpit. She gunned the engine and shouted above the roar. "You better strap in tight cause we're gonna do some aerobatics. The California border's swarming with choppers."

She waited for her two goggled passengers to nod. "Oh yeah, one other thing. You try anything up there and so help me God, I'll drop you in the Colorado River!"

She jammed the throttle forward and accelerated through the opened hangar doors. Seconds later, the red biplane lifted off the dirt strip into the darkening sky, headed for the orange clouds above the Arizona desert.

Chapter 15

Ringley Adams

"Dad, you okay?"

Fletcher put down his fork and smiled at his son. "Just tired."

Robert folded his napkin and placed it beside his empty plate. He breathed a contented sigh and smiled at his mother. "You haven't lost your touch, Mom. Nobody makes French lamb chops like you."

"I second that." Franklin wiped his black beard and leaned back in his chair, his hands resting on his bloated stomach. "How about you, Dad? Bet you eat like this all the time."

Fletcher started to speak, but Estelle cut him off.

"This is the first time we've sat down as a family since you guys left for summer session. Your dad and I would explode if we ate like this every night. Usually, it's just a sandwich or some soup in front of the TV."

Fletcher nodded and picked up the fork. "Sorry about the old appetite. I'll finish it later." He took a bite of lamb and rested the fork on his plate.

Robert leaned toward him. "So, what's going on?"

Fletcher shook his head. "You know I can't say anything."

"Looks pretty serious."

"It'll be okay."

"They say it's some kind of virus."

"Probably, but that's good news."

"Good?"

Fletcher pushed his plate aside and rested his arms on the table. He hesitated and spoke softly. "The virus's lethality works in our favor. To put it bluntly, a virus can't survive on dead hosts. With everyone dropping so fast, it'll probably die off in a few weeks. Kind of gruesome, but that's how it will end."

Fletcher noticed his wife glaring at him across the table. He leaned back and raised his hands apologetically. "I'm sorry. I shouldn't have—"

She stood up, her hand clutching the napkin. "Why be sorry? It's only a few thousand victims. Look at the good side. The virus will starve to death. How encouraging. How goddamn encouraging!"

"Estelle, I—"

"Damn you!" She threw the napkin on the table. "Is this what you sacrificed nineteen years for? To play politics while innocent people die?"

"Enough!" Fletcher slammed his fist on the table. The stress and lack of sleep had finally taken their toll. He gritted his teeth and watched her storm out of the dining room.

"Dad?"

Fletcher felt a warm hand on his arm. He glanced to his left and saw Robert staring at him.

"You okay?"

Fletcher's anger melted. He gripped his son's hand and felt his eyes well up with tears. "She doesn't understand. No one understands."

Franklin slipped beside his dad and rested a hand on his shoulder. "We're with you, pop. All the way."

Fletcher stared at the empty space across the table. He sighed and lowered his head. "I'm going to tell you something that has to stay between us."

Franklin patted his dad's shoulder. "It's in the vault."

They spent the next two hours in the study listening to their dad's description of the meeting with Tarver. When Fletcher broke the news about taking over CDC, Robert's eyes lit up. Franklin stared at his father, his jaw hanging open.

"Well, what do you think?"

Robert glanced at his brother who had broken into a beaming smile. He turned toward his dad, his brown eyes aflame. "Hell yeah, pop. Go for it."

That was all Jonathan Fletcher needed to hear. He embraced his two sons and shuffled upstairs. It wouldn't be easy breaking the news to Estelle, but she'd come around. After nineteen years in hell, Jonathan Fletcher had hit the lottery. He picked up the cell phone and placed a call to California.

. . .

Marianne eased the throttle and shouted over her shoulder. "I'm gonna do a low pass over those lights. Looks like a diner or something. See if you can pick up a name. I can't make out the sign in this haze."

Karl gripped the cockpit's cowling and leaned toward her. "How do we land if you can't see anything?"

"Shut up and check those lights! What do you expect for three hundred bucks? In a couple minutes, we'll be down and I'll be outta here. And you boys can go save the world, Hallelujah!" She jerked the stick to the left, dropping the biplane into a steep left bank.

Karl hung on for dear life as the biplane circled the colored lights. He swiped his sleeve across his goggles and squinted at the neon sign glimmering through the haze. When he tried to lean over the cowling, a sharp slap on the back stopped him cold.

"Watch it! You're pinching expensive property."

"Sorry about that."

Thala cursed under his breath and slid his numbed legs to the right. After three hours dodging mountains, electric towers, and surveillance aircraft, his nerves were shattered. Add the hundred seventy pound weight on his lap, and he was ready to throw in the towel.

Marianne glanced over her shoulder. "Well?"

"Looks like *Rudy's*. Can you drop any lower?"

"We're too low. Too many hills and towers. I'm taking us up." She pulled back the stick and gunned the throttle, lifting the biplane toward the full moon above the hills.

Thala grimaced and shouted at their helmeted pilot. "What kind of move is that! Do you want to kill us!"

"Hold your horses, big guy. I gotta check my maps. My eyes aren't what they used to be."

Thala glared at her. "What kind of pilot are you? Just find a damn strip and set this piece of junk down. If I'm going to die, I'd rather do it on terra firma."

Marianne switched on a flashlight and shuffled through her maps. She squinted at a paved road winding along the ocean, then glanced back at Karl. "Hey, blondie, does your computer work?"

"Yeah, probably."

"Look up Rudy's Diner off Highway One in San Clemente. See if you can get a map-info plot to that address you're looking for."

Karl snatched the laptop out of Thala's bag and turned it on. It only took a minute to come up with the directions. He leaned forward and shouted above the engine. "Two miles north of the diner on Highway One. Off Pico toward the ocean. Looks like a cluster of private homes."

"Hang on."

Karl's left shoulder slammed into the cockpit's wall as the *Marianne* rolled into a steep right bank. "Are you nuts! You almost threw me out of the plane!"

"Hang on, fellas. I'm almost outta gas. I'm gonna set her down on that marginal road off the main highway. It looks deserted in the moonlight."

Karl shook his head. "How does she know? She can't see a damn thing."

"Shut up, this was your idea." Thala gripped his seat and watched the plane's nose dip toward the gray strip of road glowing in the moonlight. With the engine throttled down, the only sound was the wind whistling through the propeller...

. . .

Adams gripped his left arm and fought the pain radiating through his chest. A bead of sweat trickled down his forehead. He yanked the bottle of nitro capsules from his pocket and crunched one between his teeth. The surge of adrenalin rushed through him like a soothing wave.

He'd spent the last hour gazing at the nightmare on television. People running for their lives. Bodies scattered in the streets. Stunned survivors probing the corpses for loved ones. A flood of bio-suited military pouring out of trucks to drive back the screaming crowds with bayonets. Lunge and thrust! Thrust again! The horror! For God's sake, they were innocent civilians! The military had no right attacking its own citizens!

A reporter tried to calm an hysterical woman who had witnessed the deaths of her husband and children. The woman kept screaming the same words. "Not them! Take me! Please, God! Take me!" They were pushed away from the camera by the relentless troops. Rifle shots could be heard in the distance as panic broke out along the Monongahela River. And all the while, the same message scrolled across the bottom of the screen...

...At least forty dead in outbreak near Pittsburgh... Survivors tell of massacre...Friends and relatives seen dropping like flies...No warning or explanation... Global death count remains classified...Experts believe it's astronomical...

"Enough!" Adams aimed the remote at the television and pressed the off button. The screen went black, filling the room with darkness. The screams and violence faded, replaced by the sound of surf crashing on the beach.

He spun around in the chair and looked at the stars shining through his opened patio doors. It was nine o'clock in San Clemente. He rested his head against the leather and closed his eyes.

He was nearly asleep when an annoying buzz snapped his eyes open. He sat up in the chair and turned on the reading lamp. "About time, dammit." He snatched the cell phone off the cocktail table and pressed it against his ear. It took a few seconds for the warbling to clear.

"Mr. Adams?"

"Yeah."

"It's Fletcher."

"Took you long enough."

"I've talked to Starburst. They're willing to pay whatever you ask. The biggest concern is time. We need a solution before this thing goes any further."

Adams squeezed the phone. "You don't need a solution. You need a miracle."

"Cut the crap, Mr. Adams. Can you stop it?"

Adams took a strained breath. "Deposit ten million to my Swiss account. When I verify it's there, you'll have your solution."

"That's a lot of money."

"You're asking for a miracle. They don't come cheap."

Fletcher hesitated. *"Five now. The rest when we have the solution."*

Adams' face turned red hot. The blood pounded against his temples. "If I don't see that ten million by tomorrow night, you can forget your miracle, and your fucking world!"

"You're playing with fire, Mr. Adams. I suggest you—"

"Go to hell!" Adams jammed his thumb on the phone's off button. "Damn you! Damn you all!"

His chest tightened. The pain was returning. He rested his head against the soft leather. His hand groped for the lamp switch. The room was dark again except for the stars. A cool breeze swept across his face from the opened doors. The only sounds were the grandfather clock ticking in the foyer and the waves rushing on the beach. So soothing. So peaceful. No one to bother him. Only the soft darkness and sweet sounds of the sea. And all that money waiting for him in Switzerland. His eyes fluttered and closed.

A harsh ring snapped him awake. He switched on the lamp and squinted at the grandfather clock. Ten o'clock, an hour gone in the blink of an eye. So little time left, and so much to do. He pushed out of the chair and staggered across the living room to the foyer.

He stared at the paneled door beneath the staircase. In the past three months, he must have unlocked that door a thousand times. Not surprising. His life's work was behind that door. A secret so deadly, it threatened the human race.

It had begun quite innocently. A simple re-test of the seventeen year sample. He had performed the test annually for sixteen years, each time with the same harmless result. Nothing detected. Zero lethality.

He'd almost decided to skip the test this year. No sense wallowing in the past. Better to go fishing. Then again, there was that indescribable high from revisiting the discovery of the ages. When his book came out next year, he would finally reveal his secret, and the human race would enter a brave new world that exceeded the wildest dreams of the alchemists. An impregnable barrier had been shattered. Ringley Adams was God.

His hand groped for the key in his pocket. He unlocked the door and stepped into the darkened laboratory. The only light came from the hissing gray screen on the lab table.

He walked to the table and sat down, his eyes fixed on the screen. His trembling finger pressed the CD recorder's "play" button.

His mind drifted back to the re-test three months ago, and the frightening revelation that had eluded him for sixteen years. If it weren't for his drunken stupor, he wouldn't have accidentally smeared a drop of his own blood on the slide from a small cut on his finger. He recalled his shock when his live blood cells withered and died on the electron microscope's screen. And that bright flash exposing his deadly creation for the first time in sixteen years.

The killer was alive! After sixteen years in hiding, it had emerged from its cloak of invisibility to reveal a monster two hundred fifty times more deadly than the original.

He recalled the frightening moment he saw the compound flash on the electron microscope's screen, and his gasp of horror when the laser spectrograph revealed a six magnitude increase in lethality. Through an unexplained flaw in his formula, the invisible killer had not died, but had instead propagated to super lethal parts-per-million.

He remembered placing the call to Menchen, his strident voice pleading for emergency funds to develop an antidote before it was too late. Then the rejection and harsh warning.

You're living in the past, Herr Adams. Starburst is only a memory, and so are you. There is no danger. There never was. You're hallucinating. Imagining things. Now listen carefully. Don't ever contact me again. I warn you, Herr Adams. Never call me again or you'll regret it to your dying day.

Adams looked down at his clenched fists. The Judas had turned on him. The warning was clear. If you value your life, never call this number again.

But that wasn't enough for Herr Menchen. For three months, Adams had been barraged with threatening phone calls. He hadn't slept since that night three months ago when he made his plea for funds. He couldn't take it any longer. They were driving him mad!

A sharp pain radiated through his chest. He snatched another capsule from the bottle and crunched it between his teeth. It only took a second for the nitroglycerin to take effect. He slumped in the chair and stared at the three drained tubes leading to the electron microscope's viewing chamber. The first tube had contained his own blood, drawn one hour ago. The second, dead blood drawn from a white rat subjected to his lethal creation.

He squinted at the third tube. Its purple liquid had been drawn from the flask stored in the small refrigerator in the corner. The flask was unlabeled except for a piece of tape containing a smudged word and date. He remembered lifting the flask out of the refrigerator and sucking a few drops of purple liquid into the tube while staring at the smudged words...

Antidote
August 2, 2013

He flicked a bead of sweat off his forehead. So complex, yet so simple. If the sodium and amyl-nitrite mesons had successfully bonded with their sodium-thiosulfate counterpart, the resulting antidote would put an end to the nightmare spreading across the globe.

Simple? What a laugh. Without funding, it had taken him three precious months to perfect the required dosage using all his funds to rent precious minutes on Stanford's linear accelerator. A hair too little or too much, and the antidote would be useless. There was no room for error.

He glanced at his watch. Six minutes had passed since the test's completion. Time for the moment of truth. He depressed the play button and squinted at the deadly flash as his healthy blood cells were assaulted by the greatest killer since the bubonic plague. Through the flash, he could see the antidote flooding downward toward his dying blood cells, its purple wave engulfing the screen like a redeeming angel, the same purple wave that had created the killer seventeen years ago. And now—finally—the answer.

His thoughts were shattered by a ringing in the foyer. He glared at the screen as the doorbell went off again. He pressed the pause button and stormed out of the lab.

"Yes?"

"*We're private pilots. Had to make a forced landing. My friend hurt his leg pretty bad. Can you help us?*"

Adams squinted at the bruised face peering down at him from the closed circuit monitor above the door. He pressed the talk button and shouted at the intercom. "I'm not well. Try the next house. It's only a hundred yards down the road."

"*I'm worried about my friend. I think he's going into shock. I'd call for help, but my cell phone broke in the crash.*"

"You crashed?"

"*Pretty bad one. About a mile down the beach. Please, if I can leave my friend with you, I'll go somewhere else for help.*" The man pushed back his leather flying helmet and stared at the camera.

Adams glared at the monitor. "I'm sick. Can't take any stress. Go away."

"*But—*"

"Go!"

Adams watched the bruised face turn away from the minicam. Seconds later, the automatic floodlight kicked off.

Good, they were gone. Now he could get back to—

His eyes focused on the monitor's flashing red light. Something had broken the electronic beam on top of the front gate. They were breaking in! Fletcher had sent in the CIA!

He switched to the minicam above the front door, flooding the steps with bright light from the activated beam. It took a few seconds for the camera to adjust to the brilliance.

He studied the monitor. Nothing unusual. Just empty steps and gravel. Maybe a short in the system, or an animal crawling on the wall. Hell, check it tomorrow.

He started to turn away and froze as a shadow moved across the gravel. It was on the steps now, and another behind it.

Adams gasped as the bruised face came into view. They were out there! On the other side of the door! He pressed the intercom button and shouted at the two intruders. "What the hell do you want?"

"We need to talk, Mr. Adams."

Adams glared at the face in the monitor. A sharp pain shot through his chest. He gripped his left arm and pressed the intercom button. "I told Fletcher we could work it out. There's no reason for this. All I need is a few minutes. It's going to work. Just give me some time."

"Let us in, Mr. Adams. We need your help. The world needs your help."

"Go away, dammit! Before I call the cops!"

Karl held up the CD. *"Go ahead, Mr. Adams. I'm sure they'll want to see this. You know, the little secret inside the flashing light?"*

Adams' head was spinning. He ripped open his shirt and gasped for breath. "I didn't mean any harm. The idiots didn't listen to me. It's not my fault!"

"Forget that crap and open the door before we break it down!"

Adams ran into the living room and ripped open the bottle of nitro capsules, spilling them on the floor. He could hear the two men slamming against the front door. *The gun! Get the gun!* He started for the desk beside the window, but froze when a terrific pain shot through his chest and arms. "God, no!"

The room was spinning. He couldn't breathe. He heard splintering wood as the door burst open. The floor rushed up at him, and everything went black...

. . .

"Mr. Adams?"

Adams squinted at the blurred face peering down at him. He tried to sit up, but a knifing pain stopped him cold.

Thala leaned toward him. "You're in bad shape, Mr. Adams. Those nitro capsules won't help. You need emergency surgery on that heart."

"Water…"

Karl ran into the kitchen and returned with a glass of water. He handed it to Thala and watched his friend lift Adams' head to the glass. The aging scientist gulped the water and fell back on the couch, gasping for breath.

Thala looked at Karl with foreboding eyes. He shook his head and put the glass on the cocktail table. "What happened, Mr. Adams? How did it come to this?"

Adams gripped Thala's shirt and pulled himself up. He groaned and slumped against the couch. "Fletcher sent you?"

Thala shook his head. "Never met the man."

Adams looked up in surprise. "Then, who are you?"

Karl sat beside the shaken scientist. "We're with CDC. I spotted your little concoction during a blood test under an electron microscope."

"Test?"

"I injected dead blood into a drop of my own. Quite a show."

Adams stared at him. Could it be? A mere mortal conducting the same test with the same result? He squinted at Karl through bloodshot eyes. "How did you find me?"

Thala reached into his bag and lifted out the internet print. He unfolded it and handed it to Adams. "Came across you in a file search. I remembered attending your lecture at Berkeley in ninety-five."

Adams stared at the familiar diagram.

"I traced your address from a call you placed to Mr. Fletcher. It wasn't easy getting here, but I'm beginning to think it was worth it."

Adams locked his bloodshot eyes on Thala. "You expect me to help you? Get the hell out of here. I've got problems of my own."

Karl glared at him. "So I gather. Well, you're not alone. They tried to kill me. My friend too. We've been lucky so far, but they won't mess up again. We know too much. Sound familiar?"

Adams rubbed his chest. "They're going to kill me?"

"If your heart doesn't give out first. Come on, Mr. Adams. We don't have much time."

Adams stared at Karl. "I'm dying?"

Karl leaned toward him. "Give us some help, Mr. Adams. Give the human race some help. You don't want to check out carrying this kind of baggage. Might be bad for you on the other side. Know what I mean?"

Adams closed his eyes and listened to the sea.

"Mr. Adams?"

His eyes snapped open. "Why should I trust you?"

Karl nodded at the TV. "Because we're the two terrorists everyone's after. Tell me, Mr. Adams. Am I a terrorist?"

Adams scowled at him. "You broke in. Now you're trying to get my secret before you kill me. Close enough."

Karl fought his anger. "If that were true, you'd be full of pentothal by now. Come to your senses, man. Like it or not, we're in the same boat."

Adams turned his head away. "Go to hell."

Thala gripped Karl's arm. "Let's search the place and get out. I've had it with this creep."

Adams' face reddened. "You call me a creep? You're all going to die and you call me a creep!"

Karl pushed off the couch and looked down at the trembling scientist. Last try, old chum. Better make it good. He rested his hand on the couch and leaned toward Adams. "I'm not much for religion, but I hope I'm standing there with the other seven billion when you cross over." He stood up and started for the foyer.

179

"Wait!" Adams pushed off the couch and stood up on shaky legs.

They helped him to the door beneath the stairs and watched him slip the key in the lock. He gripped the doorknob and hesitated. "When you walk through this door, nothing will ever be the same." He swung the door open and stepped into the dark room.

It only took a second for Karl to recognize the electron microscope's frozen video screen. He edged toward the screen, his eyes focused on the purple mass flooding the blood cells. "What is it?"

"Salvation...Armageddon...it depends on one's point of view." Adams dropped into the chair facing the screen. "How much do you know?"

"Just what we told you."

Adams rested his finger on the play button. "They meant well. If their chemical process worked, it would save millions of starving people. The resulting agricultural boom would change the face of the Third World. No more hunger. No more poverty. An impoverished continent rising from the ashes. Villages resurrected from the dead. Food for the children. Hope for the future."

Karl rested a hand on Adams' shoulder. "Who were they?"

"They came to me after my presentation at Berkeley. Everyone laughed at me, but not them. They gave me money. Everything I needed. Materials, equipment, the latest technology. Hell, we even rented an atom smasher in California." He looked up at Karl. "Imagine, a whole month bombing my brew with plutonium radiation. Know what that costs?"

Karl stared at the distraught scientist. Could this be happening? Two days ago, he was ready to throw in the towel and head back to York. Now, he was standing beside a madman in a multi-million dollar home overlooking the Pacific, a madman who was about to reveal a secret so deadly, it threatened humanity. He leaned toward Adams and spoke softly. "Who were they, Mr. Adams?"

"Starburst."

Karl's eyes widened. He felt Thala press against him. "You know them?"

"I'm not sure. I remember a name in FDA's database. Star something." He looked down at Adams. "Am I right?"

Adams grimaced. "What are you going to do to me?"

"You need to get to a hospital, Mr. Adams. And we need to get out of here. Just give us something and we'll call the paramedics before we go."

Adams looked up at Karl with desperate eyes. "You're not going to kill me?"

"Just give us something and we're outta here."

Adams looked down at his trembling hands. "Maybe we can help each other. If I give you something, will you be my poison pill?"

Karl knew what he meant. Poison pill was an espionage term for protecting oneself through concealed evidence against one's enemy. Evidence that could be triggered in the event of one's death at the hands of that enemy.

"Well?"

Karl felt Adams' eyes burning into him. He nodded and forced a smile. "Like I said, we're in the same boat."

Adams pressed the CD player's eject button. "Take this disk, and the flask in the refrigerator. There's a loose floorboard in the back of my bedroom closet. Take the metal box under the floorboard. It has everything you're looking for. When they come for me, I'll tell them that you—" Adams' eyes bulged. He gagged and gripped his throat. "I...can't...breathe!"

"The nitro!" Karl pushed Thala aside and seized the bottle in Adams' hand, but it was empty.

They helped Adams off the chair and laid him on the lab floor. Karl lifted the old man's eyelids. The pupils had receded, leaving two bloodshot eyeballs. "He's going into arrest. We need adrenalin!"

Thala didn't wait for the end of the sentence. He bolted through the lab door and rushed back with his medical bag.

He ripped open a fresh syringe and jammed the needle into a vial of adrenalin. It was too late for an injection in the arm. He watched Karl tear open Adams' shirt, exposing the old man's bare chest.

Thala positioned the needle under the sternum and jabbed it in while depressing the plunger. There was no reaction.

They applied mouth-to-mouth and heart massage for almost fifteen minutes. Karl was about to take over when Thala pulled him away. "What the hell are you doing?"

"He's gone."

"No, there's still a chance. Get out of the way."

Thala's grip tightened. "Listen, man! Don't you hear them?"

Karl looked up at the ceiling. The ominous sound was unmistakable. Choppers, closing from the sea. He stood up and seized the disk off the lab table. His eyes darted to the small refrigerator in the corner. He yanked open the door and snatched the purple flask off the shelf. "That jeep in the drive must be his. See if you can find the keys. And take these." He handed Thala the flask and CD.

"Where are you going?"

"We need that box."

"Are you crazy? They'll be down in a minute." Thala cursed under his breath and started for the door. He hesitated and looked down at the man lying on the floor. "I'm sorry, Mr. Adams. God forgive you."

He ran out of the lab and charged through the broken front door. In the distance, twin beams of light were converging on the estate, their ominous vibrations echoing off the cliffs.

The twin choppers landed on the beach at 11:04 p.m. Hampsted led the charge across the sand, his hand clutching the nine millimeter inside his jacket. With Adams' neighbors only a hundred yards to either side, the search and seizure must be done quickly. The first team would break into the estate and sedate Adams while the second ransacked the interior for any journals, documents, or chemicals. The first shock came when they saw the metal security gate hanging off its hinges. From its outward lean, it had been rammed open from the inside. The second shock came when they found Adams lying on the lab floor.

True to their orders, team one stuffed Adams in a body bag and carried him across the beach to the waiting chopper. Elapsed time: one minute, twenty-two seconds. Team two had already begun the interior's strip search.

At three minutes, forty-seven seconds, team two exited the house with the tubes, recorder, and chemical apparatus used for the test. Behind them, Hampsted did a final walkthrough, his flashlight scanning the slashed couches and broken furniture for anything of value. The watches and jewelry had been removed, as had Adams' wallet and personal possessions. It would look like a cult killing, probably drug related.

With sirens blaring in the distance, Hampsted shined the flashlight into the opening beside the dislodged floorboard in the bedroom closet. He glared at the square silhouette in the dust beneath the floor—the spot where the box had rested. A quick probe under the floor with his gloved hand, and he was running out the door toward the waiting choppers. Behind him, the first phosphorus bomb ignited in the living room.

At four minutes, fifty-eight seconds, the twin choppers lifted off the beach and headed out to sea. Behind them, three red bubble lights flashed on the road leading to Adams' home. The distraught neighbors had placed 911 calls only two minutes earlier, but the police weren't even close. They drove through the broken front gate toward the home, their eyes fixed on the twin choppers fading to the south. By the time they reached the front door, the foyer was engulfed in flames. Seconds later, the windows burst in brilliant fireballs. The call went out for fire assistance, but it was overwhelmed by the flood of alarms coming in from the beach communities to the north, where dozens were dropping in their tracks from the unknown killer. No explanation or safe haven. The angel of death had reached Southern California.

Chapter 16

Unmasked

Ralph Moran dropped the metal scoop in the sink and eyed the bowl of neapolitan ice cream on the kitchen table. He dug a spoon out of the kitchen drawer and sat down beside his favorite flavor. The only sound was the refrigerator's soft hum. He smiled and took a generous bite. It was good to be home.

It was ten p.m. in La Jolla. The unexpected flight had only taken a couple of hours in his new *Gulfstream*. Good thing he'd told Charlie to lay over at Love Field instead of Dallas-Fort Worth. Not easy getting air traffic clearance with the nation on terror alert, but Charlie's security contacts had taken care of that. Moran took another bite while recalling the past four hours.

The Dallas meeting had terminated abruptly when news of the local outbreaks reached IBM's Richardson facility. The mysterious virus had devastated three towns along the Trinity River before hitting Dallas. At least a hundred were dead. No warning or explanation. No pattern or footprint. A proud city on the verge of panic. National Guard troops moving in, with martial law declared.

Moran lowered the spoon, his black eyes gazing into space. He would never forget the final moment in the Richardson conference room when the stressed executives accepted his proposal for improved hyper-plasma memory. His surge of elation when the last dissenter slumped in his chair, grudgingly nodding approval. Then the interruption and shattering warning. Charts and graphs flung aside as the shaken executives scrambled for the door. The wail of sirens from downtown Dallas as waves of olive drab trucks and choppers converged on the great city. So sudden. So frightening.

Moran grimaced. A year's worth of preparation wiped out by a crackling intercom. Cost to *Moran Software*, forty million dollars, not to mention the ten years it had taken off his life. He dug his spoon into the ice cream and wolfed it down.

He was cleaning the dish in the sink when he heard his wife step into the kitchen. He turned and gave her a sheepish smile.

"Thank God." Anne wrapped her arms around him and rested her head on his chest. "I was so worried. The National Guard's intercepting aircraft all over the country. There are rumors of shoot downs."

He forced a smile and lifted her chin with his finger. "It'll take more than a few jets to keep me away from you." He kissed her softly on the lips. The silence felt so good. So warm and secure. He hugged her and listened to the refrigerator's hum.

"Jeremy's not doing so well."

He eased away and looked into her tear-filled eyes. "He knows?"

Her eyes flickered with anger. "That damn internet. He knew about his dad before me." She shook her head. "I still can't believe it. Karl was in bad shape, but this? Was it the alcohol? Drugs? Money? How could he do this to innocent people?"

Moran took her in his arms and felt her tremble against him. "Easy, sweetheart. Just take it easy. We'll get through this. We'll make it."

She pushed away and looked at him with pleading eyes. "What about Jeremy? This mess is tearing him up. How could a father do this to his son?" She broke down while her husband tried to find the right words.

"I'll talk to him."

She shook her head. "I tried that. He acted like I wasn't there. He just sits up there with that computer and smelly iguana."

"It'll be okay. He needs a father's words."

She nodded and wiped her eyes. "I was watching WNN. There must be two hundred outbreaks across the world. At least thirty here in the states." She hesitated. "The hospital called. They want me to come in."

"What?"

She forced a smile. "I'm a doctor, remember?"

"You're going?"

"It's my job."

He leaned against the counter. "I don't know, honey. Better to let the military deal with it. They have that protective gear."

She sighed. "It'll only be for a shift. Make me feel better." She glanced at the empty dish in the sink. "What happened in Dallas?"

He looked down. "They shut down the facility. Pulled everyone out."

"I saw the news. I was so scared when they closed down the broadcast. What about the city?"

Moran rested his hands on the counter. "Last thing I saw was National Guard trucks headed into downtown. Lots of choppers overhead. Then Charlie grabbed me and shoved me in the car. Next thing I knew, we were taking off."

She eased against him and gave him a hug.

"I think I'll stick around for awhile." He kissed her on the forehead. "Maybe you should too."

She sighed and patted his hip. "There's some ham in the refrigerator. Want a sandwich?"

He broke into a smile. "Sounds good. Let's see if our son wants one." He started for the hallway and froze when the doorbell went off. "Who the hell's that? It's almost eleven." He shook his head and walked to the front door.

"Mr. Moran?" The agent flashed his photo ID.

Moran squinted at the card. "FBI?"

"Yes, sir." The agent glanced at Anne who had stepped beside her husband. "May we come in?"

Moran nodded and led the two dark-suited agents into the living room. He gestured nervously toward the couch and waited for them to sit down before dropping into the chair across from them. Anne rested a hand on her husband's shoulder and stared at the two agents.

The senior agent leaned forward and clasped his hands. "It's late, so I'll be brief." He looked at Anne. "We have reason to believe your ex-husband may try to contact you."

Anne squeezed Ralph's shoulder. "You know this?"

The agent nodded. "We're offering you twenty-four hour protection. It's the wise thing to do. To be blunt, it's common for an estranged husband to seek revenge on his ex-spouse. Not a pretty picture, given Mr. Frankton's capabilities."

Moran patted his wife's hand. "You didn't answer her question. Do you have evidence?"

The second agent leaned forward and met Ralph's glare with his own. "You know what this man has done. If we can nail him, we'll have a shot at the others. It's for the good of your country—and yourselves."

Moran sank in the chair.

"We'd like to place a few monitoring devices on your property. It'll only take an hour to set them up. It's for your protection."

Moran sighed. "Okay, but no longer than necessary."

"Of course." The agent stood up and headed for the door, followed by his associate. When they reached the door, the agent turned and handed Moran a card. "Call us anytime. We'll have men at your door within seconds." He patted Moran's arm. "Thank you, Mr. Moran. You're doing the smart thing."

Anne watched them climb into their car and drive away. The agent's words echoed in her ears.

Moran slipped his arms around her. "You okay?"

"I don't know."

Moran kissed her softly on the ear. "I'm going to talk to our son."

Jeremy's room was at the end of the upstairs hall. Moran leaned against the door and knocked gently. No response. He frowned and shouted above the din of rock music. "Jerry?"

The music stopped.

"It's Ralph, can I come in?"

Jeremy unlocked the door and swung it open. His eyes were bloodshot and his blond hair needed a comb.

Moran forced a smile. "I just got back. Thought you might want to join us for a sandwich."

"No thanks."

Moran's smile faded. "Maybe we can talk for a minute."

"About?"

"I think you know."

"If it's about my dad, it's none of your business."

Ralph fought a rush of anger. "Okay, then we'll talk about you." He pushed Jeremy aside and stepped into the room. The first thing that caught his eye was Bernie glaring at him from his cage.

"What are you doing!" Jeremy slammed the opened door against the wall. "This is my room. You have no right cutting into my space."

Moran's face twisted in a scowl. Forget anger management. The little punk needed discipline. He took a menacing step toward his stepson. "Who do you think you're talking to? Is this all the thanks I get? I've never tried to cut into your space, but you're pushing the envelope, kiddo."

"Then throw me out. You'll be doing me a favor."

Moran clenched his fists and looked down to avoid eye contact. He'd come through too many hard times to take this crap from a pubescent twelve-year-old. If he had his way, the little creep would be out the door in thirty seconds.

Unfortunately, life isn't that simple. He took a calming breath and blurted out his little speech. "I'm sorry about your dad. I know it must hurt, but for God's sake, don't take it out on me. I didn't plan this. We're all trying to find answers."

Jeremy stepped back and leaned against the opened door. "That's it?"

Moran's face flushed. "Except for one thing. That doorbell was the FBI. They're covering the house. They think your dad might try to hurt us." He watched Jeremy's face go blank. "So like it or not, we're in this together. Your mom, me, and you." He brushed past the shaken young man and stormed down the hall.

.   .   .

Thala squinted at the clock on the dashboard. Five hours had passed since they skidded away from Adams' estate. The choppers and sirens were gone, replaced by the sound of waves. He looked up at the big dipper and listened to the sea, and he heard his daughter's voice...

The ghosts, Papa. I don't like them. Make them go away.

His black eyes glistened. He remembered the last time he saw Xolisile standing beside her mother and sister, her brown eyes locked on him. Then, that horrible moment in Pretoria Prison when he heard her screams, and saw the pigs torturing her. Oh, God...

He stiffened and fought back the tears. No time for sorrow, Doctor. You're in it now, up to your neck. There's work to be done—impossible work—and you're all that's left except that madman sitting beside you. He looked at the moonlit ocean while recalling their escape.

He'd barely cleared Adams' front door when the choppers touched down on the beach. He remembered jumping into Adams' jeep, his eyes fixed on the line of flashing red lights coming down the beach road. The darkness echoed with sirens and the roar of choppers. He jammed his foot on the gas pedal as Karl scrambled into the jeep, a metal box dangling from his hand.

With cop cars closing from the front, and certain death on the beach behind them, there was only one chance. He skidded the jeep off the gravel road and plowed across the sand into the black, churning surf. By steering the jeep through the surf, he eliminated their tire tracks until he swerved into the rocks, a mile down the beach. His crazed maneuver had saved their lives. Another desperate act learned in apartheid South Africa.

His thoughts were interrupted by the sound of rustling papers. He sighed and turned toward the man seated beside him. "Well?"

Karl squinted at the notebook in his lap. He could barely read the scribbled text in the dim glow of the dashboard's map light. His eyes burned from two hours of digging through the documents in Adams' metal box. He closed the notebook and looked at the sea.

"You okay?"

Karl rubbed his eyes. "When I was in Somalia and Willapa Bay, I had this weird feeling. I couldn't put my finger on it, until now."

"Feeling?"

Karl rested his head against the seat. "Bodies and food scattered across the village in Somalia. Dead fish and birds lying on the shore of Willapa Bay. Dead fish at Trinity. But no pests."

"Pests? You mean coyotes and vultures? There were plenty of them at Trinity."

Karl cracked a smile. "I'm not talking about wild dogs and birds. Come on, Doc. What's the one creature you always find around the dead."

Thala shrugged. "Rats?"

Karl nodded. "In two years, I've seen too many crisis sites across the globe, most of them in godforsaken places. Searing heat. Frigid cold. Rain. Wind. Drought. But it didn't matter to the rats. They were always there, chewing on the dead...until now."

Thala leaned against the wheel. "Go on."

"I was right about Starburst. A privately-held chemical manufacturer based in Stüttgart. Founded in nineteen-ninety-four by a man named Gunthar Menchen and two associates. They'd developed an improved strain of warfarin that wiped out the competition. In ninety-five, they landed three billion bucks in spraying contracts from the top five agricultural firms."

Thala looked down at the notebook. "You're talking about the pesticide?"

Karl nodded. "Warfarin's been around since fifty-five. Developed at the University of Wisconsin. Supposedly the safest rodenticide ever made. A coumarin derivative. The rats eat it and die from internal hemorrhage. Pure, organic compound. Dissolves harmlessly into the environment in a matter of days."

"So?"

"Eco-safety has its drawbacks. Conventional warfarin was so safe, the rats became immune. That meant big problems for the agricultural firms. They'd spent billions developing new strains of genetically-engineered wheat for use in the Third World. Drought resistant, bug resistant, the whole nine yards. They'd planted the wheat in Asia, Africa, and South America after getting huge advances from the UN. Everything was going well until the rats moved in. That's when the agricultural guys found out their warfarin was useless."

Karl frowned while recalling the dead rats in upstate New York. "The wheat was all the little guys had. With the warfarin compromised, the rats had a feast. By ninety-five, they were eating it faster than the natives. In another year, the crops would be wiped out." He looked up at the stars. "That's when Menchen and his boys came out with their enhanced warfarin. Great timing. They were able to dictate lucrative terms while guaranteeing their brand would do the job. Another victory for technology."

Thala looked at the sea. "I remember the spraying, except it was in ninety-six. I was in Kenya on assignment with CDC when the planes dropped it on the crops. It made big headlines on Al Jazeera. The salvation of the Third World, and all that. From the sound of things, it worked pretty well. I remember a photo of dead rats piled in heaps beside a wheat field. The agricultural companies were using bulldozers to collect them. There must have been millions." He looked at Karl. "I don't get it. Millions of dead rats for thousands of villagers saved from starvation. Seems like a good trade."

"Yeah, except for one thing." Karl looked down at the notebook. "In ninety-five, Starburst set up test sprayings in Kenya and Somalia. The contracts were already signed when they realized their improved warfarin had degraded to zero potency. An unexplained flaw in their organic formula. To put it in King's English, they were in deep shit. Three billion dollars worth. When the agricultural companies discovered the new warfarin was useless, Starburst and its three partners would be wiped out."

Thala felt a chill. "Adams?"

Karl nodded. "Remember his little speech about the guys that believed in him? Well, their names were Menchen, Nakashima, and Schoenfeld. The founders of Starburst. They were the guys that met with Adams at Berkeley in ninety-five. Three desperate men looking for a miracle."

Thala's eyes widened. "You're telling me he pulled it off?"

Karl gripped the notebook. "It took Adams seven months to convert his theory into reality. The man was insane, but he was brilliant, and Starburst gave him everything he needed. He produced a revised strain of lethal warfarin in late ninety-six. That's the stuff you saw them spraying in Kenya."

"Get to it, Mr. Frankton."

Karl took a deep breath. "This is the hard part. I've gone over Adams' notes twice. There's no mistake. I don't know how he did it. Maybe it was the radiation treatments at Stanford University. Maybe the cyanogenic mesons released from the irradiated apricot pits. Maybe the isotope he used for the transmutation. Hell, to his dying day, Adams didn't know the answer. It's in his diary's final entry, dated yesterday."

Thala stared at him. Transmutation? Mesons? Radiation? Isotope? These were the words of alchemists and their contemporaries. Names like Becquerel, Curie, and Rutherford. Nuclear scientists that had pushed the envelope of established principles. Dreamers that had broken the barrier of the impossible.

Karl glanced at Thala's medical bag. "If I'm right, that little flask of purple liquid is the fruit of Adams' labor. An irradiated compound that saved Starburst's ass, but damned the human race to extinction. Now, it might save us all. How's that for an epitaph?"

Thala slumped in the seat. "I've always considered myself an intelligent man, until now. What are you saying, Mr. Frankton?"

Karl opened the notebook to a scribbled drawing. "Recognize it?" He held it close to the map light.

Thala stared at the drawing in horror. It was the same blurred structure they saw on the video screens at Trinity and Adams' home, only this picture had chemical symbols. Thala leaned closer and placed his finger on the interlocked chains of letters, numbers, and symbols.

"I spent three months in FDA's approval labs, and six more in Atlanta's Level Four. In that time, I studied every lethal brew known to man, but nothing like this."

Thala looked at him. "It's impossible. The damn thing's a mutation. It can't be what's out there."

Karl stared at the picture. "I'm afraid it is, Doc. When Starburst bought Adams' services, they opened the door to hell. I'm no biophysicist, but it's clear from this diagram that he gave them their miracle. A killer rodenticide that wiped out the rats in their tracks. Only problem was the legal issue. Adams couldn't use banned ingredients because of the ecology laws, but he had no choice. There just wasn't enough time to come up with something that met all the rules. So he went in a different direction."

"Different?"

"He used his knowledge of sub-atomic mesons to develop a transmutation catalyst, a kind of cloaking device that blended the killer ingredient with its host so deeply, the killer became invisible to detection, like a chameleon taking on the color of its environment. The damn thing attacks red blood cells, takes away their oxygen, and blends into the dead cells so it can't be detected."

Thala slumped against the wheel while recalling the flashing light on the screen, and the blurred mass inside it. "Then…that thing inside the light is warfarin?"

Karl locked his bloodshot eyes on him. "It's more than that, Doc. It's a blend of warfarin, Adams' radioactive catalyst, and the ingredient that dropped those rats in their tracks. The same ingredient they've sprayed around the world for the last seventeen years. The ingredient that was supposed to degrade to zero lethality within three months after spraying. But it didn't. Something in Adams' catalyst reversed the ingredient's half-life decay. Instead of decomposing, it's grown stronger with each passing year. Strong enough to kill a person in less than a minute." Karl hesitated. "You were right, Doc. It's in the water…and it's invisible."

Thala forced out the words. "You know what it is?"

"Adams was desperate. He'd entered a forbidden world and couldn't turn back."

"What is it, Mr. Frankton?"

Karl closed the notebook and looked at the sea. "Cyanide."

Thala couldn't speak. He slumped against the wheel, his black eyes frozen on the man beside him.

"It's in the oceans, rivers, and streams. It took care of the rats. Now it's gonna take care of us. After seventeen years, its parts-per-million are moving into the red zone. That's what happened in Somalia and Willapa Bay. That's what dropped those migrants at Trinity. And that's what's happening across the world. Some die from drinking it. Others from inhaling it. At seventy-eight degrees, it becomes a deadly vapor, just like in a gas chamber. Only this cyanide is undetectable. You take a whiff, convulse, and drop dead."

Karl stared at the medical bag. "That little flask of purple liquid is Adams' eleventh hour attempt to change his legacy. A long shot at an antidote that might break through the cloaking agent and neutralize the cyanide." He glanced at the stunned Zulu. "Watch that flask, Doc. It's our last chance."

Chapter 17

Seize the Moment

Fletcher placed the call to Samuel Tarver at ten o'clock on the morning of August 3rd. Twelve days had passed since the outbreak in Somalia, but that didn't matter just now. After nineteen years of struggle, Jonathan Fletcher had been offered entry to the world's most powerful inner circle, and he wasn't going to blow it.

"Yes?"

"Jonathan Fletcher for Mr. Tarver."

"Yes, Mr. Fletcher. Please hang on."

Fletcher listened to the silence on the other end. The only sound was the clock ticking on his desk. A few seconds seemed like eternity.

"Hello, Jonathan. Good news?"

Fletcher forced out the words. "I've discussed your offer with my family and I'm ready to proceed, if you want me."

"That's great news, Jonathan. I'm glad for both of us."

"Yes, sir."

"Tell you what. Meet me in my office at two thirty. We'll break the good news together."

Fletcher felt a chill. "You mean, to the President?"

"None other. Takes three to tango on this one. I'm sure he'll approve, but we want to dot all the i's. He's a good man, Jonathan. He'll ask some tough questions, but I've got you covered. Just use your usual diplomacy and everything will be fine."

Fletcher grimaced. "Yes, sir."

"We need to put this mess behind us. I'm convinced you're the right man for the job."

"Yes, sir."

"At two thirty then. Goodbye, and thank you."

Fletcher pressed the off button and gazed at the portrait of Estelle and the boys. It had been a hard night, with occasional sobs from his beloved wife. He almost had her convinced when the sirens went off. Nothing but a false alarm along the Potomac, but it was enough to shake her.

Estelle had never blown up at him before, and it really hurt. He pressed the auto-dial button while recalling her stinging words...

Don't you see what's happening? The world's coming apart and you're worried about a promotion? What happened to you, Johnny? What happened to the man I loved?

He remembered her flicking on the TV with the air raid sirens howling in the distance. WNN was covering the latest crisis sites via a split screen. The shaken anchor tried to stay calm while WNN's field reporters took turns describing the chaos around them. Hand-held cameras swept downtown Detroit for signs of life, but the only movement came from military patrols in their white and silver bio-suits. Michigan Avenue was strewn with abandoned cars from yesterday's panic when the killer swept through an afternoon rock concert at Hart Plaza, just north of the Detroit River, dropping fleeing teenagers in their tracks.

The news was even worse in Charleston where ambulances lined the street in front of the million dollar town homes facing the harbor and Fort Sumter. At least fifty body bags had been removed from the homes since the first 911 call.

WNN switched to the devastation in London where two hundred were reported dead on the east end, and a hundred more in Whitehall, including a dozen MP's who had collapsed en route to their morning trains.

Seventy had died on the docks of Marseille. Burly laborers seen clutching their throats and falling to their knees as if collared by an invisible hangman's noose.

One hundred fifty crisis sites across the globe. Troops pouring into the cities. Rumors of looting and shoot outs. Panic sweeping the towns and villages along the world's rivers and coastlines. Martial law declared. No end in sight.

Fletcher felt the phone vibrate in his hand. He pressed the plastic to his ear and waited for the familiar warbling to clear.

"Where are you?"

"*South of San Clemente. We found Adams' jeep in a cul-de-sac near a golf course. We think they stole another car and headed south.*"

Fletcher felt a trickle of sweat roll down his forehead. He'd received Hampsted's crushing news four hours earlier. Adams was dead. Frankton and Thala were still loose. And the worst news of all. Adams' formula and documents were missing.

"*You there?*"

"Go ahead."

"*There's no way they can break out. If they try to cross the border, they're dead meat. I have choppers covering the inland desert. It's only a matter of—*"

Fletcher squeezed the phone in a death grip. "Listen to me, Parker. In five hours, I'm meeting with Tarver and the President. They're going to offer me the number two slot at CDC. Do you know what that means?"

"*Director of Operations? I thought you were cashing out?*"

"Forget all that. In five hours, I'll be the fifth most powerful man on earth. The only thing that can screw it up is the two terrorists you can't seem to find. If they get to the media with that evidence, we're the ones that'll be dead meat. My international contacts don't like press coverage. They'll come down on me with a sledge hammer. And if I go—you go."

"*Now just a damn—*"

"I'm warning you, Parker. I want them taken by midnight along with the disk, formula, papers, and anything else they dragged out of Adams' home. Pull it off and you'll be rich beyond your wildest dreams. Screw it up and your history."

Fletcher pressed the phone to his ear and waited for a response.

"You'll have them, but I have a question."
"Yeah?"
"I've been getting reports on the fatalities. This thing is more serious than I thought. Just for the record, does all this ladder-climbing crap matter with people dropping like flies?"
Fletcher clenched his fist. "You still don't get it, do you? You're it, Parker! The fucking archangel! If you mess this up, we're finished!"
"We?"
"The human race, you idiot!" Fletcher pressed the off button and collapsed in the leather chair, his eyes locked on the portrait of his family.

Three thousand miles away, Parker Hampsted vented his anger on his men. "Whatever it takes, we nail them today! Stay tight with the choppers! Disregard nothing! I want their faces on every newspaper and television screen in Southern California! Now move!"

With two hundred agents deployed between San Clemente and the Mexican border, Hampsted's command car raced down Interstate 5 toward San Diego. If his two targets tried to escape into the desert, his choppers would stop them cold. If they tried to double back toward LA, they'd have to run a gauntlet of agents and police armed with the latest detection and communications technology. There was only one direction now, and it was south.

Hampsted rested his head against the rear passenger seat and stared at the Pacific. In a few days, this mess would be over and he'd be on a jet to Tahiti. After thirty years of hazardous duty with the FBI, CIA, NSA, and "private" sector, he was fed up with the spineless worms that had replaced the legends he respected. Gone were the likes of Casey, Baker, Gates, Poindexter, Liddy, and Ashcroft. Instead, he had to deal with career politicians like the man who had just chewed him out. Hell, if it weren't for the money, he'd fly to DC and strangle the arrogant slime with his bare hands.

He took a deep breath and felt his eyes closing. Let it go, man. Just take care of business and you can buy that sixty foot schooner and set sail for Tahiti, Bora Bora, and a thousand lesser isles across the South Pacific. Dark-skinned beauties, good rum, sun-swept beaches, and a well-oiled typewriter to bang out your memoirs.

A smile crept across his lips. Better use an alias on those memoirs. Don't want any unpleasant visits from past associates. Yeah, that's it. An obscure name no one will recognize. Something like, Ringley Adams.

Hampsted's head slumped to the side as his command car sped past the first exit sign for La Jolla. If he'd known better, he would have taken that exit, and the right turn down Ardath and Torrey Pines Road toward the wooded cove where a white SUV was nestled beneath the palms. Inside the SUV, two men huddled together watching a television broadcast from San Diego. The news anchor's voice was subdued while he described the latest report of devastation coming out of Los Angeles where three hours earlier, thousands of men, women, and children had fled their homes in Watts, Westwood, Santa Monica, and Venice. Many had died in the streets, their futile gasps accompanied by a faint hissing sound emanating from the sewers beneath the city. An ominous sound like escaping steam. An invisible sound. The sound of death.

The television station broadcasting the devastation was KFMB. The gray-haired anchor was Milton Sarvan...

. . .

"Mr. Sarvan, you have a call."

Sarvan chugged the shot of bourbon and placed his finger on the intercom. "Who?"

"Not sure. He says it's about the outbreaks. Says he has something important."

Sarvan rubbed his tired eyes. "Hell, it's just another sicko trying to cash in on this mess. You should know better. Tell him to take a walk."

"*Yes, sir.*"

Sarvan flicked off the intercom and collapsed in the chair, his black eyes gazing at the worn face in the mirror. He hadn't slept in days. At sixty-seven, there wasn't much left in the old tank.

He glanced at the news sheet lying on the dressing table. Hard to believe the words on that yellow paper. More like a blurb for a sci-fi movie than the real thing. New York in panic. Chicago under martial law. Los Angeles swarming with National Guard. Mass deaths in New Orleans. St. Louis evacuated. Miami overrun with looters. All because an invisible killer had descended on the planet like a biblical plague. In his forty-nine years of journalism, Sarvan had never seen anything like it. And it was getting worse.

He rested his head against the chair and closed his eyes. The next newscast was thirty minutes away. Just a few minutes of peace and quiet. Not too much to ask.

He was nearly asleep when the intercom went off with an annoying buzz. He sat up and fumbled for the button. "Yeah?"

"*I'm sorry, Mr. Sarvan. I think you should talk to him.*"

Sarvan's face twisted in a frown. "This better be good, Larry. I'm damn tired."

"*Yes, sir.*"

"Well?"

"*He says he's one of the terrorists.*"

And I'm supposed to believe that?"

The voice hesitated. "*He sounds pretty convincing.*"

Sarvan poured a shot of bourbon and stared at the phone's blinking red light. "Dammit, Larry. You're going to put me in a grave."

"*I'm sorry, sir.*"

Sarvan chugged the bourbon. "Put him through." He placed his hand on the receiver and snatched it off the hook. "Sarvan here."

"Mr. Sarvan?"

"Who is this?"

"Karl Frankton. We need to talk, Mr. Sarvan."

"So talk."

"I prefer face-to-face."

"Come to the station and ask for me. I'll be here."

"Sorry, can't do that. I'll meet you tonight at La Jolla cove. Scripps Park. North end of the parking lot. Eleven o'clock sharp."

Sarvan gripped the phone. "Do you know how many calls I get like this? You expect me to risk my life in a curfew because of a crank phone call?"

"I think so."

Sarvan's face reddened. "Nice try, whoever you are. Pleasure talking with you."

"Wait, Mr. Sarvan. I listened to your broadcast this morning, and the little intro about your days in Vietnam. Purple heart. Pulitzer-winning war correspondent. Consumer crusader. Defender of the people. Peabody winner. Well...is it true? Or is it just a bunch of media hype?"

Sarvan fought his anger. "Who the hell are you?"

"I told you, and my time's up. I'm betting my life on you, Mr. Sarvan, and a lot of other lives. I'll be at the park at eleven. If you're not there by eleven fifteen, you'll never hear from me again."

"And I'm supposed to consider that a threat?"

"No, it'll just mean I'm dead. Goodbye, Mr. Sarvan."

Sarvan listened to the silence on the other end. He hung up the phone and leaned back in the chair, his eyes staring at the face in the mirror. Hell with him. The jerk's an imposter. Too many important things going on to risk your life chasing shadows. Let it go, Milton. Let it go.

His eyes fluttered and closed. A pleasant, numbing sensation crept through him. Good to sleep. Not a care in the world. Just let everything go...

His bloodshot eyes snapped open. He sat up in the chair and glared at his watch while cursing the day he became a newsman.

. . .

Karl stuffed the cell phone in his pocket and stared at the windshield.

"Think he'll come?"

Karl frowned. "If he does, he won't be alone. He's too smart to risk his life on a stranger's phone call."

Thala sighed and pushed the driver's door open. He crawled out of the SUV and shuffled past the junipers toward the cliff overlooking the Pacific. It was eight a.m. in Southern California.

Karl jumped out of the SUV and followed his friend up the path to the sea. For a moment, they stood side-by-side, looking down at the waves crashing on the rocks. It was a beautiful summer morning. The rising sun beamed down on their shoulders from a cloudless sky. A brisk, cooling breeze swept against their faces. They could taste the ocean on their lips.

Hard to believe what was happening around them. A nation driven to its knees. A world on the brink of panic. All because three greed-driven men and a crazed scientist had created a monster that threatened to turn the planet into a gas chamber.

Thala looked down at the deserted patches of beach between the rocks. He stiffened, as if listening to something.

"You okay, Doc?"

Thala's eyes flashed. "My family loved the sea. We were on a beach like this when the Afrikäners came. That was the last time I saw my family before..."

Karl lowered his head while recalling the night in the motel room when the Zulu spilled his guts about South Africa, the Afrikäners, and the nightmare no man should live. He nodded and forced out the words. "I'm sorry, Doc. I wish I had your guts."

Thala brushed away a tear. "You underestimate yourself, Mr. Frankton. Because of you, we're standing on a beach in Southern California with the government ready to close the book on us. I'd say you've taken a stand."

Karl shook his head. "Blind ambition, Doc. It's always gotten me in trouble."

"I think it's more."

"More?"

Thala looked at the sea. "None of us are very brave until we have a cause. For me, it was my wife. Before I met her, I was a happy-go-lucky kafir in a desolate place called Kwa-Zululand. She changed my life the first night we made love on the beach. She gave me a reason to live. To be more than myself." He looked down at the rocks. "What changed you, Mr. Frankton?"

Karl sighed. "Don't know, Doc. You figure it out."

Thala smiled. "Already have."

Karl knelt down and snatched a blade of grass. He opened his fingers and watched it disappear into the wind. "I have an idea. You with me?"

Thala shrugged. "Why stop now."

"That PC of yours. Does it burn CD's?"

"I think so, but I've never used it for that."

"Come on, Doc. We've got work to do." Karl stood up and shuffled down the dune.

.   .   .

The limousine picked up Fletcher at his Georgetown home at 1:11 p.m. He tried to say goodbye to his wife, but Estelle had locked the door to her room. Not exactly a congratulatory sendoff for the man who would soon be CDC's Director of Operations. Fletcher managed a moment with his sons before heading out the door.

"She'll be okay, Dad. She's just shook like everyone else."
Fletcher embraced Robert and smiled at Franklin. "Try to make your mother understand." He reached out and grasped Franklin's wrist.

Franklin's eyes filled with tears. "You're going to stop those guys, right? You're going to end this mess?"

Fletcher squeezed his son's wrist. "You can count on it." He embraced Franklin and headed out the door toward the waiting limo.

His two sons watched the limo pull away from the house, accompanied by two police motorcyclists. Above them, Estelle Fletcher watched the limo disappear around the corner, and she said a prayer. In the distance, air raid sirens wailed a chilling tune as the latest rumors of terror swept the nation's capital.

Chapter 18

Homecoming

"Mr. President." Fletcher extended his hand toward the imposing figure standing on the presidential seal.

Manis gripped Fletcher's hand. "Good to see you, Mr. Fletcher. Samuel tells me you've reached a decision."

"Yes, sir." Fletcher hesitated. "If you're in accord, I'd like to accept."

Manis eyed his guest. "Let's talk." He gestured toward the powder-blue couches flanking the fireplace.

Fletcher felt Tarver's hand on his back. He followed Tarver to the couch on the left and sat beside him. The President sat on the opposing couch, his brown eyes trained on Fletcher.

Manis reached into his jacket pocket and pulled out a folded paper. He flipped it open and handed it to Fletcher. "I just received this from the Pentagon. The death count's doubled."

"Doubled?"

Manis nodded. "It's getting ugly. The secret service is advising me to clear out of DC." He leaned forward, his brown eyes flickering with anger. "Imagine that, the President of the United States blowing town in time of crisis. Are they nuts?"

Fletcher stared at the paper. Two thousand dead in twenty-seven countries. Twice what it was yesterday. Instead of doubling in a week, the death rate had doubled in one day. Panic was breaking out in Paris, Madrid, Rome, Moscow, and a dozen other foreign capitals. Eleven American cities were under martial law. No end in sight. No clue to the invisible killer. The terrorists were still loose in Southern California, the extent of their network unknown. Condition—red.

"This can't go on, Mr. Fletcher."

Fletcher handed the letter to the President. "No, sir."

"Well, what are you going to do about it?"

Fletcher glanced at Tarver, but there was no encouraging smile, no helpful interjection. Tarver stared at him, his hands folded in his lap.

Fletcher felt a rush of anger. *Idiot! They're setting you up!* He looked at the President who was glaring at him with those piercing brown eyes. The only sound was the clock ticking on the mantle.

Manis shrugged impatiently. "Well?"

"I have some ideas."

The President's face reddened. "Ideas? You have to do better than that. We're going public in an hour. National press core. Worldwide media. The whole works. They'll need some good news from their new hero."

Fletcher looked at him in shock. "The media?"

"Of course. That's the way it's done. You should know that by now. First, we introduce you to the nation. Then, we turn you loose to work your magic. Samuel tells me it shouldn't take long with all those agents in the field." Manis leaned closer, his brown eyes blazing. "He's right about that, isn't he? You're close to nailing those madmen?"

"Yes, sir. But then we have to—"

Manis raised his hand for silence. "No buts, Mr. Fletcher. That's unacceptable for the future Director of CDC. You must be decisive—convincing. We have a near panic on our hands. The damn thing's coming unglued. The people need someone to reassure them." He hesitated, his eyes focused on Fletcher. "Like it or not, you're the man. No turning back. You're in it now, up to your eyeballs."

Fletcher looked down at the coffee table. Nineteen years of hell for this? The glorious moment he'd waited for? To sit in the Oval Office with two of the biggest dirt bags he'd ever met? To take the fall for them?

He took a deep breath and looked at the President. He needed time to think—to figure a way out of this mess. Gotta buy some time. Nothing new, he'd done it before. He stuck out his chin and nodded. "I'm ready, sir."

Manis reached out and slapped Fletcher's knee, his face beaming. "At-a-boy. I knew you wouldn't let me down." He glanced at Tarver. "Well done, Samuel. Looks like you picked the right one."

Tarver stood up and gestured for Fletcher to do the same. He shook the President's hand and patted Fletcher's shoulder. "Come on, Jonathan. They're expecting us in the media room."

Fletcher gave him a feeble nod and started for the door.

"Mr. Fletcher?"

Fletcher looked down at the President's extended hand. He clasped it and forced a smile.

"Remember, they'll expect good news." The President released his grip and walked toward the most powerful desk on earth.

Fletcher's head was swimming. He followed Tarver and the security guard down the blue carpeted corridor to the elevator. The next thing he knew, they were sitting in a small office just off the media room.

He glanced at his watch. Three thirty. In a few minutes, the President would introduce him to the press core. Cameras from every major news organization would focus on Tarver as he stepped forward to accept the President's vote of confidence in front of the American people.

Following his speech, Tarver would turn to his new Director of Operations and make the announcement, then step back and gesture toward the microphone, and Jonathan Fletcher would become the fifth most powerful man in the world.

The President's words rang in his ears. *No turning back. You're in it now, up to your eyeballs.* He looked across the table at Tarver. A young lady was applying makeup to Tarver's face to reduce the glare from the camera lights.

Tarver brushed her hand away and gestured for her to leave. He watched her disappear through the door.

Tarver leaned toward him. "Are you okay?"

Fletcher nodded. "A little nervous."

"That's expected."

"Yes, sir."

"Maybe you should call your man in Southern California."

Fletcher froze, his eyes locked on Tarver.

Tarver shrugged. "It's important to stay on top of things. Mr. Hampsted should be close to wrapping things up. Give him a call."

Fletcher stared at him in disbelief. He dragged the cell phone out of his pocket and punched Hampsted's autodial code. *My god, he knows everything. Parker blew the whistle. The man I trusted for eight years just cut my throat.*

The cryptic warbling cleared.

"Parker?"

"Yeah?"

"Anything?"

"You said midnight. I still have eleven hours."

Fletcher swallowed hard. "I'm at the White House. Going on the air in a few minutes. Thought you might have some news."

"I told you, we'll get it done. Now quit bugging me. I've got work to do."

Fletcher squeezed the phone. "Do you know Samuel Tarver?"

There was no response.

Fletcher pressed the mouthpiece to his lips. "I won't ask again."

"I've done some work for him. Hell, I knew him before you. Sort of helped his career, if you know what I mean."

Fletcher's grip tightened. "You should've told me."

"You didn't ask. Besides, in a few hours, my job will be done and everyone will be happy. And we'll all be rich, right?"

Fletcher felt a twinge of pain in his chest. "Let me know when it's done." He punched the off button and stuffed the phone in his pocket.

Tarver leaned forward. "Nothing?"

Fletcher shook his head.

"I wouldn't worry. Parker will take care of business. He's a good man."

"He's a parasite."

Tarver smiled. "Maybe, but you wouldn't be here if it weren't for him. He green lighted you to be my successor. Said you were the perfect candidate. Cunning, ruthless, loyal. The big three in this zoo."

Fletcher sank in the chair while recalling his wife's words.

"Must warn you though. Parker called me this morning with a little concern. Something about you threatening him." Tarver frowned. "Not wise, Jonathan. We need men like Parker to take care of the nasty stuff. They're the foot soldiers that make things happen. Must treat them with respect."

Fletcher forced out the words. "Then, you know?"

"About Starburst? Adams? The warfarin? Of course. And Frankton too. And his friend."

"Does the President know?"

Tarver shook his head. "That's not the way it works. We don't bother the top dog with details."

Fletcher looked down. "Because he doesn't want to know?"

"Very good, Jonathan. That's why I picked you. After nineteen years, you've seen it all. The good, bad, and ugly. Lots of the latter. You're the perfect man for this job." Tarver pushed back from the table. "Unfortunate how these things happen, but Menchen and his cohorts meant well. I'm convinced of it."

Fletcher gathered himself. *Buy time, man. Buy time!*

"I wasn't in the loop until Hampsted phoned me from Corpus Christi. Hell, I'd just taken over and was suddenly faced with the worst nightmare imaginable. That's when I decided to find someone I could trust. Someone who could turn things around." Tarver forced a nervous smile. "I'm right about you, aren't I, Jonathan?"

Fletcher returned the smile. "Yes, sir."

"Just do your job and everything will work out. In a year, you'll live like a king. You're family too." Tarver reached into his pocket and pulled out a folded paper. "Here's your speech. Don't substitute a word. When they ask questions, just listen to the little bird in your ear and you'll be fine."

"Bird?"

Tarver handed him a tiny earphone. "Excuse the expression, but stick this in your ear and your little bird will take care of the rest."

The door opened and a nervous young intern popped his head in the room. "Five minutes, gentlemen."

Tarver eyed the man seated across from him. "We better get that makeup lady back in here. You're sweating pretty heavily.

Fletcher didn't hear him. He was recalling Estelle's tirade, and the faces of the dead on WNN.

"Sure you're okay?"

Fletcher nodded and stuffed the folded speech in his jacket pocket.

.   .   .

Bernie scrambled across the cage, his amber eyes trained on the flies swirling inside the opened jar. He leaned back on his haunches and waited for the perfect moment to strike.

The first two flies never had a chance. The iguana's sticky tongue flicked them out of the jar with lightning precision. Invigorated by his snack, Bernie backed away and proceeded to pick off the other escaping flies as they darted out of the jar, his tongue lashing out at them in deadly thrusts.

When he was sure the jar was empty, the iguana raised his head and blinked at the young man towering over him. A quick swipe of his tail and Bernie was waddling back to the corner of his cage for a rewarding dunk in the water basin.

Jeremy closed the cage door and eyed his pet of one year. He loved Bernie almost as much as he loved his dad. They were so alike, his dad and the iguana. Fiercely independent, tenacious, and proud. A little weather-beaten, but still standing.

He glanced at the photo taped to the wall beside his bed. It was the last picture of him and his dad, an auto shot taken from the floor of his dad's apartment in Atlanta.

He leaned against the dresser and stared at the picture. God, what he'd give to be back in that rundown flea trap with his dad, instead of this high-priced prison his mother called home. She and Ralph could have their designer furniture and custom interiors, their fancy clothes and prestige cars, their phony parties and false friends. He'd dump the whole mess in a heartbeat if he could only be with his dad.

He heard a rustle and looked down at the cage. Bernie was looking up at him, his amber eyes shining in the reflected light. Jeremy knelt beside the cage and smiled at his four-legged friend. "How about it, Bern? Ready to blow this cage? Maybe we can find dad out there. I bet he could use a couple friends right now."

He felt a tear roll down his cheek. It was eight o'clock in La Jolla and the sirens were wailing in San Diego. The evening curfew had begun. Any unauthorized civilian caught in the streets would be subject to immediate arrest. Any resistance would be dealt with harshly.

He pushed off the floor and looked at the PC on his desk. Ralph had bought him the Septium 2000 on his twelfth birthday, another feeble attempt to win over his adopted son. The latest and best, Ralph had told him. Just like you, kid. Just like you…

He sat down and stared at the black screen. What a line of bull. Ralph was the most pathetic creature he'd ever known, a goal-driven man too obsessed with his career to care about a stepson. If Ralph had his way, this room would be empty. If it weren't for mom, ol' Ralph would have kicked out his stepson months ago.

He looked down at his clenched fist. How could she do it? How could she dump dad for a jerk like that? Didn't she care about her son? Was she so caught up in her success that she'd forgotten her own son? He grimaced and pounded his fist on his lap.

For a moment, he just sat there, glaring at the screen. The sirens faded and everything became silent except for the gentle hum of the PC. He sighed and rested his hand on the mouse, causing the screen to come alive with a sweeping view of Manhattan's skyline, it's center magnified to reveal a close-up of the Chrysler Building's stainless steel crown.

He'd created the screen saver from the photographs his dad took three years ago when they celebrated mom's graduation from Columbia. A better day. A happier day.

His eyes drifted to the opened closet where a dismantled PC lay on the floor beneath his clothes. His dad had given him the PC four years ago, a gift for his son's eighth birthday. It was useless now, its memory chips burned out, its megahertz dwarfed by the new Septium generation of hyper-plasmic computers. But that old, beat up PC would stay with Jeremy Moran forever, a lasting reminder of the father he loved.

He brushed away a tear and sat up in the chair. Enough self-pity. Time to check out the nightmare sweeping the globe. Maybe there would be an update on his dad and the other guy. He clicked the mouse and shuddered. What if they'd been captured? What if they were—

He was startled by a beep. An e-mail alert? He clicked the "read" icon and stared at the screen in disbelief. Was this some kind of cruel trick? Impossible. No one knew that codeword. No one, except—

He clicked the mouse, his eyes trained on the message...

Hey Jeremy,

What a mess. Too bad you can't come down to the school to shoot some baskets. Ask your mom. Maybe she'll let you out for a couple hours before curfew. We need a sixth for some three-man hoops. Anything's better than sitting on your butt with nothing to do.
Let me know by 5,

Bernie
(oops...sorry...forgot the time. Oh well...maybe tomorrow)

Jeremy's eyes brightened. He yanked open the desk drawer and seized a ragged piece of paper. He unfolded it and stared at the string of letters, numbers, and symbols scrawled in pencil. He'd scribbled them on the sandwich wrapper last year when he and his dad were together. He didn't know it then, but that random string of characters would become their only way of communicating once his mom married Ralph Moran.

He keyed the characters while recalling his dad handing him the decryption software disk. Then the demonstration and tests as he keyed secret messages and decrypted them while his dad stood beside him, his warm hand resting on his son's shoulder.

He stared at the screen, his eyes glistening with tears. He had learned so much from his dad, but most of all, his dad had taught him the meaning of love. He positioned the cursor over the "decrypt" icon and clicked the mouse.

The screen flashed as the message dissolved and a new one took its place. He leaned closer, his heart pounding. Yes! Thank God!

Hi Son,

I wish it didn't have to be this way, but I don't have much time. I'm sure they're monitoring your communications, so I hope the ol' cryptograph still

works. I'm here, son. Only a few minutes away.
From the looks of that car parked outside your
house, you've got FBI or whatever watching the
Morans with eagle eyes. I need to see you, but it's a
little tight. If you're with me, here's the scoop...

Jeremy studied the rest of the message, and read it again
before clicking the "destruct" icon. The message blurred to
nothingness, replaced by the Chrysler Building's stainless
steel crown.

He stared at the Manhattan skyline. The PC's clock read
8:20. Time for a tough decision. A half dozen FBI agents
stood between him and his dad. He gritted his teeth and
pushed up from the desk.

.   .   .

"See that?"

Agent Palmer sat up and blinked at the dark windshield.
"What you got?"

"Looks like something moved out there." Agent Minchak
leaned closer to the windshield, his eyes trained on the moonlit
shadows covering the Moran residence.

Palmer reached for the cup of cold coffee on the console.
"Want me to check it out?"

"No, but stay awake. This damn breeze is making the
shadows move." Minchak snatched the microphone and
pressed the talk button. "Red tail to blue tail. Detecting some
movement on the north perimeter. Anything on the motion
detectors?"

The radio crackled. *"Looks like a stray cat. The infrared
spotted a four legged animal hunched in the bushes. We'll
take a look."*

"Ten-four." Minchak snapped the mike into its holder and
glanced at his watch. It was nine o'clock in La Jolla, three
hours before shift change. He could hear sirens in the
distance. The latest outbreak had struck only twelve miles

away in Solana Beach. Things were getting a little tense in Southern California.

Minchak eyed the two yellow plastic bags lying on the back seat. They were unzipped, revealing oxygen masks and bio-suits. Two oxygen tanks lay on the floor beneath them. He frowned and slumped in the seat.

"Any word from your family?"

Minchak shook his head. "Not since Monday."

"They're still in LA?"

"Don't know. I keep getting Joan's answering machine. Can't reach her on her cell." Minchak glared at the darkness. "How about you?"

Palmer looked down. "My wife's been reassigned to the San Francisco office. I talked to her today. She's okay, but Frisco's on the edge of blowing up. That outbreak at the Embarcadero really shook 'em."

Minchak looked down at his watch. "Where the hell's blue tail? How long does it take to find a cat?"

Sixty yards away, Agent Tabor had abandoned his monitoring truck to check out the stray cat. Behind him, Agent MacArdo had stepped out of the truck for a quick leak. Had he stayed at his infrared monitor, he would have spotted the two-legged flash darting across the screen. As for the stray cat, Agent Tabor was two minutes from discovering the large lizard sitting in the bushes outside the Moran's home. In that time, the lizard's owner had crawled down a drainpipe and covered the quarter mile to the park behind the house.

. . .

"Dad?" Jeremy pushed through the bushes and listened for a response. This had to be the place. He couldn't have messed up. He took a nervous breath and edged closer to the moonlit soccer field. It was 9:10 in La Jolla.

"Hello, Jerry."

Jeremy wheeled around and stared at the figure standing in the shadows. The man stepped closer, his stubbled face glistening in the moonlight.

"Dad!" Jeremy charged into his father's arms.

"Oh, Jerry." Karl hugged his son and fought the tears. "It's good to hold you. I'm so sorry..."

They clung to each other and remembered better times. Nothing was said. Nothing had to be. The only sound was the breeze rustling through the leaves.

Jeremy felt his dad push away. He squinted at the tear-stained face smiling down at him.

"You okay?"

Jeremy nodded and wiped away a tear.

"I don't have much time. Gotta be someplace at eleven. Those agents will be looking for you."

"I wish we had more time."

Karl nodded through his tears. "Guess it's not in the cards for guys like us. I don't know who wrote the book, but it looks like we drew the short straws." He smiled and rested a hand on his son's shoulder. "How's ol' Bern?"

"Hangin' in there, like me."

"Well, that makes four of us."

"Four?"

"A guy I ran into along the way."

Jeremy looked up at his dad. "The guy in the news?"

"Yeah."

"Do you trust him?"

"With my life...just like you." Karl patted his son's shoulder and led him into the bushes.

Karl knelt on the ground and fumbled for the penlight in his pocket. He switched it on and unbuttoned his shirt. "Here's your birthday gift." He reached inside his shirt and dragged out a brown envelope.

Jeremy took the envelope, his blue eyes trained on the sealed flap. "What is it?"

"A surprise."

Jeremy dug his finger into the flap, but his dad stopped him. "Open it when you get back. Better that way." He forced a smile. "Think you can make it?"

Jeremy nodded. "What about you? What are you gonna do?"

Karl gripped his son's arm. "I'll be okay. We'll all be okay."

"I love you, Dad."

"Me too, Jerry. Me too..." Karl embraced his son and broke down.

.　.　.

Moran was stunned when he opened the door and saw the two agents straddling his stepson. "What the hell?"

Agent Minchak patted Jeremy's shoulder. "We found him wandering near Torrey Pines. He really had us shook. Thought he might be—" Minchak caught himself.

Moran glared at his stepson. "What's this all about?"

Jeremy looked down at the lizard in his arms. "Bernie crawled out the window when I wasn't looking." He looked up at Moran with defiant eyes. "I went after him."

"Just like that?"

"Hell, what do you care? We were doing you a favor."

Moran felt the blood rush to his face. He grabbed his stepson's shoulder and yanked him into the house.

"You okay, Mr. Moran?"

Moran looked at Minchak with apologetic eyes. "I'm really sorry about this. Things have been a little strained. I think it's time for some discipline."

Minchak smiled at the young man holding the lizard. "No problem, Mr. Moran. Don't be too hard on him. These are rough times for us all, not to mention a twelve year old." He stepped back from the door. "Gotta be patient with these young ones."

Moran forced a nod. "Thanks for your understanding. It won't happen again." He watched the two agents shuffle toward their car. Behind him, the walls reverberated from a slamming door.

He turned and glared at the stairs. His face was red hot. "We're not done, dammit!" He slammed the front door and charged up the stairs. He was nearly to Jeremy's door when Anne stepped out of the steaming bathroom, a white robe wrapped around her.

"What's wrong?"

Moran fought the rage seething inside him. She hadn't heard a thing in the shower.

She gripped his arm. "What is it, honey?"

He frowned and slumped against the wall. "Your son almost got blown away chasing that damn lizard down Torrey Pines Road."

She looked at the closed door in shock.

"The FBI just brought him home. Good thing they didn't—"

"My God." She leaned against him and felt his hand on her waist.

"I can't take any more. I've tried everything with him. I didn't expect any miracles, but he hates me for God's sake." He rubbed his forehead. "What does he expect from me? What am I supposed to do?"

He started for the door but she blocked him. "No, honey. This isn't the way. Let me talk to him. You need to cool down. Please—"

He held her close and listened to the rock and roll music blaring from Jeremy's room. Oh, if he could just have ten minutes with that little punk. No more coddling. No more turning the other cheek. From now on, it was hardball.

He took a deep breath and waited for the anger to subside. *Easy, old man. She's right, this isn't the way. It'll all work out. Things will be better tomorrow. This mess will probably be over and you'll be back on the phone with IBM. Some last minute scheduling and you'll be airborne to Dallas to resume that meeting. And when they sign on the dotted line, you'll be forty million bucks richer. The perfect time for that long overdue family vacation. A great chance for some father and son bonding. Maybe a windjammer cruise to the south seas. Or a mountaineering expedition to the Andes.* He felt his body relax against her. Everything would work out. Everything always works out. He placed a finger under her chin and kissed her passionately. "I want you, babe. I want you real bad."

Her warm tongue found his. He felt her hand slip between his legs. All was well again. Tomorrow would be a better day.

And while they made sweaty love in their master bedroom, the angel of death prepared to eliminate them and seven billion others from the face of the earth. Ringley Adams' devilish concoction had reached critical mass.

Chapter 19

Angel of Death

"It's almost eleven."

Karl nodded, his eyes fixed on the moonlit sea. A stiff breeze had picked up, filling his nostrils with the smell of fish and plankton. It was a good smell, a hopeful smell. He scooped a handful of sand and remembered the day at Martha's Vineyard when he gazed at the sea, and felt the warmth of the woman he still loved.

Thala knelt on the sand. "You okay?"

"Guess so."

Thala glanced at the moonlit bluff behind them. "I don't like those shadows. They could pick us off like sheep."

Karl shook his head. "They won't kill us without interrogation."

"You mean, torture?"

"They have to be sure no one else is involved."

Thala glared at him. "I spent twenty-five years trying to forget Pretoria, and you're telling me I'm going to be tortured to death in Southern California. Thanks a lot, Mr. Frankton. You just made my day."

Karl scooped another fist of sand and scanned the moonlit beach. "Keep the faith, Doc. We're not done yet."

Forty minutes had passed since they staggered onto the beach at Point La Jolla after a frantic escape from the Moran's Torrey Pines estate. If not for Thala's skilled handling of the SUV, Hampsted would be interrogating them now. With FBI prowl cars closing from the rear, the Zulu cut a new road through the park behind the Moran's home, dodging trees and bushes all the way.

When they skidded out of the trees onto La Jolla Shores Drive, they were confronted by a line of flashing red lights approaching from the south. In that instant, Thala recalled a similar chase in Kwa Zululand twenty-six years ago when Afrikäner jeeps bore down on him and his comrades, their headlights flashing in the darkness. He'd learned a valuable lesson from that frightening moment in South Africa. Do the unexpected. If all escape routes are blocked, make one.

The SUV nearly turned over when Thala gunned the accelerator and veered down a dead end road, blasting over a dune and plowing through the soft sand until the SUV churned into the ocean and sank beneath the waves.

The rest was a blur. Two men scrambling out of the surf, one carrying a dead PC, the other a black medical bag. The desperate run along the beach with their ears vibrating from the sound of approaching choppers. The beach flooded with the choppers' piercing searchlights. The sand erupting as the first chopper touched down while they cowered behind a cluster of rocks. Their shock when the chopper suddenly lifted into the starlit sky and retreated down the beach toward San Diego. Then, the exhausting two mile dash through the sand and rocks until they collapsed on the beach below the cliffs of Point La Jolla.

Karl looked down at the brown envelope on his lap. He opened the flap and glanced at Thala. "Give me the samples."

Thala dug into his medical bag and pulled out two small plastic tubes. He handed them to Karl and watched him slip them into the envelope. Karl closed the flap and sealed the envelope's metal clasp. He rested the envelope on his lap and looked at the sea.

"You had a good talk with your son?"

"It was good to hold him."

Thala clasped the tiny bible dangling from his neck. "It's good to hold your children. In the end, that's all we have."

"I wish we had more time."

Thala felt his eyes well up with tears. He rested a hand on Karl's shoulder. "I know that feeling. It's a bit late for me, but we can still finish this for your son."

Karl gripped the Zulu's hand. "I wish your children were here. I think they'd be proud of their father."

Thala forced a smile. "Don't go soft on me now, Mr. Frankton. I like you the other way."

Karl shook his head. "Some combo. An aging Zulu and a recovering alcoholic sitting on a beach with a tube of sub-atomic soup that might save seven billion people. Wonder what the odds are in Vegas."

"It doesn't matter. The house always wins."

Karl brushed Thala's hand off his shoulder. He scrambled to his feet and stared at the bluff behind them.

"Something?"

"I'm not sure. Thought I heard a car on the gravel."

Thala looked down at his watch. Eleven p.m. He stood up and followed his friend up the rocks, the medical bag dangling from his hand.

It took a few minutes to scale the bluff. Thala climbed over the ledge and stood beside his friend, his eyes squinting at the twisted, moonlit trees of Scripps Park. Everything looked quiet. No movement. No sound, except the waves crashing on the rocks below.

Karl gripped the envelope while cursing himself for not picking up a gun along the way. Then again, what would he do with it? He was a healer—a physician. Guns belonged to murderers. He glanced at his watch. Six minutes past eleven. No sign of life.

"Well?"

Karl frowned. "I don't know. Maybe we—"

Karl froze. A shadow was coming toward them from the trees. Instinctively, he stepped back toward the ledge, his arm dragging Thala with him. If it was a trap, they might have a chance to scramble down the rocks to the beach. Pretty thin, but it was all they had.

The shadow was thirty feet away when it stopped. The only sound was the waves.

"Mr. Frankton, is that you?"

Karl squinted at the shadow. "Who are you?"

"Sarvan. You're Frankton?"

"Yes."

The shadow moved closer. "Let's get this over with before some crazed guardsman blows us away."

Karl felt Thala press against him. The message was clear. No turning back. After three days dodging the most powerful intelligence force on earth, it was time to make a stand. Karl edged forward until he could see Sarvan's gray beard in the moonlight. The anchorman wasn't smiling.

"Well?"

Karl shifted the envelope to his left hand. "I'm glad you came." He extended his right hand, but Sarvan wasn't in a handshaking mood.

"Get to it, Mr. Frankton. I have a broadcast in an hour."

Thala stepped beside Karl while eyeing the news anchor. "We need some light to show you what we have."

Sarvan nodded. "My car's back there. Gotta be careful with lights. They have hi-tech sensors on their vehicles. Can pinpoint a headlight with their GPS satellites." He started to turn away, but Karl grabbed his arm.

"No, stay here. I have a penlight." Karl knelt down on the grass and gestured for Sarvan to join him. The newsman frowned and knelt beside him.

Karl opened the envelope and shined the light on it. He reached inside and pulled out the first plastic tube. "This is tainted blood from one of the victims at the Trinity River near Houston. I used it to conduct a test with my own blood." Karl pulled out the CD. "Check this recording with any legitimate biologist. We programmed it to freeze at the instant the cyanide assaulted my blood cells."

Sarvan looked at him. "Cyanide?"

225

"I don't have much time, Mr. Sarvan, so I'll be brief. The details are in these documents." Karl dug his hand into the envelope and pulled out a stack of papers. "There was a company called Starburst. They developed a rodenticide that made them billions. Only problem was the rats became immune, so Starburst got desperate and contracted a biophysicist to bail them out. The man's name was Ringley Adams, a deranged genius who developed a radioactive catalyst that made the cyanide undetectable in its victim's blood." He hesitated and eyed the stunned newsman. "You getting any of this?"

Sarvan looked down at the papers in Karl's hand. "And this is documented?"

"Yeah—in these papers—and a bit more." Karl handed Sarvan the papers. "The first sprayings were conducted seventeen years ago. Adams figured the cyanide would decay within a few months, but something went wrong. The damn thing got stronger, and it's been getting stronger ever since. It's spread through the planet's eco-system. Through the oceans, lakes, and rivers. It's reached critical mass—ten parts per million—and we're all going to die unless we get this to the Centers for Disease Control." Karl reached into the envelope and pulled out a second plastic tube marked with a purple dot. He held it in the flashlight's beam, making a shadow on Sarvan's face.

The stunned reporter eyed the tube, then looked down at its twin resting on the envelope with the CD. His eyes darted to the papers in his hand. "My God, if you're telling the truth—" He jumped to his feet and backed away, his terrified eyes glaring at Karl.

"What's wrong?"

Sarvan shook his head. "I didn't know."

Thala felt a sudden chill. He squinted past Sarvan and saw a line of shadows racing toward them. His black eyes locked on the reporter. "You scum! You call yourself a human being! You're nothing but a low-life parasite!" He grabbed

Karl's shoulder and yanked him up. "It's a trap! The pig set us up!"

"Freeze, Mr. Frankton!"

Karl snatched the tubes and CD off the ground and turned for the ledge, but the tranquilizer darts had already found their mark. One in the chest, two in the leg. He managed a few more steps before the dizziness swept over him. Instinctively, he reached for Thala, but his friend was already down from five darts in his back. He dropped on his knees and felt a firm hand grip his shoulder—and the world went black.

The flak-jacketed agent stood up and waved his Uzi in the air. "We've got them, sir. Pulses are okay." The agent backed away and stared at the shadow approaching from the trees.

Hampsted stepped into the moonlight, his eyes glaring at the two bodies on the ground. A smile crept across his face. He knelt beside Karl and squeezed his wrist until the twin tubes rolled out of Karl's opened palm onto the ground.

Hampsted picked them up and motioned for the agents to train their flashlights on the ground. He snatched the CD and backed away, his eyes focused on the shaken reporter. "I think you have the last thing I need."

Sarvan stared at him, his hand clutching the papers. "Are they alright?"

Hampsted nodded. "Just unconscious from the darts. Same stuff we use on animals. Appropriate, don't you agree?"

Sarvan's eyes blazed with anger. "We have a deal, remember? I give you the terrorists and you give me the story."

Hampsted nodded. "Correct, and that's just what I'm going to do." He stuffed the tubes and CD into Thala's bag. "Now, if you'll just give me those papers, the deal will be complete."

Sarvan glared at him. "What the hell are you doing? Those tubes belong to me. And so does that CD."

Hampsted shrugged. "You're mistaken, Mr. Sarvan. You won't need them for your story. You're going to make history. A real American hero. You're a veteran, right?"

Sarvan felt his stomach churn. "What does that have to do with it?"

Hampsted stepped back. "A lot, Mr. Sarvan. With you being a war veteran, I bet they'll bury you at Arlington." He reached inside his jacket and pulled out a nine millimeter. Sarvan stared at him in disbelief. "Are you nuts? I'm wired, you idiot. You think I came here without cover? You think I trusted the government? Hell, I learned that lesson in 'Nam. Now give me those tubes and I'll be on my—"

The first bullet hit him between the eyes. The second caught him in the heart as he staggered backward. The third was an extreme prejudice shot to his left temple as he lay motionless on the ground.

Hampsted reached down and yanked the papers out of Sarvan's frozen hand. He ripped open Sarvan's bloody shirt, revealing a small transmitter taped to his ribs. "Nice try, Mr. Sarvan. Too bad we jammed your little broadcast. Your friends only got static." He straightened up and sneered at the dead reporter. "Don't feel bad. I do this for a living. Know all the tricks. Besides, you should thank me. I just made you a hero."

Hampsted wiped his prints off the gun and knelt beside Karl. He placed the gun in Karl's hand and pressed Karl's fingers on the grip and trigger. "Thank you, Mr. Frankton. I knew you were good for something." He stuffed the gun in a plastic bag and nodded at the two agents standing in the moonlight. He watched them drag Karl to the car parked in the shadows. Thala would take a bit longer, but the end was in sight.

Hampsted picked up Thala's medical bag and shined the flashlight on the area while backing toward the car. Yes, everything was in order. The police would find Sarvan's body in the morning, Karl Frankton's final act of terror before he and his cohort met their downfall in the Palomar foothills. He broke into a smile. Let Tarver and Fletcher play their political games. Next stop—Bora Bora.

. . .

Estelle Fletcher was nearly asleep when her husband slipped into bed and wrapped his arms around her. He held her close and whispered softly in her ear. "Can we talk?"

He waited for a response, but the only sound was the electric clock humming in the darkness. He was about to give up when she gripped his arm.

"Are the boys asleep?"

"I think so."

She rolled over and stared at him with those baby blues. "Sure you want to hear this?"

"No, but go on."

She frowned and uttered a deep sigh. "I watched that debacle on television. I even recorded it and watched it again to make sure I wasn't hallucinating." She hesitated and brushed away a tear. "Don't you see what they're doing? They've found their scapegoat. If you don't get out now, you'll never get out."

Fletcher looked down. "Think I don't know that?"

Her eyes filled with anger. "Then get out, Johnny. Get away from Tarver, Manis, and the rest of that scum. They caused this mess and now they're trying to dump it on you. Don't let them do it. Let's blow DC while we can. We have enough money. We'll sell the house and buy that cottage in Maine."

He forced a smile. "I thought you didn't like Maine."

"I don't, but anything's better than this. I'll do anything to get away from those vermin."

His smile faded. "I wish it was that easy. If I pull out now, they'll use every dirty trick in the book. Even go after you and the boys. It'll be the end of us."

Her blue eyes burned into him. "What are you saying?"

"There are things you don't know. Baggage I picked up along the way. They'll use it on me, and my family."

Her grip tightened. "Baggage?"

229

He looked into her eyes, and he suddenly knew the terrible price he'd paid for his climb to the top. If he told her the truth, their marriage would be finished, and so would he.

"Johnny?"

He felt her fingers dig into his flesh. It was coming at him too fast. He needed time to think. Time to work things out. Don't blow it, man. Just a little white lie to buy some time.

He rolled on his back and stared at the darkness. "You're right, sweetheart. I'm just looking for an excuse. Nothing's worth losing you and the boys."

Her eyes brightened. "You mean that?"

"More than you know. That meeting with Manis showed me the light. I've had it."

"Then, you'll tell them?"

"I'm scheduled to meet with Tarver tomorrow afternoon. I'll break the news to him then."

"That, you're leaving?"

"As soon as I clean things up. Can't just walk away after nineteen years. Gotta give them time to put things in order, especially with what's going on. It'll take a few weeks, but that should be enough." He took her in his arms. "We'll put the house up for sale and find that cottage by the sea, and we'll be done with them."

"Oh, Johnny." She rolled on top of him and buried her lips on his. He could feel her breasts heaving against him. Her lips and tongue were all over him. She was so hot, and he was so hard. It was good to be young again. Good to make love again.

When he finally climaxed, Jonathan Fletcher was a new man. He had bought precious time to figure out his next move. His wife loved him. His sons loved him. His path was set.

He lay on his back, glaring at the darkness. Those fools on Pennsylvania Avenue didn't know who they were dealing with. He had come too far to be screwed by a bunch of amateurs. Once he got his hands on Adams' formula, he'd turn the tables on them. Nothing like a little blackmail to even the playing field. And the price? Hell, Adams had blazed that trail. Ten million, tax-free, in a Swiss account. And of course, the proverbial poison pill to keep the pigs from changing their minds. Maybe a sample of the formula stashed away in a nondescript postal box, along with a few juicy documents from Adams' file. And an ominous letter of condemnation triggered for mailing to the nation's major newspapers if Jonathan Fletcher didn't make his daily call to the appropriate party.

Yes, it would all work out. When it was over, he'd buy that seaside cottage in Kennebunkport for his beautiful wife, and a new life would begin. No more midnight meetings. No more boot licking. No more dirty work. He'd be free, dammit. Free!

He glanced at the digital clock on the nightstand. Two thirty? Where the hell was Parker? If he'd blown it, they were doomed.

A chill shot through him. What if Parker hadn't blown it? What if the scum had nailed the two targets and given Adams' formula to Tarver? Without the formula, there would be no bargaining chip, no poison pill, and all would be lost. Estelle's prophecy would come true. Her husband would become another slave in the world's most corrupt bureaucracy, doomed to live out his remaining years in disgrace as Samuel Tarver's lackey.

He slipped off the bed, taking care not to awaken her. He could smell her perfume. She looked so beautiful lying naked in the shadows, her breasts heaving gently. He draped the sheet over her and backed away.

She was all he had. The only person he could trust. If he lost her, he might as well put a bullet in his head. Unacceptable, dammit! He slipped on his robe and headed downstairs.

The study was stifling from DC's latest heat wave. He cursed under his breath and shuffled to the Victorian door behind his desk. Damn air conditioning system. He should have replaced it years ago. No sense worrying about it now. They'd only be in the house a few more months.

He pushed open the door and reeled from a blast of heat and humidity. It would probably break 100 tomorrow. Hell with it. He closed the door and sat at his desk, his hand groping for the cell phone. No sense using the lamp in this damned heat.

He snatched the phone off the desk and stared at its illuminated dial. A bead of sweat trickled down his forehead. He punched Hampsted's calling code and waited for the warbling to subside.

"Yeah?"

He leaned forward and pressed the phone to his mouth. "Well?"

"It's over."

Fletcher's eyes lit up. "You've got them?"

"Affirmative. We're on the way to a safe house near Mount Palomar. Should be there in a couple hours."

Fletcher collapsed in the chair, his eyes staring at the darkness. "That's good news. I was getting worried."

"Hell, it's not midnight yet. Get your time zones straight. I'm the one in the field. We operate on my time, remember. That's standard procedure."

Fletcher restrained himself. "Yes, of course. Sorry."

"So, that's it?"

"Does Tarver know?"

Hampsted hesitated. *"What kind of question is that? You know the way it works."*

Fletcher clenched the phone. "I thought I did, but maybe it's time for a refresher. Just how many people do you brief?"

"After nineteen years, you should know that. Nothing personal, it's just a question of rank. Gotta keep everyone happy."

Fletcher leaned forward, his face hot with anger. "So, you brief him first. Is that how the damn thing works?"

"I wouldn't put it that way, but that's pretty much it. Hell, I thought you knew."

"I do now."

Hampsted's voice sharpened. *"Then know this. Samuel Tarver has been your boss since the mess at FDA. He was the invisible higher-up you exchanged e-mails with. The one who gave you FDA's terms regarding Frankton's contract. That's when Tarver decided to groom you for the top job at CDC."*

"You expect me to believe that? Tarver wasn't even in the picture when that happened?"

"Wasn't he? You think these things happen by accident? My assignment was to help you the same way I helped Tarver before you. Only problem is I'm tired of wet-nursing a bunch of bureaucratic wanna-be's. That's why I'm getting out."

Fletcher brushed a bead of sweat off his forehead. "Sounds like you've been at this some time."

"I guess you could say that."

"You must have helped a lot of wanna-be's."

"A few."

"Tell me, Parker. Was one of them the President?"

"That's classified."

Fletcher dug his fingers into the phone.

"I don't have time for this melodramatic crap. We need to get on with more important things. I need your okay to terminate these two jerks after interrogation."

Fletcher grimaced. "Do what's necessary."

"There's more."

"Go on."

"I need to sterilize this mess. A few others must be removed to eliminate any exposures. Specifically, the two guys that worked with Thala at Trinity, and Frankton's associates at Willapa Bay and Somalia. Agreed?"

Fletcher looked down at his clenched fist. "Yes."

"One of them's waiting for us at the safe house. She thinks we're going to reward her for helping us track down Thala and Frankton. She's real good with computers, the way

she GPS'd Thala's web searches. Helped cut the time to track them down. Too bad she's so ambitious. Can't trust people like that. Know what I mean?"

"Do it, dammit. Whatever is necessary."

"Calm down. You think I like this? You bureaucrats are all the same. Real big shots until it's time for the dirty work. That's when you need me so you can look the other way."

Fletcher pressed his mouth to the phone. "Maybe so, but for the record, I think you like it. I think it turns you on."

Hampsted exploded. *"Know something, big shot? I'm sick of your hypocrisy and I'm sick of you. I don't think you'll last much longer."*

Fletcher sat up in the chair, his hand gripping the phone. "Is that it?"

"I'll call you at zero-nine-hundred, my time. Things should be wrapped up by then. Think about the best way to make the transfer. From what I've seen, I have everything Tarver and his boys need to save their skin. Even a little extra. These documents will guarantee all the money we need from those overseas contacts of yours. Hell, will they be shook when you break it to them."

Fletcher stared at the darkness, unable to speak.

"You got all this?"

"Yes."

"One last thing. We split whatever you get, fifty-fifty. And no games. I'll be in touch…"

Fletcher dropped the phone on the desk and fell back in the chair. The illuminated clock on the mantle read 2:45. In the distance, he could hear sirens. Or was it the screams of the dead?

He sat motionless, his eyes gazing at the clock. Time was short and he was losing the biggest fight of his life. Can't give up now. Not when you're so close.

He sat up and rested his arms on the desk. There was only one answer. He had to eliminate Parker before it was too late. It was the only way. He would let Parker do his dirty work, then advise Tarver that the bastard was threatening to blackmail the team. That Parker was trying to set up a poison pill. That the only solution was termination with extreme prejudice.

He rubbed his tired eyes. After nineteen years of bureaucratic ladder-climbing, he was about to make the biggest play of his life. Timing would be everything. He must somehow get his hands on Adams' formula, get rid of Parker, and use the formula to free himself from Tarver and Manis before they got their hands on it. It was risky, but there was no other way. If he failed, and Tarver discovered his attempted betrayal before he had the formula, Jonathan Fletcher's fate would be worse than Karl Frankton's because the targets would include his wife and sons.

He looked up at the portrait above the mantle. He couldn't see their faces, but he knew they were looking down at him. "Please, God. Not them."

He collapsed in the chair, his eyes filled with tears. Enough for tonight. He couldn't think straight. Besides, those unnerving sirens were getting louder. Shut them out, dammit. Shut everything out.

He felt his eyes closing. Not enough energy to make it upstairs. No matter. His wife was out cold from the best sex she'd had in months. His sons were asleep in their bedrooms, probably dreaming about the women they'd have after their dad's big promotion.

A smile crept across his face. Go to sleep, man. Go to sleep and quit worrying about this garbage. Everything will work out. It always has. It always will.

His head drooped to the side. A sweet numbness ebbed through him. The sirens faded. He was home in Portland, Maine, a sixteen-year-old teenager with a heart full of dreams…

Johnny, quit reading all them books and come do your chores.

He closed the law book and rested it on the stack of books beside his bed. He would read them all before he took them back to the local library. Then he'd take out three more and do the same, cause Johnny Fletcher wanted to be somebody. Let the other kids play their stupid games and chase the young girls. He wasn't going to waste a minute of his precious life.

No way could his mom understand. She was a plain woman, but a loving mother. When his dad pulled out on them, she cried a lot and thought her son would fill his dad's shoes. Can't blame her for thinking that, but Johnny Fletcher had a different plan. He was going to read every damn book in that library until he went to college and became a lawyer. Then he was going into politics to move up the ladder with the power boys. And when he reached the top, he'd take good care of his mom, and anyone else who helped him along the way.

But not his dad. No way, dammit. His dad would be toast. He'd fry the scumbag for abandoning him and his mom. And he'd fry anyone else who opposed him. And that's the way it would be…

Fletcher's eyes snapped open. What was happening? Those sirens? And screams? He swung the chair around and looked out at the garden. The darkness flashed with red lights. The sirens were deafening. He heard a voice crackling through a loud speaker. The words were all too clear…

"Evacuate! Evacuate immediately! Proceed north toward the flashing red lights!"

He sat up and stared at the clock. Four a.m.? Was this some kind of nightmare? Maybe a fire? That's it, someone's house was on fire.

He bolted off the chair and ran out of the study. He was halfway across the living room when he heard Estelle's screams.

"Johnny!"

"I'm here! It's okay!"

"My God, Johnny! Look outside!"

He heard Estelle running across the upstairs hall. A door slammed open at the top of the stairs.

"What's wrong, Mom? Where's Dad? Where the hell is Dad!"

Fletcher stared at the red light flashing through the foyer window. He charged at the front door and jiggled open the lock. He could hear Estelle and the boys running down the stairs behind him. He pulled open the door and stared at the street in horror.

People were running in all directions, some clothed in pajamas, others barely clothed at all. Many had fallen, their partially-clothed bodies sprawled on their lawns and driveways. He stumbled down the front steps and raised his hand in front of his face to block out the flashing lights, and he saw the face of hell.

Two bio-suited men raced toward him, spare tanks and suits dangling from their arms. He backed away from the two specters. What kind of hellish nightmare was this? People running for their lives? Bio trucks rumbling by, their snorkels sampling the air? And now, this? Two men racing toward him with spare tanks and suits? No, this wasn't happening. You're having a nightmare. Snap out of it, man!

"My God, Johnny! My..."

He felt a hand on his shoulder and spun around. Estelle had dropped to one knee, her eyes bulging as she gasped for air. Behind her, Robert had collapsed beside his brother on the hall floor, his hands clutching his throat.

"Estelle!" Fletcher reached for his wife, but someone seized him around the waist and pulled him back. "Let me go!"

"Calm down, Mr. Fletcher. We're here to help you. Put on this mask. We'll get you and your family out of here."

Fletcher slapped at the mask and broke away. He ran past the second bio-suited agent and dropped on the front steps beside his unconscious wife.

"Please, Mr. Fletcher! There's no time!" The agent reached for him, but Fletcher swiped at the agent's hood, forcing him to back away.

Fletcher tried to lift her, but a searing pain stopped him. He gripped his chest and collapsed on the steps. "God, no!" Her blue eyes were frozen on him. A trickle of saliva rolled down her cheek. She tried to clutch her throat, but her hand fell short. There was no relaxation. Her body was stiff and motionless, as if frozen in a photograph.

He crawled past her into the hall where his two sons lay on the floor. Robert was motionless, his body drawn into a fetal position. Franklin's body convulsed as if jolted with electricity. His hands tore at his pajama top, exposing his distended neck muscles. His brown eyes bulged from their sockets, like the eyes of a man dropped from a gallows. His face was blue. He convulsed a final time, then fell silent beside his brother, his face frozen in twisted terror, his glazed eyes staring into space.

Fletcher managed to huddle against his two sons before rolling on his back, his hands clutching his throat while his lungs tried to overcome their paralysis. With the dark veil of death closing over him, he listened to the screams coming from the street as his friends and neighbors succumbed to the invisible terror that had erupted from the Potomac River, spreading northward through the upper class neighborhoods of Georgetown, Embassy Row, and Upper Northwest, DC.

Like his fellow victims, Jonathan Fletcher had been too caught up in his life to grasp what was coming. As the paramedic's words faded in his ears, he finally knew the truth. Cyanide doesn't care about political battles or human emotions. It just reacts to nature's laws and becomes a deadly gas at 78° F. It was judgment day, and the nation's capital was a gas chamber.

"Got a pulse?"

"No...he's gone. My God, we just lost the number two man at CDC."

Chapter 20

78°

Menchen pressed the off button and stared at the darkened screen. The only light came from the computer console. The only sound was his strained breathing. He rested his head against the leather chair and closed his eyes. The darkness felt cool and comforting...

He tensed from his beeping watch. It was high noon in Salzburg. Nicole and Gretta would soon return from their morning stroll around Mönchsberg hill. They hadn't disturbed him when they left. Nicole probably thought her husband had awakened early to make some overseas calls. Best to leave him alone.

He'd spent the morning in his study, his eyes glued to the terror unfolding four thousand miles away. First came the reports of late night joggers collapsing along the Potomac River, their hands clutching their throats. Then, helicopter videos of automobiles scattered across the Roosevelt Bridge, their occupants slumped against the windows. No movement. No signs of life.

The first comprehensive report was telecast twenty minutes ago by *Reuters*. The virus had struck Washington, DC at two a.m., killing hundreds of unprotected civilians who were seen staggering through Potomac Park, their hands tearing at their throats.

After devastating the river's north shore, the virus moved inland toward Foggy Bottom, the Ellipse, and the White House. With the Secret Service suppressing all news of the President's status, the coverage shifted to the city's northwest quadrant where the plague reached the affluent community of

Georgetown, and its renowned university. While classified, the death toll was believed in the thousands. Reports of bodies in the streets flooded the airwaves. The National Guard was called in to control the terrified citizenry. Bio-suited troops poured out of their shrouded trucks in a futile effort to evacuate the civilian population as the plague continued its ravaging march inland, aided by high winds from a sudden thunderstorm. Bodies could be seen as far north as Mt. Pleasant.

At four thirty, a cold front swept through the nation's capital, breaking the oppressive heat wave that had engulfed DC for two weeks. In minutes, the sultry temperatures plunged into the sixties, and the unexplainable happened. As quickly as it had come, the plague faded away.

Menchen took a painful breath and punched two codes into the console. In seconds, his associates' pagers went off, alerting them to the urgent message flashing on their screens...

We must talk immediately.
GM

The first call came from Schoenfeld. Nakashima responded minutes later, his voice filled with concern.

Menchen punched them into conference mode and pressed the intercom button. He waited for the green light before speaking. "Are you there, gentlemen?"

The intercom crackled with their voices.

"I have grave news."

"About the crisis in the US capital?"

Menchen recognized Schoenfeld's voice. He leaned toward the intercom and spoke deliberately. "It appears we have lost our overseas contact. He lived only a short distance from the Potomac River. Rotten luck. He was just appointed to the number two position at CDC."

For a moment, there was no response. Schoenfeld finally broke the silence. *"So, we're flying blind over there?"*

"I'm afraid so."

Schoenfeld hesitated. *"Best to do nothing. If we get involved, we might expose ourselves."*

Nakashima spoke up, his voice filled with anger. *"How can you say that, Schoenfeld-san? If we don't get involved, the world health authorities won't have a chance. It will take them months to isolate the cyanide and develop an antidote. By that time, it will be too late."*

Schoenfeld's voice harshened. *"You make too much of this, Yoshio. I'm merely suggesting we develop an alternate plan while pursuing a new contact in the United States. That will take a few weeks. There will still be time for resolution without creating undo risk for ourselves. That's the smart play. The scientific play."*

Menchen listened for a response from Nakashima, but there was none. He sat up in his chair, his elbows resting on the conference table. "It seems we have a disagreement. Since we're in this together, it falls on me to cast the deciding vote."

Schoenfeld exploded. *"I won't go along with any insane ventures. I'm not going to prison over this. We may be in this together, but that doesn't include suicide."*

Menchen grimaced. "I'm afraid it's more serious than that. I've studied Yoshio's charts. The news of the past week is irrefutable. However it happened—whatever quirk of nature brought us to this moment—we've opened Pandora's Box. I'm convinced we're on the brink of disaster."

"No—you're overreacting. The damn thing will die out on its own." Schoenfeld's voice softened. *"Listen to me, Gunthar. I'm only asking for two weeks. Is that too much to give a friend?"*

Menchen shook his head. "I'm sorry, Magnus. I'm afraid we don't have that long."

The silence was overwhelming. It was as if the connections had been severed. Nakashima finally spoke. *"What should we do?"*

Menchen reached for a piece of paper lying beside the console. He snatched it off the conference table and crushed it in his hand. "An hour ago, I received a phone call from a Mr. Hampsted in California. It seems he has the antidote and the two terrorists. He wants to make a deal."

"And you trust him?"

Menchen looked down at the crushed paper. "I've checked on him. An associate of Mr. Fletcher. Quite capable, if you know what I mean. He knows everything, Magnus. We don't have a choice."

Schoenfeld's voice grew strident. *"Kill him!"*

"Not advisable. To be blunt, Mr. Hampsted is holding the cards. If we try anything, he'll give the evidence to the media."

Nakashima cut in. *"How did he find us?"*

"I don't know, but anyone that good must be respected."

Nakashima hesitated. *"How much, Menchen-san?"*

"Ten million. Not much to put this behind us. Think of it, gentlemen. For your one third contribution, Mr. Hampsted will stage the appropriate discovery of Adams' formula. With the formula in CDC's hands, the epidemic will be suppressed in a few months, and we can go on with our lives, minus perhaps a few million people."

Schoenfeld sighed. *"And you'll let him walk away with ten million and a promise?"*

Menchen grimaced. "Come to your senses, Magnus. Mr. Hampsted has everything...Adams' notes, letters, and the formula. If you haven't grasped it, we're being blackmailed."

"Then...we're finished?"

Menchen shook his head. "I don't think so. I believe Mr. Hampsted will honor his commitment. He just wants to enjoy the rest of his life."

"Like us, Menchen-san?"

"Exactly, Yoshio. Just like us. Oh, I'm sure he'll protect himself with the appropriate poison pill...but that's acceptable. It will create a standoff which I am quite happy to live with. An unholy alliance, if you will."

"*It's suicide, dammit!*"

Menchen frowned. "No, Magnus. It's good business. My vote is to negotiate with our new friend in the states."

The only response came from Nakashima. "*Agreed.*"

Menchen listened to the silence. "Magnus?"

"*Suicide...*" Schoenfeld's connection went dead.

"So be it. I'll contact Herr Hampsted immediately."

"*Stay well, Menchen-san.*"

Menchen listened to the second click. He rested his finger on the off button and stared at the darkness.

.   .   .

He was standing on a bluff overlooking Morningside Park and the Manhattan skyline. Above him, St. John's bell tower came alive with a crescendo of melodic chimes. He squinted at the bright sun beaming down on him from the cloudless sky. A cool breeze brushed his face, filling his nostrils with the scent of spring flowers.

"Well, what are you waiting for? Take the picture already. I need to get this cap and gown back by one."

He stared at the beautiful woman smiling at him from the trees, her blond hair ruffling in the breeze. "Anne?"

"Come on, honey. I'm not in the mood for games."

He stepped closer, trying to make sense of the apparition. She gave him a puzzled frown. "You okay?"

He glanced at the camera in his hand. "I don't know."

"Hey, Dad, what's wrong?"

A warm hand slipped into his. He looked down at the blond-haired boy peering up at him. "Jeremy?"

The boy flashed a smile. "Who else, Spiderman? Come on, take the picture so we can go to Grams. This suit is killing me."

244

He felt his wife's hand grip his arm. "Maybe you should sit down. The heat might be getting to you."

"No, this isn't happening. I shouldn't be here. None of us should be here." He pulled his arm away and stepped back toward the trees.

"Karl?"

"No, stay away. You're not real. None of this is real..."

"Where the hell are you going!"

He spun around and saw his sister glaring at him from the steps of their farmhouse, a white paper in her hand. Morningside Park was gone, replaced by a rain swept Pennsylvania cornfield.

"This is how you repay me? By sneaking out and leaving a damn note?" She crushed the paper in her fist and flung it at the ground. "Damn you! After all I've done for you. I swear to God, you walk out on me and we're finished!"

He couldn't speak. This was no dream. It was a nightmare. The worst nightmare of all. He turned toward the open gate at the end of the path."

"Wait, Karl!"

He ignored her and ran through the gate...

"Hello, Mr. Frankton."

He froze. Ringley Adams was standing in a dense fog, his bloodshot eyes burning into him. The air smelled from death—dank, cold, and stale. Everything was covered with thick, gray fog.

Adams' face twisted in a sneer. "You really blew it, Mr. Frankton. Because of you, seven billion people are going to die. Can't blame that on me. I gave you the ball and you dropped it. You have a lot of explaining to do, if you know what I mean."

"No...you're dead."

"Right on, Mr. Frankton. And so are you...and the rest of us. All seven billion." Adams retreated into the fog. "Too bad about the human race. Wonder what takes over. Maybe the roaches and ants. Maybe some rats that became immune to the cyanide. Now that would be sweet revenge. The rats make it, and we don't. All because a washed-up alcoholic named Karl Frankton dropped the ball. How about that for a legacy?"

"Damn you!"

"And you too, Mr. Frankton. See you in hell. I'll be the one laughing when you drop in." Adams backed into the mist and disappeared…

"Wake up!"

A harsh voice echoed in his ears. He looked around, but there was only cold, spinning darkness.

That light? Like a train coming at him in the night. The ultimate rush. Getting bigger now. A blinding beam shining in his eyes. And that voice ringing in his ears.

"Snap out of it!"

He winced from a sharp slap on the face.

"I think he's coming to. Hey, Frankton, you with us?"

He blinked at the blurred face in the light, and felt a sobering chill. If this was hell, he was staring at the devil. Parker Hampsted was looking down at him, his face filled with rage.

"Nice nap?"

He tried to speak, but his throat felt like sandpaper. He swallowed hard and forced out the words. "Hello, scum."

A rugged hand seized him by the hair and snapped his head back. He tried to move, but his hands were tied to the chair's legs.

Hampsted leaned forward until they were nose-to-nose. "Make you a deal. Answer one question and you can go back to sleep."

Karl glared at him. "I'm not tired."

"Then you die the hard way, like your friend." Hampsted backed away, revealing Thala tied to a chair across the room. Mandu's swollen face was covered with bruises. Blood trickled from his mouth and nose. His head rolled from side to side, as if he were in extreme pain.

Karl strained against the ropes. "What did you do to him!" Hampsted looked down at Thala's writhing body. "Your friend's a real trooper. From his history, he's taken plenty of torture. We gave up on the strong arm stuff. Tried a little LSD with electro-shock." Hampsted scratched his head. "Gotta give him credit. He's a tough one, but he won't last long."

Karl tugged at the ropes anchoring his hands and feet to the chair.

"You're wasting your time, Mr. Frankton. Ours too." Hampsted glanced at the two white-shirted agents standing off to the side.

Karl slumped in the chair. Through the corner of his eye, he noticed one of the agents drawing a clear liquid into a syringe. The other was stripping an extension cord. In another minute, they'd wire him up and inject the LSD. No way could he stand that kind of torture.

Hampsted reached down and snatched a black bag off the floor. "I believe this belongs to your friend." He nodded to one of the agents who flipped a switch connected to a wire coiled around Thala's chest. Thala let out an agonizing cry while convulsing helplessly from the voltage coursing through his body.

"Stop it, dammit! What kind of animal are you!" Karl lunged at Hampsted, chair and all, but a quick punch from one of the agents knocked him to the floor.

"Easy, Mr. Frankton. You need to look good for your visitor. She's come a long way to see you." Hampsted whispered something to the agent and watched him slip through the door. He nodded for the second agent to turn off the electricity surging through Thala's body. The agent flipped the switch, forcing a hellish cry from Thala who convulsed a final time before collapsing in the chair, his head drooped forward.

Hampsted grabbed Karl by the hair and pulled him off the floor until he was sitting upright in the chair. "There you go.

Shouldn't greet your guest lying down." Hampsted gave Karl's hair a painful twist before releasing his grip with a hard shove.

Karl clenched his teeth and stared at his unconscious friend. *God, please let him die. He's suffered enough. This is my fault. I dragged him into this mess. Better they torture me instead of Mandu. He's my friend, dammit! The only friend I ever had!*

The door swung open and a young woman stepped into the room. Karl stared at her in disbelief.

Susan Cayman tried to force a smile, but the blood on Karl's face stopped her cold. She glanced at Thala and let out a gasp.

Hampsted rested a hand on her shoulder. "Sorry, it's the unpleasant side of my job. Remember, we're dealing with two sicko's that have killed lots of people. We need to know if others are involved."

She took a calming breath and nodded. "What are you going to do to them?"

Hampsted shrugged. "Finish the interrogation and take them back to DC. I thought you might want to be in on the action, given what you've done for us."

Karl glared at her through his swollen eyes. "You're with them?"

She shrugged and looked at Hampsted. "Well, am I?"

Hampsted gave her a reassuring nod. "If you help us now, we'll be eternally grateful."

Her face brightened. That was all she needed to hear. She turned toward Karl, her eyes flashing with the same blind ambition she'd shown in Somalia. "Come on, Karl. Tell them what they need to know. Make it easier on yourself."

His blue eyes burned into her. "Are you nuts? Do you know who you're dealing with? You just committed suicide."

His words went right past her. The moment was too intoxicating to waste on the pleadings of a captured terrorist. After eleven years of hard work and groveling, Susan Cayman had finally found her angel, a hard-nosed ex-CIA agent with ties to the right people. No way would she blow it. Just extract a few words from Mr. Frankton and she'd be on her way. Promotion, money, first class travel, and a plush office in Atlanta. Then, that magic transfer to the nation's capital for a shot at the top job. Unlike Raquel Carson with her jaded past, Susan Cayman knew how to play the game. Before she was done, she would become the youngest director in CDC's history. All she had to do was squeeze a little information from the washed-up alcoholic tied to the chair in front of her.

She rested her hand on the chair arm and leaned toward him. "So, how did you do it? Level Four? You spent enough time down there. A dozen visits in the past year. Plenty of time for a man with your insight and intellect to conjure up the deadliest virus in history. But what about the funding? Where did you get the money to clone it? Al Qaeda? Blue Brigade? Shining Path?"

She pushed away from the chair and folded her arms, her brown eyes trained on him. "There's only one thing I don't get. How can someone with so much potential end up like this? What drove you to it? Booze? Drugs? Sex?"

Karl tried to speak, but the words wouldn't come out. She didn't know! She thought it was a virus! The fool! The poor, ambitious fool!

She leaned closer. "Tell them, Karl. Who else worked with you? We know about Dr. Thala, but there must be others. Was it Dolstadt? Kremler? Masters? Buckley?" She hesitated. "Tell you a little secret. I always suspected Nihalla. You spent so much time with him in the van, going over those samples." She glanced at Thala. "Yeah, it makes sense. Two oppressed blacks and a washed-up alcoholic venting their hatred on a helpless world." She thrust her face at his. "It was Nihalla, wasn't it? He was the other one."

Karl looked into her brown eyes.

"It was him, wasn't it?"

"Idiot! You're toast!"

She reeled back from his sudden outburst, her face spattered with saliva. She wiped off the saliva with her sleeve and turned to Hampsted. "It's Nihalla."

Hampsted stared at her, his eyes flickering with anger. "Why?"

"Because of the pattern. Oppressed Third World blacks. Disillusioned alcoholic. It all fits."

Hampsted looked down. "That's all you have?"

She looked at him in surprise. "It couldn't be the others. No motive. Hell, ask them."

Hampsted glanced at the agent who had brought her in. "That might be difficult. They're all dead."

"Dead?" She stepped back against the door, her eyes filled with terror. "What happened to them?"

Hampsted shrugged. "Accidents, Ms. Cayman. I'm sorry, I thought you might help us."

Her hand groped for the doorknob. "But, I did?"

"No, Ms. Cayman. But don't feel bad. It wouldn't have mattered."

She forced a trembling smile. "You're playing games. It's a test, right?"

"Afraid not."

She turned and gripped the knob with both hands as Karl's words rang in her ears. *You're toast!*

The agent jammed his nine millimeter against her head and squeezed the trigger, driving her face against the door. She turned and gawked at him in stunned terror before sliding down the door in a heap.

Without batting an eyelash, the agent placed the gun against her left temple and put a second bullet into her brain. Karl watched in horror as the agent felt for a pulse and backed away.

"So, Mr. Frankton. You've killed another one. Too bad we couldn't save her when we rushed your little hideaway." Hampsted wiped a drop of spattered blood off his cheek. "Tell you what. Let's take a little inventory." He reached into Thala's medical bag and pulled out the confiscated tube of tainted blood. "Exhibit A." He placed it on the table and reached into his pocket. "Exhibit B." He lifted out Adams' folded notes and placed them on the table beside the tube. "C." He pulled out the CD and placed it on the table. "And finally, D." He dug into the bag and pulled out the purple-dotted tube. "Hmmm—it seems we're missing the other two tubes of antidote. See the way it's marked one-of-three? Perhaps you can shed some light on that."

The mustached agent ripped open Karl's shirt and wrapped the bare wire around his chest. The other agent put away his nine millimeter and picked up the syringe. He pointed it at the shack's wood ceiling and squeezed off a few drops of LSD.

Hampsted leaned closer. "I'm waiting for an answer, Mr. Frankton. It seems we've come full circle. Remember how we met at Hartsfield? Your assignment was to help us uncover the virus, and you have. Hell, you even found the cure. So, if you would just tell me where those tubes are, you can die in peace."

Karl winced from the sweat trickling into the cuts on his face. He glanced down at Susan's lifeless corpse, twin streams of blood pouring from her head, her brown eyes gazing into space. He heard a faint groan from his friend in the shadows. *Don't wake up, Mandu! Don't wake up!*

He felt the agent rip open his sleeve. Only seconds left before Adams' prophecy came true. His heart hammered against his chest. It wasn't the dying that scared him. What if Adams was right and seven billion raging *homo-sapiens* met him on the other side? The human race, for God's sake! The whole planet venting their wrath on the one man who could have saved them!

Hampsted gripped his hair. "Last chance, Mr. Frankton. The tubes, please."

The needle pricked his left arm. His body tingled from the first jolt of electricity—and he felt his fear turn to anger. Karl Frankton had risen from obscurity to chase his dream, only to have it crushed in a Bethesda lab. With his marriage and career destroyed, he had drowned his sorrow in booze, only to be re-awakened by a newspaper article while en route to his final assignment. Was it an accident? Twist of fate? Or was it a wakeup call from whoever or whatever watches over this beautiful planet and its fragile occupants. A wakeup call to fight back.

The agent pressed down on Karl's shoulder. He felt the needle going into his arm. Hampsted backed away, revealing a rusted thermometer attached to the door jam.

Karl's eyes locked on the twin tubes lying on the table. If this was the end, make it a good one, dammit. For Mandu, Jeremy, and the other seven billion. But most of all—for yourself. Come on, Frankton. Fight back!

Before the stunned agent could react, Karl lunged forward at the table, his shoulder catching it as he went down. The impact was enough to topple the plastic tubes onto the floor.

The two agents were on him in a flash, pounding at him, choking the life out of him. He felt the tubes under his heels. Take the shot, Frankton. Do it! He let out a groan and smashed his right heel on one of the tubes, spraying blood against the wall.

"Get him up!" Hampsted watched them sit him upright beside Thala. The enraged agent reached for the plug lying on the floor and jammed it into the wall socket. "Okay, Mr. Frankton. Forget the LSD. We'll do it the hard way."

Karl watched Hampsted place his trembling hand on the transformer dial. One twist and it would be too late. "Wait! I'll talk! We buried the other two tubes in the rocks below the cliff! I can tell you where they are!"

Hampsted slid his hand off the transformer dial and glared at the man he had grown to hate. "You have ten seconds."

Karl looked up at him. "That should be enough."

"What?"

"It's a little warm in here, don't you think?"

"Time's up, bastard." Hampsted placed his hand on the dial.

"Yeah...real warm. Must be over seventy-eight."

Hampsted heard a stifling groan and looked to his left. One of the agents was clutching his throat, his eyes bulging out of their sockets. The other was leaning against the wall, gasping for breath.

Hampsted turned toward Karl, his eyes suddenly filled with terror. He looked down at the blood spattered on the floor. "What did you do? What the hell did you—" His hand slid off the dial and gripped his shirt collar. He couldn't breathe. Everything was spinning. A searing pain ripped through his chest. He fell back against the table and sprawled across it, his body convulsing from cyanide vapor.

Karl held his breath and tore at the ropes. He ripped his hand free with superhuman strength and clawed at the ropes around his feet. *One chance!* He dived for the unbroken tube and glared at the purple dot.

He dug into the medical bag and yanked out a syringe and needle. He jammed the needle into the tube and filled the syringe with blessed purple liquid. His lungs were exploding. In another second, he'd take a fatal gasp.

He crawled beside his friend and plunged the needle into Thala's calf. He yanked it out and stuck the needle into his own arm.

He couldn't hold back any longer. He took a convulsive breath and jammed the syringe to the hilt. *Outside! Now!* He gripped Thala's shirt and dragged him toward the door, chair and all. He was so dizzy. His chest was on fire. He kicked Susan's lifeless body out of the way and pulled open the door.

The warm night air struck his face, but he couldn't take a breath. He dragged his friend through the dirt and felt his legs collapse. The ground slammed against him. He gazed at the stars and felt the world slipping away, and he forced out the words.

"I tried, Jerry. God knows...I tried..."

Chapter 21

Bernie

Camden Dunbar leaned against the Plexiglas window and looked down at the Washington Monument. The capital seemed so peaceful from up here, but Dunbar knew better. Below that haze, the streets swarmed with bio-suited troops, police, and paramedics combing the city for dead.

There was no pattern to it. Some areas had been left untouched, their panicked occupants cowering in their homes. Other sections had been devastated with fifty to one hundred percent lethality.

But the strangest thing was the killer's mysterious exit when the cold front swept through the city seven hours ago. There had to be a connection, some link with the high winds and temperature drop.

Dunbar was attending an 0130 briefing at NORAD when the shocking news hit the conference room. Harold Franklin Manis, Forty-fifth President of the United States, was dead, his life taken by the plague that had assaulted the nation's capital.

Manis and his beloved wife, Ellie, had died in their bedroom at the White House while scores of secret service agents tried to save them, only to succumb beside their fallen president.

The victims included Dr. Paul Nimrod, longtime physician and friend to the President; Pam Carey, the President's personal secretary; Juliette McAvee, the President's famed speechwriter; Zeke Flatley, Secret Service Agent-in-Charge; and thirty-seven members of the White House staff and security force.

The killer had spared no one, even claiming the White House's fabled head chef, Steven Postly, and his cadre of gourmet cooks as they prepared breakfast for the morning's crisis meetings. Five members of the President's cabinet had been lost, struck down in their suburban homes while they slept. And the names were still coming in.

Dunbar was snapped from his thoughts by the pilot's voice crackling on the intercom. *Air Force One* would land at Dulles International in five minutes. From there, *Marine One* would transport Dunbar to the Pentagon where he would address the surviving members of the President's cabinet, the congressional leadership, the joint chiefs, and the directors of the nation's security agencies. No media would be allowed.

Dunbar dropped back in the seat, his eyes trained on the blue notebook in his lap, and its prophetic gold emblem. The Presidential Seal glared back at him, its eagle talons grasping a cluster of arrows and olive branch.

He glanced at his watch. Three minutes past eleven. In exactly fifty-seven minutes, he would take the oath of office at the Pentagon.

All visual and audio recordings would be restricted to the military press core. Following the ceremony, he would be escorted to the Pentagon's media room for a public reenactment of his oath. Through blue screen and special effects, the ceremony would appear telecast from the steps of the Rose Garden, as if everything were under control. Fact is, the White House and all surrounding buildings were off limits to anyone not in a bio-suit.

"Are you alright, sir?"

Dunbar looked at Dean Stanley, the President's Chief of Staff who had taken the seat across from him. If not for a twist of fate, Stanley would have been at the White House when the plague struck. Instead, he had taken his wife to the Hamptons for a weekend escape, only to be whisked to La Guardia by the secret service, then flown by military jet to Indianapolis,

Indiana for a rendezvous with *Air Force One* and its shaken Vice President.

After barely having enough time to share their grief, the two men were lifted into the morning sky by *Air Force One*, bound for the nation's capital. Not much time for Stanley to brief the Vice President of the United States on the perilous state of the nation's government, and the human race.

Stanley leaned forward and spoke softly. "Would you like something? Maybe a little water?"

Dunbar shook his head and looked out the window. "Helluva time to take over."

"Yes, sir...helluva time." Stanley frowned and eased back in his seat. "Did you get a chance to read the notebook?"

Dunbar rested his hand on the blue leather cover. "She makes it sound hopeless."

Stanley forced a smile. "She's caustic as hell, but if anyone can stop this thing, it's her." He sighed and looked out the window. "So, we'll say a little prayer and listen to what she has to say."

Dunbar looked down at the notebook. The first page contained Raquel Carson's latest lethality projections. If she was correct, and a cure wasn't found within a month, the virus would be too widespread to rein in. Carson's fatal warning was typed in bold letters at the bottom of the page...

The human race will cease to exist by Spring, 2014, eight months from now...

Dunbar clutched the notebook and stared out the window. "One month. Not much time for an incoming president to work a miracle."

"No, sir."

"Some legacy."

Stanley reached out and patted him on the knee. "We're with you, sir. All the way."

Dunbar's gray eyes welled up with tears. "What should I do, Dean? What the hell should I do?"

Stanley gripped his seat as *Air Force One* rattled from its touchdown at Dulles International. He looked out the window at the military vehicles rolling alongside the huge jet. "Be bold, Mr. President. Put your best people on the front line. It'll give you time to come up with something." His blue eyes locked on Dunbar. "The people need a leader. Riots are breaking out in the cities. Thousands are fleeing to the countryside and mountains, but they just keep dropping, wherever they go." He clenched his fist. "Be their leader, Mr. President. Right or wrong, act decisively. Show them you're in charge. It's your best shot."

Marine One landed on the Pentagon grounds at high noon. Vice President Dunbar and Dean Stanley were escorted from the chopper by a cordon of marines carrying two spare bio-suits, should they be needed.

Dunbar stepped into the massive underground war room at 12:07 amidst a round of thunderous applause and shouts of encouragement from the people who had risen from their chairs at the black circular table. He recognized their faces and acknowledged their applause with nods of gratitude toward Fenton Maladay, Secretary of Defense; Cheryl Milliken, Secretary of State; Matthew Langston, Secretary of HUD; Clayton Morehead, Director of National Security; Colling Tors, Director of the CIA; Corey Whitman, Director of the FBI; Marvin Tate, Director of Civilian Defense; Sarah Hotchkiss, Director of the Red Cross; General David Stoyer, Chairman of the Joint Chiefs of Staff; Matthew Dean and Langston Hall from the Congress; and the recently appointed CDC Director, Samuel Tarver. Standing beside Tarver was Raquel Carson, Director of CDC's famed Department of Infectious Diseases, her eyes worn with fatigue, her fingers resting on a gray notebook. The notebook's contents were identical to Dunbar's.

Stanley escorted the Vice President to an empty chair beneath the Presidential Seal. Twin viewing screens flanked the seal, each one tracking incoming fatalities by nation. The tabulations were increasing every thirty seconds. Dunbar stood in front of his chair and scanned the solemn faces at the circular table. He recalled Stanley's words. Whatever twist of fate had brought him to this moment, Camden Dunbar was about to become the most powerful man in the world. He took a deep breath and spoke softly. "Before we begin, please join me in a prayer for our president, nation, and planet." He lowered his head and listened to the silence. "Thank you."

It only took a minute for Chief Justice MacIntyre to administer the oath of office. Dunbar stared at the Chief Justice while repeating the solemn words, his hand resting on a bible. He nearly broke down when the Chief Justice shook his hand. He didn't hear the applause and shouts of encouragement. He was too shaken to hear anything. A farm boy from Nebraska had just become the most powerful man on earth, yet he felt helpless against the microscopic creature threatening him and his seven billion brothers and sisters.

Dunbar gestured for the attendees to be seated. He waited until they were down before glancing at the viewing screens.

The death count in South America had reached five thousand. It was over three thousand in Europe and North America, with China close behind. Africa led them all with twenty thousand, but India was closing fast with fourteen thousand. The global death count exceeded fifty thousand.

Dunbar glared at the Chairman of the Joint Chiefs. "General Stoyer, please have someone turn off those screens. I know it's bad, but there's no sense rubbing my nose in it." He watched Stoyer look over his shoulder at the control room window and slash his finger across his throat. The twin screens went black.

"Thank you, General." Dunbar sat down and eyed the people seated around the table. His attention focused on the newly appointed CDC Director. "Mr. Tarver?"

"Sir?"

"I'm sorry for the loss of Mr. Fletcher. I know his death came at the worst possible time."

Tarver looked down. "Yes, sir."

"Where do we stand with the terrorists?"

Dunbar's directness caught Tarver off guard. He glanced at the FBI and CIA Directors while fumbling for an answer.

Dunbar leaned toward him. "Are you alright, Mr. Tarver?"

"Yes, sir. I'm awaiting confirmation."

"Confirmation?"

Tarver blurted out the words. "At two thirty this morning, I received a communication from my lead agent that our men had cornered the terrorists at a remote shack in Palomar, California and were preparing to engage them."

"Yes?"

Tarver hesitated. "I've lost contact with my agent. I've asked the FBI and CIA to send in choppers."

Dunbar's face reddened. "When did you make that request?"

Clayton Morehead cut off Tarver. "An hour ago."

"Hour?" Dunbar glared at Tarver. "You waited nine hours?"

Tarver couldn't speak. He felt the room closing on him.

"Well?" Dunbar's eyes burned into him.

"Mr. President, we have our best men up there. Experienced men with backgrounds in espionage and law enforcement. I didn't want to distract them."

"I see." Dunbar eased back in his chair, his eyes trained on Tarver. "Can I ask you something?"

"Of course, sir."

"What agency do you represent?"

"Sir?"

"What agency, Mr. Tarver?"

Tarver stared at the President. "CDC, sir."

Dunbar's eyes flickered with anger. "Then what are you doing with ex-CIA and FBI agents? Aren't you supposed to cure people and leave the dirty work to Clayton?"

Tarver leaned forward, his brown eyes locked on the President. "Sir, I was ordered to use whatever resources necessary to bring down the terrorists."

"By who, Mr. Tarver?"

Tarver hesitated. "President Manis, sir. I thought you knew."

Dunbar looked down at the notebook. "Well, I do now. Thank you, Mr. Tarver." He watched Tarver ease back in his chair.

For a moment, nothing was said as the new President flipped through the notebook. He looked at Raquel Carson. "These figures are pretty scary, Ms. Carson. Sure you aren't overreacting?"

Carson dug her fingernails into the chair. After three nights without sleep, the President's cutting words were the last thing she needed. She mustered every ounce of control left in her exhausted body while managing a tremulous, "Yes, sir."

The President closed the notebook and folded his hands. "So, what do we do?"

Carson glared at the President while Samuel Tarver stood up and rested a hand on her shoulder. "Sir, this is my responsibility. Let me say—"

"Shut up, Mr. Tarver."

Tarver reeled from the President's words. "Sir?"

"Shut up and get out." Dunbar nodded toward the MP guarding the door. "I need people I can trust, Mr. Tarver. Now please leave the room."

Tarver stared at the President in disbelief. He gathered up his papers with a trembling hand and shoveled them into his attaché case. He patted Carson's shoulder. "We'd better go." She nodded and reached for the notebook on the table.

"Where are you going, Ms. Carson?"

She looked up in surprise. "Sir?"

"You haven't answered my question."

President Dunbar watched Tarver leave the room, accompanied by the MP. His decision to kick out Tarver was anything but divine inspiration. In those brief hours with Dean Stanley on *Air Force One*, the first item covered was Samuel Tarver, a megalomaniac who would do anything to become the next President of the United States, even at the expense of the human race. Interesting priority for the nation's CDC Director.

Dunbar didn't have time to probe the source of Stanley's information. Had he, the revelation would have been intriguing since it involved a double, if not triple, agent who trusted no one. An agent whose only goal was to retire to the South Seas with a wad of money and sixty foot schooner. A paranoiac named Parker Hampsted.

Raquel Carson folded her hands. "Mr. President, I'm not sure what to say."

Dunbar shrugged. "Say what's in your heart, Ms. Carson."

Carson looked down for a moment, then rose to her feet, her eyes focused on the blackened screens. "Let's see those numbers."

Dunbar frowned. "Ms. Carson, I don't see the value of—"

"Reality, Mr. President. Since we started this meeting, two hundred have died." Her eyes flashed with anger. "My prior calculations projected two thousand dead by the end of week two. We've exceeded that by forty-eight thousand. At that rate, we'll have a quarter million dead at the end of month one. Then, hyper-geometric progression to finality. Estimated time—eight months."

The President's face reddened. "Answer my question, Ms. Carson. What can you do about it? Or did I make the wrong decision?"

"Sir?"

"To put you in charge of this mess."

Her eyes widened. "Me?"

The President leaned toward her. "I need you, Ms. Carson."

She sat down, her eyes fixed on him. "I didn't expect this."

The President forced a smile. "Neither did I."

She looked down at the notebook in disbelief.

The President leaned closer. "Do I have to beg?"

Her head snapped up. "I'll call an immediate teleconference with our field teams and overseas contacts." She looked at Director Morehead. "We need those terrorists alive."

Morehead glanced at Tors and Whitman. He grimaced and stood up. "Mr. President?"

Dunbar nodded. "Of course, Clayton. Whatever it takes." He watched his three security directors gather their papers and head for the MP at the door.

"Wait!" General Stoyer stood up, his hand gripping a black telephone. The empty cradle lay on the table in front of him, its black finish throbbing with a red glow. He lowered the phone and looked at the President. "Sir, this is from the control room. Something's coming in on the internet. Some kind of broadcast."

"Broadcast?"

"A virus of some kind. They're not sure how it got downloaded to us, but they say it's coming in everywhere." Stoyer frowned. "Sir, it appears to be from the terrorists."

Dunbar stared at the general. "Can you patch it in?"

"Yes, sir."

All eyes focused on the screens beside the Presidential Seal. The gray static cleared, revealing a man standing in bright sunlight. His face was drawn beneath his blond ruffled hair. He wore khakis and a denim shirt, unbuttoned at the collar. As the camera zoomed in, they could see cuts and bruises on his unshaven face. And there was something else. The sound of waves rushing against a shore.

Tors returned to his seat and fumbled through his attaché case. He yanked out a photograph and glanced at the screen. "That's him. The one called—"

"My name is Karl Frankton. My friend, Dr. Thala, is working the minicam. Sorry for the poor quality, but it's the best we can do. I don't have much time, so here goes."

"We're not terrorists, only two men who were in the wrong place at the wrong time. Or maybe it was the right time. I'll let you figure it out."

"I spent two years at CDC as part of a cover-up deal negotiated with a man named Jonathan Fletcher. I'd uncovered an FDA plot to release an unsafe AIDS drug called M-13. When I tried to turn the evidence over to the press, the drug's manufacturer threatened my family, so I cut a deal to prevent the drug's release. I guess the pharmaceutical boys were pretty upset. My attorney warned me they wouldn't rest until my name was etched on a tombstone. Nothing new about that. Greed does that to people, especially when they lose lots of money."

"What the hell is this?" Stoyer turned to give the cutoff signal, but the President raised his hand.

"Let it go, General. I want to hear this."

"But, sir—"

Dunbar glared at him. "I want to know how he came up with that name."

Stoyer frowned and dropped back in his chair.

"The boys at CDC were about to cut me loose when I stumbled across something at the Trinity River near Houston, Texas. That's when I met Dr. Thala." Karl shaded his eyes and squinted past the camera. *"Show them your face, Mandu."*

The picture jiggled as Thala came into view. He stepped in front of the camera and nodded. *"I'm Dr. Mandu Thala. I've been with CDC for twenty-five years. My record speaks for itself. Check it out if you don't believe me. Then ask yourself why a dedicated physician and pathologist would suddenly turn on his brothers and sisters after fighting so long to protect them? I assure you, every word Mr. Frankton says is true. I don't like him very much, but we're in this together, and we don't have much time. Excuse me, I have to steady the camera."* Thala stepped out of the picture, leaving Karl standing in the sunlight. The camera focused on Karl's haggard face.

"In 1996, a German chemical firm named Starburst began spraying a rodenticide called Terra Verde. By the time they were finished, large sections of Africa, Asia, and South America had been blanketed with their product. According to the World Health Organization, their sprayings killed a billion rats and saved thousands of third-world villagers and migrants from starvation. The Starburst symbol was everywhere, and everyone should have lived happily ever after."

Karl looked down at the stack of papers in his hand. *"Everything I'm about to tell you is documented in a sub-program that will kick in at the conclusion of this message. We've scanned every document the rodenticide's creator stashed in his San Clemente home. The sub-program includes the rodenticide's formula, and a possible antidote that might stop the killer. If you want a sample of the antidote, you can trigger a second sub-program from the icon at the end of this message. The sub-program contains a map leading to two tubes of the antidote. That is…if this message has gotten to the right people."*

The camera closed on Karl's face. *"That's the problem, you see. We don't know how far the corruption has penetrated our government. We don't even know if we have a government. From what I've seen, there isn't anything left except a bunch of puppets dangling on a string. The puppeteers are men with names like Schoenfeld, Menchen, and Nakashima. Powerful, obsessed men more dangerous than any terrorist."*

Stoyer's face twisted in a scowl. "He's not making sense. A real schizoid. He's all over the map."

Dunbar raised his hand for quiet. "Calm down, General. I want to hear the madman out."

Karl held up the stack of papers. *"So, here's the punch line, whoever you are. The invisible killer sweeping our planet isn't a virus, bacteria, or terrorist germ. It's a product of man's greed, a bionuclear nightmare that made Starburst's owners rich while implanting a time bomb that has finally gone off. You can't see it because of the sub-atomic cloaking agent developed by its creator, a chameleon-like catalyst that conceals the rodenticide within the blood cells of its dead hosts."* Karl shook his head. *"Brilliant, but deadly."*

He lowered the papers. *"Well, that's about it. We're headed south to San Diego. Not sure what we'll do. There's a TV commentator named Sarvan. Maybe we'll try to turn everything over to him. It's worth a shot."* He hesitated, as if struck by a thought. *"Actually, I know someone else down there. With some luck, I might get through to him. Either way, it's goodbye from two guys that tried to make a difference. Hope you make it."*

Karl's eyes flashed as he forced out his final words. *"Goodbye, Jeremy. I'll always be with you. If things work out, remember your ol' dad. And remember that he didn't quit. And if things don't work out…I'll be waiting for you on the other side…"* The twin screens flickered and went blank.

The President looked at his three directors of security.

Tors shook his head. "It's a trick to divert our attention. The man's delusional."

"No."

All eyes focused on Raquel Carson who had stood up from her chair, her eyes locked on the twin screens. The room flashed with colors from the letters and charts scrolling across the screens. But one image didn't fade. It seemed frozen, its spectrographic map shrugging off the other images.

"My God." Carson rested her hands on the table.

Dunbar squinted at the brilliant rainbow of colors. "What is it?"

She shook her head. "The fools finally did it. Oh, how desperate they must have been. So much money at stake. They had to be sure."

Dunbar leaned toward her. "Ms. Carson?"

She rubbed her forehead and looked down at the notebook. Her words were barely audible. "Cyanide. They spiked the rodenticide with cyanide. That's what killed the rats. That's what's killing us."

Dunbar pushed up from the table and turned to the screens. The flow of documents had ceased and only the spectrographic rainbow remained. He stepped to the left screen and touched the colored bands. "Cyanide?"

Carson eased beside the President. "It's had seventeen years to spread across the planet. Through the water tables, creeks, and streams. Through the lakes, rivers, and oceans. It's everywhere, and it's reached critical PPM."

"PPM?"

"Parts per million. At ten PPM, cyanide is lethal. Five milligrams per cubic meter, and you're dead."

Dunbar stared at the screen. "Then, that's what hit us last night?"

She sighed and looked up at the screen. "Cyanide is extremely volatile. It reaches vaporization at only seventy-eight degrees Fahrenheit. It was over seventy-eight last night. The cyanide must have reached critical PPM in the Potomac."

Dunbar turned toward her. "It's still there?"

Carson lowered her head. "It's everywhere, Mr. President."

The room was dead silent. In a few seconds, that silence would turn to panic. The President backed away from the screen and stared at her. "What should we do?"

Carson locked her eyes on Morehead. "Those two men are our only hope. If we don't take them alive—"

"What in God's name is that?" Corey Whitman was standing at the table, his finger pointing at the screens.

Sarah Hotchkiss stood up and rested her hands on the table. "My God. It's—"

"An iguana. Maybe three years old from the looks of the crest." Carson leaned on the table and stared at the forked tongue flicking out at them.

The President backed away from the screens. "How about that. The world's on the brink of extinction and I'm looking at a lizard." He turned to General Stoyer who was frozen in his chair, his eyes gazing at the screens. "General Stoyer, please have your control room click on that lizard."

"Sir?"

"Do it, General. That's your icon."

At first, there was no reaction as the seated members arose from their chairs, their eyes fixed on the scaly creature flicking its pink tongue at them. Then came the red cursor, positioning itself on the iguana's eye. Why pick an eye? Ask General Stoyer. Maybe it seemed more military that way. Either way, the room came to life when the control room attendant clicked his mouse.

The iguana disappeared, replaced by a map of Scripps Park and the beach where Karl and Mandu buried the two tubes of Ringley Adams' antidote. A red "x" marked the spot.

Stoyer couldn't take anymore. He rose to his feet, his eyes filled with anger. "It's a hoax. A damn hoax!"

"Hope you're wrong, General. For all our sakes." Raquel Carson nodded to Morehead. "Well, what are we waiting for?"

The room exploded with sliding chairs and voices shouting into cell phones. Colling Tors dialed his contacts at Interpol and delivered a firm message. "At all costs, arrest the men called Menchen, Schoenfeld, and Nakashima. This is a priority one, international alert. The men called Gunthar Menchen, Magnus Schoenfeld, and Yoshio Nakashima must be apprehended with all possible speed."

Corey Whitman stood beside his CIA counterpart, his cell phone patched to the choppers closing on "Site Y" on Palomar Mountain. Whitman's change of orders stunned his field team. The two terrorists must be taken alive and brought to the Pentagon for interrogation. All resistance must be overcome with nonlethal measures. Under no circumstances must the terrorists be harmed.

And while they shouted orders, President Camden Dunbar stared at his Chief-of-Staff, and for a moment, saw a smile on Dean Stanley's face. It was too soon to know if the miracle had come. The President lowered his head and said a prayer.

Chapter 22

A Good Sound

The morning sun burst over Mt. Palomar, accompanied by yelps of coyotes returning from their night hunt. The critters raced across the rugged terrain, their noses pointed at the shadows beneath the cliffs.

There was no time for rest. They must reach their caves before the sun flooded the valley, for daylight meant the return of their mortal enemy, the two-legged creature called man.

They scampered toward their caves, the sun rising behind them, their yellow eyes glancing at the hills for the threatening glint of a rifle barrel.

But there would be no shooting today. No sickening thuds from the hunter's impacting bullets. It seems their enemy was also fleeing for his life. Through his insatiable greed, man had created a pesticidal killer that threatened his very existence. He had gone too far. The hunter had become the hunted. Man and dog were one.

A warm breeze swept through the brush, accompanied by the pack leader's high-pitched howl. The mangy dog crept out of the brush, its ragged coat covered with burrs. The coyote slinked across the sunlit clearing, its nose sniffing the air as it edged toward the cabin.

The coyote's ears pricked up from a creaking sound. It glared at the cabin's opened door. The air smelled from death. The animal lowered its head and moved closer.

The coyote was almost to the door when it dropped on its haunches, its eyes trained on the two bodies sprawled in the dirt. It raised its head and emitted a ghostlike howl. Behind it, the coyote's brothers and sisters crawled out of the brush, their hungry eyes staring at the two bodies.

The coyote slinked closer to the first body, crouching low to sniff the man's hand. It hesitated and sniffed again. It's head snapped back. Warmth! The man was alive! The coyote sprang backward as the man convulsed and rolled on his stomach. The stunned animal chased its brothers and sisters into the brush where it spun around and dropped low, its eyes peering at the man in the dirt. The man clenched his fists and began coughing violently. Slowly, deliberately, he pushed off the ground and sat up on his knees, his body swaying in the breeze.

Karl gasped for breath and fought the waves of dizziness sweeping through him. He remembered dragging his friend into the warm, night air before the suffocating pain brought him down. Then, the blackness as he uttered a final prayer for the human race, and for the son he loved.

He looked down at the man lying beside him. There was no movement. No sign of life. He dropped down and pressed an ear against his friend's chest. Through the dim light, he spotted the coyote staring at him from the brush, its head tilted to the side as if trying to grasp what was happening. The animal let out a guttural howl and bolted past him, followed by its brothers and sisters. There would be no killing today.

Karl detected a faint heartbeat, barely audible above the rustling brush. He loosened Thala's ropes and flung the chair aside. "Wake up, dammit. You're not checking out on me now. We're gonna finish this together." He gripped Thala's shirt and gave it a violent shake.

There was no response.

"Damn you!" Karl straddled his friend and pressed his fists against Thala's chest. Then came the mouth-to-mouth he once administered as a paramedic in Manhattan. He continued the frantic ritual until the dizziness overtook him. A final press on Thala's chest and he collapsed on his back, his eyes staring at the blue sky.

Karl Frankton had lost his friend. Drawn together by fate, the two pathologists had waged a desperate fight against man's most hideous creation. Now, only one could go on. He sat up and glared at the cabin. The self-pity was gone, replaced by a firm resolve. He had faced betrayal, disgrace, and death, and had survived. He was alone, but the stakes were too great to quit now. *On your feet, Frankton. You're not dead yet.*

He started to push off the ground and froze. A hand clutched his wrist. A cold, black hand. He yanked his arm away and slid backward, his eyes locked on the man lying in the dirt.

Thala coughed and rolled on his side. He leaned on his elbow and squinted at the man beside him.

"Mandu?"

"That you, Mr. Frankton?"

Karl's eyes filled with tears. "I'll be damned."

"What happened?"

Karl couldn't speak. For a moment, they just stared at each other. Finally, Karl pushed off the ground and stood up on shaky legs. He bent over and gripped his knees, waiting for the dizziness to clear.

Thala glanced at the cabin. "Where are the others?"

Karl ignored him and stumbled through the cabin door. Seconds later, he burst from the cabin with Thala's black medical bag dangling from his hand. He collapsed in the dirt, his hand clinging to the bag.

"Where's Hampsted?"

"Inside."

Thala looked at the opened door.

"He's dead, with three others."

"Dead?" Thala rubbed his aching head. "I don't remember anything except a nightmare about Pretoria. Someone was dragging me through the dirt."

"It was me."

"You?"

"You were out cold. They were gonna finish me, so I took my best shot and crushed the Trinity blood tube. I guess the cyanide did the rest."

Thala looked at the cabin. "But, we were in there too?"

Karl looked down at his bloodstained arm, and at the empty syringe lying in the dirt. "Before I blacked out, I injected us with the antidote. Then I dragged you out here and said goodbye to this cruel world."

Thala's eyes widened. "It worked?"

"Guess so."

"My God."

"Yeah, something like that."

Thala slumped on his elbow. "What are we going to do?"

"Don't know. Haven't gotten that far."

Karl rolled on his back and stared at the flock of vultures circling overhead. A coyote's howl echoed through the hills. And there was something else. A faint vibration coming from the east, and it was growing stronger.

Karl staggered to his feet and helped his friend up. They leaned against each other, their eyes focused on the sunlit ridge above the cabin. The vibration had become a roar.

The first chopper burst over the ridge, its radar spears protruding below its armored nose. Then came the second, and third.

"Karl Frankton?"

Karl squinted at the chopper hovering above the cabin. The loudspeaker blared a second time.

"Is that you, Mr. Frankton?"

Karl felt Thala press against his shoulder. "Guess this is it."

"Yeah."

Karl watched the chopper descend on the clearing. Two marines jumped out dressed in battle gear. The lead marine glanced at the opened cabin, then glared at Karl with hardened eyes. "Anyone in there?"

Karl nodded. "Four dead."

The lead marine gestured toward the cabin and watched his comrade approach the door, covered by the two marines that had dropped out of the second chopper. Seconds later, the marine burst from the cabin and gave a nod. "Four dead, sir."

The lead marine spoke into a small headset and pressed the earpiece with his finger while receiving orders. His other hand grasped an automatic rifle, his finger tight on the trigger.

The marine's head snapped up. "Come aboard." He gestured toward the first chopper.

Karl didn't move. His eyes were trained on the automatic rifle. If they both rushed the marine, one might seize the gun and get off a burst before it was over. Better to go down fighting than die from a shot of curaré.

The marine gestured a second time. "Come on, Mr. Frankton. The President wants to see you."

The words rang in Karl's ears. "Who?"

The marine's face twisted in a scowl. "President Dunbar."

"Dunbar? He's the Vice-President?"

The marine shook his head. "President Manis died last night, along with two thousand others."

Karl stared at the marine in shock.

The marine stepped toward him. "We don't have much time." He stepped to the side and pointed the M-16 at the chopper.

Karl reached for the medical bag, but one of the marines had snatched it. He glared at the marine and pointed a trembling finger at the bag. "Easy with that. It's all we've got."

The marine lifted the bag toward Karl. "What's in it?"

"Your life, soldier. All our lives."

Karl started for the chopper and felt Thala grab his arm. He turned around and forced a smile. "Come on, Doc. I feel lucky today."

As they climbed into the chopper, a young man in La Jolla stared at his PC screen, his blue eyes focused on the latest rerun of his dad's recording. A micro disk passed from father to son had turned the tide of battle, its global web broadcast engineered by two men who refused to quit.

The days ahead would be hard. Many would die, including the three men who unleashed Adams' deadly creation on mankind. Nakashima, Schoenfeld, and Menchen would succumb by more conventional means. Two suicides and a fatal heart attack in a darkened study while a wife and daughter slept.

When the chopper rose into the morning sky, Karl heard an animal's cry coming from the shadows below the mountain. He leaned toward the window, but the marine nudged him back in the seat.

"It's just a coyote."

Karl nodded, his eyes filled with tears. "It's a good sound."

The coyote howled at the three choppers fading into the haze. When they were gone, it retreated into the darkness of its cave, and waited for the moon...